MIAH

stories

JULIA LIN

Julia Lin
2013

We acknowledge the support of the Canada Council for the Arts for our publishing program. We also acknowledge support from the Government of Ontario through the Ontario Arts Council.

We acknowledge the financial support of the Government of Canada through the Canada Book Fund for our publishing activities

Cover design by Ingrid Paulson

Library and Archives Canada Cataloguing in Publication

Lin, Julia,
    Miah : stories / Julia Lin.

ISBN 978-1-894770-99-6

    I. Title.

PS8623.I49M53 2012   C813'.6   C2012-905117-9

Printed and bound in Canada by Coach House Printing

TSAR Publications
P. O. Box 6996, Station A
Toronto, Ontario M5W 1X7
Canada

www.tsarbooks.com

For my parents

Contents

Huang Family Tree

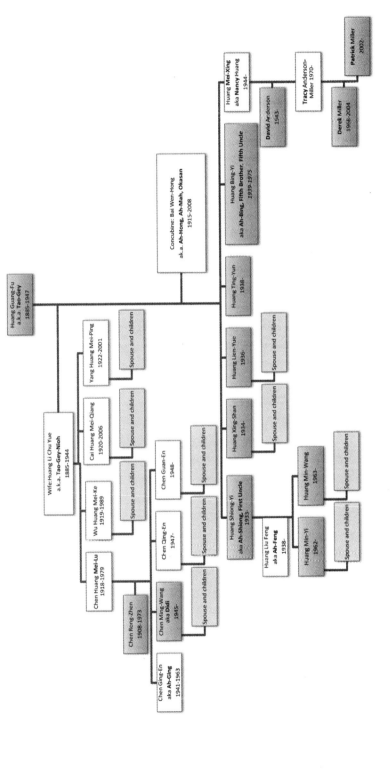

Miah

IT WAS ANOTHER BREEZY, *sunny morning in the village and I was sitting at the doorway of the living room, pretending to ride a horse while waiting for my mother to wake up so we could go pick flowers from the lane and fill the basket in our bedchamber with the petals. I heard my grandmother make a strange sound in the kitchen, like the pigs make when the men run after them with a knife.*

The man with the funny walk stumbled into the courtyard. He had lived with my grandmother for as long as I could remember and he'd always walked like one leg was shorter than the other. My grandmother tore out of the kitchen and went running after him with a bowl overflowing with something that looked like egg yolk and he was shaking her off. "Drink it! Drink it!" she kept screaming.

⌣

My mother asks me to accompany her to Taiwan for my grandmother's funeral. I was last on the island in 1975, thirty-three years ago, when I was five. My Canadian father had returned to Vancouver to arrange for our immigration papers and we stayed with my grandmother for a year on her farm in southern Taiwan. I still have a black and white photograph of myself in an oversized cotton dress, squinting in bright sunlight, standing barefoot on spindly legs under a banana tree; wisps of hair have strayed from my loose plaits, and I am holding the hand of a man whose face is hidden by the shadow of his bamboo hat.

Ah Mah dao, Taiwanese for grandmother's home. Ah Mah's farm is

1

the first home I can remember. It was where I learned the differences between grasshoppers and cicadas, frogs and toads, blazing stars and peonies, male and female Chinese deities, life and death. Where I learned that some things are not permanent and there are mysteries in the adult world not spoken of to children. Where I first heard my mother utter the words "No need to tell."

Now, as she peers at the measuring cup on the kitchen counter of our West Point Grey bungalow and adds more "stinky tofu" brine to bring the meniscus up to the correct level, my mother says, "I got good deal on ticket. You come. No need to tell anyone."

My mother is the only person I know who actually measures out ingredients for Chinese cooking as precisely as she follows new recipes for poached salmon or Cape Breton scones or maple syrup pie or tourtière or puff pastry. When I was living at home, she was chronically disappointed with my slovenly housekeeping habits; these days she is aghast at the way I throw stir-fries or spaghetti dinners together for my son and me. "Slow, slow, Tracy. Do right." Orderliness, not just cleanliness, is important to her.

"Okay, I suppose I should come. I'm just worried about leaving Patrick with Dad for two weeks. You know Patrick's never been away from me for so long before." Grains of glutinous rice trickle through the conical bamboo-leaf cup I fashioned a moment ago, and I quickly scoop up the rice from the table, hoping my mother hasn't noticed. In my teens, I used to call her the Geiger counter for imperfection, able to detect flaws in the most unlikely places.

To my surprise, my mother, who is usually hyper-vigilant when it comes to Patrick, says, "No worry. Your father take good care. You come."

She empties the contents of the measuring cup into a pot of fresh tofu, puts the lid on, then takes the cup out of my hands and expertly reshapes it. I compress my lips, exhale slowly, pick up two more bamboo leaves to form a cone, and pour rice into it. This time the bottom holds.

"Ma, do you remember when we lived with Ah Mah? You know the man who lived there with us?"

"Aiyah, Tracy, these thing in past, what good to bring up? How it help you?" she asks in her annoyed manner and gives me "the look" guaranteed to silence further inquiries.

When I was growing up, I always thought I would understand my mother when I became a mother myself. But Patrick is already six and I am nowhere close to solving the tangram that is she. Like a member of some secret Chinese society my mother has mastered the transformation of "cloak" from noun into verb.

"No need to tell…" was a refrain that I learned well, whether it was to keep silent about the small bill that she slipped out of my father's wallet, or to pretend that she wasn't home when canvassers appeared at the door, or to say "Sorry, my mother can't come to the phone right now, she's in the shower." For her, truth is a malleable substance—homemade play dough, superheated iron, genuine Chinese gold.

But it isn't just the white lies, there is also "no need to tell" about her past, her family, or even things that we did last weekend, to friends or my father's mother. One never knows how information will be used. Better safe than sorry.

She is constantly chastizing my father for divulging too much information to people "outside," meaning anyone besides our immediate family. On rare occasions, I've heard my exasperated father object. "Nancy, that's silly. What's wrong with telling my mother that we'll be away for a couple of days? What difference would it make?" "It doesn't make sense, Nancy. Nobody cares who our visitors are. There's no need to keep their names a secret." "Nancy, I'm going to put the sign up on the lawn whether you like it or not. I have a right to endorse my candidate." These are the only times I hear my parents argue.

My father has always told me, "Your mother is a courageous woman," by which he means that it took gumption for her to brave her family's disapproval by marrying a foreigner, and not just any foreigner, but a white one who not only couldn't speak Taiwanese but also had ash blond hair and skin that turned red instead of brown in the tropical sun. Back in the 1960s, foreigners could still turn heads when they walked down the dirt-paved streets of Taipei where my father was teaching at a cram school and my mother was trying her best to master English. She was determined to study abroad after finishing her undergraduate studies in chemistry at National Taiwan University, the best university in the country, she says proudly.

"Love at first sight" was the first idiom my father ever taught my mother.

When I speak to my father about the man with the limp, he says, "I'm afraid I'm not much help, honey. Your mother has never told me. All I know is that her family lived through the White Terror and some of her relatives were implicated. I really don't know the details."

I've read the history books but I'm not any closer to understanding. I know that during the "White Terror," hundreds of thousands of political dissidents were imprisoned or executed under the leadership of Chiang Kai-shek, after his Kuomintang troops, comprised entirely of Mainlanders, were chased off mainland China to Taiwan by the Communists. Martial law was imposed in May 1949 and not lifted until 1987. My mother, like many native Taiwanese of a certain age, has a deep-seated hatred of the Mainlanders, or *guah seung lung,* Taiwanese for out-of-province people.

"Half century under Japan then half century under Kuomintang . . . too much," my mother would sigh and shake her head. And that would be the end of the discussion.

But like generations of native Taiwanese who weathered colonization by the Dutch, Spanish, and Japanese, my mother has inherited "Taiwanese resilience," which has helped her acclimatize to a land where her lack of fluency in English has forced her to be a lab technician instead of a professor. Her sighs signify acceptance of her "miah,"—destiny or fate.

As an act of defiance, my mother made sure that I learned the main native Taiwanese dialect, spoken by seventy percent of the population, instead of Mandarin, the official language of Taiwan. "You are real Taiwanese, not *guah seung lung,*" she would intone between brush strokes as she readied my hair for plaiting each morning.

He had heard that it was going to happen again. He didn't want to believe it could happen twice in a lifetime but he had to face reality. Suesing was too loyal a friend to lie to him and her sources were always reliable. Last time the police had come in the dead of night. That was always the way. The "registration checks" still happened every two or three nights at 3 AM, even now, four years after his release. The police made sure all the drawers were upturned and all the neighbours heard. Idiotic pigs! Did they think there was anyone left in the village who didn't know about his troubles already? But this time he'd be prepared. He was not going back. Fifteen years was long enough.

He would never forget the night they arrested him. His mother's crying and pointless begging. Then the blinding lights. The fear. The powerlessness. The hatred. The pain. The same questions. Always the same. Time alternated between periods of calm, while he lay curled up in fetal position on his bunk, and periods of noise and blood in the interrogation room. Until the night he heard his tibia break. They finally stopped after that.

The prison guards on Green Island had no mercy for a lame man. He carried the same loads as the able-bodied. Walked barefoot on the same rocks. Slept in the same stinking cells. If he didn't have his "go diam mun hoh" to recite and give him comfort, he would have gone insane or committed suicide like so many others. He thanked the gods for his training in the Four Books and Five Classics. A man learns the depths of his resources in a place like that. Maybe the lucky ones were the ones they killed upon arrest. Better miah.

My mother and I arrive during the two-week wake. First Uncle lives here now with his wife and two sons. He leads us on a tour of the family compound: the farm has been sold, the well and pond filled in, the banana grove cut down, and the chirping of cicadas silenced. Only the kitchen, the washing room, and the living room, all along one length of the rectangular courtyard and the two rows of bedchambers along the widths remain. On the fourth side of the courtyard, a new concrete fence closes the compound off from the village road. Dusty photographs of ancestors with queues and bound feet in their traditional po-faced poses are still hung in the worship area of the living room. A bronze urn with half-burned incense sticks sits on the altar next to a walnut scroll table and two polished jumu chairs with lotus blossom designs.

"*Siuh gung. Lon siuh gung.*" Same. All the same. First Uncle nods and sweeps one arm to indicate the worship area. But it's not. Everything is smaller and dustier than I remembered.

During the tour, First Uncle opens bedroom doors to reveal mattresses and duvets that have replaced the tatami mats on the ancient, metre-high, family-sized platforms. The paving stones in the courtyard that I stepped on to go to the outhouse have been cemented over and the room where I slept with my mother has been converted into a carport for two motor scooters and a Honda CR-V. I am tall enough now to see the detailed workmanship on the carved eaves of the old buildings and, during inattentive moments, to trip over door thresholds that I used to ride as imaginary horses.

As I walk around the compound, I keep expecting Ah Mah or the man with the limp to appear. But then, remembering that world no longer exists, I try to dispel the unsettling disorientation that has plagued me since our arrival.

White squares of calligraphy paper with the character "death" have been pasted on the double teak doors, and bamboo stands bearing flower wreaths proclaim my grandmother's passing. In the living room, an enlarged copy of the photograph she'd sent us on her ninetieth birthday sits on the "soul table" along with fruits, flowers, incense, and candles; she holds her pose in a conservative western-style suit, hands folded in her lap, to be remembered by future descendents in ancestor-worship ceremonies. Everything else in the room that could be considered decorative has been covered with white cloth. Ah Mah has been dressed in seven sets of clothing in preparation for burial, and ghost money made of paper has been burned to help her on her way to the afterlife.

In the evening, clad in white ceremonial sackcloth garments, my mother and I light our incense sticks and bow to the photograph. Three women relatives in mourning clothes follow suit. One of them whispers to me, "She had a long life. Ninety-three years old. Five sons. *Hoh miah.*" Good fate.

Five sons?

But I know of only four uncles.

⌒

He was tired of living off his family's charity. He considered his options. Maybe he should try and get out of the country. But where would he go? The mainland? It was closed to the Taiwanese, and besides, after decades of separation, he doubted he would be able to find S-K Chang, his friend who moved to the mainland before the borders closed. It was hard enough trying to find a job even with his family connections here. Of course, nobody on the mainland would know that he had been a political prisoner. But they would not be sympathetic to a Taiwanese native. The Maoists only welcomed Communists. He could pretend . . .

He shook his head. Straw dream. Even if he could get across the Strait and escape the military, how would he find a job without any papers?

Maybe Japan? Again, no friends and his Japanese was rusty.

He could try hiding out in the mountains. He'd heard of men who had managed to survive for years that way. He opened his dresser and started pulling socks out.

⌒

On the day of the funeral, my mother is unconsolable and unabashedly joins in the weeping and wailing. I am reminded of the day we left for Canada—Ah Mah didn't think she would ever see her only daughter again, the child born years after her sons. But she wept in private, since our departure was supposedly a happy occasion. But I alone had seen her grief. Stretching out her hand, my mother places inside the coffin one of the gold bracelets that my grandmother had given her in Canada on her sole foray out of Taiwan. First Uncle arranges a pair of white pants next to Ah Mah's body so her spirit will be protected against unfriendly ghosts in her journey to the afterlife. Then the men nail the coffin down. I have to restrain my mother from advancing upon the funereal platform, apparently to throw herself onto the coffin.

Then eulogies and poems, chantings lead by Buddhist monks and nuns in brown or saffron robes, incense lit by mourners who fill the courtyard, cooked meats on the offering tables, hired singers and wailers, Chinese drums and cymbals, a Western marching band. Flashes of white are everywhere and it seems I will never escape the crush of leathery-skinned, black-eyed people. I link arms with my mother only to be told that I have to walk behind, and we follow the coffin bearers, towards the hills, in the direction I remember my grandmother taking when she went to gather firewood for the day's cooking.

Our orderly procession snakes through the streets in the oppressive heat and I am thankful that the geomancer had chosen a morning service, for even at ten o'clock the white garments I have worn since my arrival are damp, and sweat streams down my neck. I trudge through shimmering ripples rising from the blazing asphalt and ignore the curious stares of men with burning cigarettes, women with babies on their backs, and children licking ice cream bars as we pass their storefronts and courtyards.

I force myself to climb up the hillside crowded with row upon row of tombstones; some are modest markers on earthen mounds and others have prominently emblazoned family names on polished marble. Bold characters such as "Chen," "Chang," "Sun," and "Lee" announce the final resting places of patriarchs, concubines, first sons, last daughters, and babies with shortened lives. My white sandals are brown from the dust as we negotiate past Chinese privet shrubs in flower, stunted crab apple trees, and dry scrub grasses.

When we reach the newly prepared hole which will receive my grandmother's remains, I turn and look down and am surprised to see that we are already two-thirds of the way up the hill. Haven't I seen this view before? I shake off the eeriness that momentarily takes hold.

We throw dirt onto the coffin. We light incense sticks. We make offerings of food and sheaves of golden paper money. I watch the flames consume the replicas of appliances for the paper house that my grandmother will be able to move into in the after-world: refrigerator, television set, rice cooker, washing machine . . . gusts of hot air from the crackling fire, the smell of incense fills my nostrils, and greyish ash sticks to my face and arms.

Visions of burning replicas from another time invade my consciousness: a man's bicycle, a writing table, men's trousers, and stacks and stacks of books. Faint echoes of my grandmother's wails, my mother's sobs, and funeral chants from another age beset my already overloaded senses. The monks and nuns bow their shaved heads and begin another round of incomprehensible chanting. I long for the ceremony to end and cannot tell if my tears are for the dead or the living.

After my mother throws her last stack of paper money into the fire, she leads me away from the mourners still easing my grandmother's sojourn in the afterlife with replicas of more material comforts, to a carefully tended tomb that we had passed on our way up, situated four metres down the hill from my grandmother's grave. The taupe-tiled hemispherical tomb enclosure protrudes from the hillside like the top half of an empty eye socket. My mother's maiden name "Huang" is engraved at the top of the metre-high archway guarding the enclosure but I can't read the epitaphs that run down the two red-tiled columns at the sides of the entrance. A patch of grass lies in front of a small headstone protected by the tomb enclosure. Inside the enclosure loose rocks weigh down scraps of ghost money—remnants of offerings from the annual spring tomb-sweeping.

She lights two incense sticks and hands one to me. "Pay respect to Fifth Uncle."

⌒

They had caught him. Four days into the mountains and they had hunted him down like a wild boar, cornered him against a tree, struck him with their rifle butts, tied him with rough, braided rope. They drove

9

him through countless villages, asking "Is your leader in there? Who else knows him?" and were enraged by his silence.

⌒

My mother speaks now, as if she can only do so in his presence, as if his memory would be desecrated if she were elsewhere.

Fifth Uncle was her favourite brother, closest to her in age and temperament. He was a Chinese scholar when the Classics were not fashionable; he started teaching her Chinese brush-writing when she was only five. She learned self-control from him. "Hold your brush upright. Remember, you are the master over your mind and body." He taught her the character for "honour."

"He was so happy when Japanese left. Then so sad when Kuomintang show true colour. He thought we all Chinese, should be brother, help each other. Then he was angry at corrupt government." She pulls the rocks off the ragged pieces of paper money.

"Ah Mah so afraid when he joined resistance. Then so sad. She told him: tell truth. But he stubborn. Told nothing. Government got mad. Add five years to sentence. Ah Mah see him many time on Green Island. Long, long trip. I go with her once." My mother brushes the last bits of paper off the enclosure floor and bows her head.

Despite my dizziness and the pulsing in my temples, I place my hand on my mother's forearm and let it linger longer than I normally would. She allows it to rest.

"No one give him job when he get out. Everyone afraid. Then someone say leader come out of hiding. Police want to know where leader hiding. They ask Fifth Uncle. They keep asking." Her voice is tremulous.

⌒

They told him to "think it over" and left him in his mother's care. They would return, they said. She sent for a doctor to set the broken fingers and jaw but took care of dressing the cuts herself. The doctor said they needed to wait to determine if there was more internal damage.

Again, he vowed not to go back to Green Island.

My mother pulls some weeds from the plot in front of the tomb-stone. Her gaze turns inward and then she forces one last utterance out, "Suicide. Drank pesticides. *Pi miah.*" Bad fate.

Bubbles of white foam dribbled out of Uncle's mouth and I wanted to touch it but was afraid of Ah Mah. Besides, the two of them left no room for me to get in between. Ah Mah held Uncle's upper arm with one hand and kept pushing the bowl toward his mouth with the other.

"Let me go while I still have my honour and dignity. I want to choose my own fate."

But Ah Mah wouldn't stop pushing the bowl at him. Then the biggest shiver that I ever saw went through Uncle, and Ah Mah dropped the bowl. The little porcelain pieces looking like little flowers bounced off the paving stones and tinkled.

They put their arms around each other and Ah Mah started crying. Uncle had a beautiful sad smile on his face. I felt as if I should take my pretty petals and throw them into the air so they would fall like rain over him. As if a man like that belonged to the earth more than to himself.

Then my mother scooped me up in her arms and carried me away from the courtyard. She was shivering too. I looked over her shoulder for as long as I could. Uncle was lying on the paving stones now and Ah Mah was kneeling beside him, still crying. Uncle smiled at her and I thought he said, "Be at peace. This is my miah. I want to thank you for everything, Ma. I'm sorry if I wasn't a filial son." Ah Mah cried harder then. I saw her stroke his face.

I can't be certain but I think she must have done that until his eyes closed and the shivering stopped. But I was only a child then and memory is imperfect, like so much in life.

After the burial, when the white cloths were removed from the wall hangings in the worship area of the living room, I had seen, for the first time, a framed head-and-shoulder shot of an earnest dark-haired man with a direct gaze and serene expression. Imperfect though the process may be, I had fixed his image onto my brain.

Back home now after the funeral, I examine a faded black and white photograph, taken from my oldest album. I believe I can see his features under the bamboo hat now. I replace the faded print in the album and on the white label below the picture, next to the inscription "Tracy, age 5," I write "with Fifth Uncle, age 36." Next, I affix a copy of my grandmother's photograph on the page opposite, and wish I had with me a basket of pretty petals to throw on her. During my university days, I had been perplexed when I came upon the Japanese concept of *wabi-sabi,* perfect imperfection. Now, as I close the photo album, I finally understand *wabi-sabi.*

Ah-Ging

MEI XING AND HER NIECE, Ah-Ging, both young women, walked down the path to the pond, each balancing a straw basket of laundry against her hip. Ah-Ging led the way but occasionally stumbled over the sprawling roots of the banyan trees and would have fallen but for the steadying hand of her companion. The path had been soft with mud just yesterday but was now as hard-baked as Mei Xing had ever seen it in her eighteen years. The leaves of canna plants shimmered in the sunlight as the women brushed past the dense undergrowth beneath banana and mango trees. They reached a willow two metres away from the edge of the pond, dropped their baskets, and sat under the branches. Ah-Ging dabbed at her neck with a handkerchief from her trouser pocket.

Mei Xing fanned herself with the skirt of her dress and surveyed the pond. The sun's glare made it difficult to see the far bank. Flocks of quacking ducks and diving grebes circled the reeds nearby, but a glimmering mirror was all that was visible at the centre. She wiped her brow with the back of one hand, and thought the discomfort of the noontime heat a small price to pay for privacy—an earlier outing would have meant meeting the other village women.

She turned to Ah-Ging and said, "Tell me about him."

Her companion's eyes glowed and a faint blush, framed by her bobbed hair, suffused her mooncake face. "He's the most brilliant man I've met. And I'm not saying that just because he's my boyfriend either. All the other students think so too. Even the president of the University says, 'Young men are the future of Taiwan and we have a shining example right here.' Tell me, how many men are offered scholarships by American universities? And after their studies, how many PhDs come back to their homeland to be of service to their people, when they have opportunities overseas? He's taught me so much as my grad advisor. And when he gives a lecture, the halls are always filled. His enthusiasm is contagious. But, Ah Yi, the best thing is we love each other." Ah-Ging cast a sidelong glance at Huang Mei Xing and smiled shyly.

Mei Xing's step-sister, Huang Mei Lu—the first child born to Mei Xing's father and his official wife—had married a prosperous merchant named Chen in their village: a liberal man who had allowed his wife to visit her bedridden mother, and after the mother's death, to permit frequent visits between the two families. Three years older, Ah-Ging, Mei Lu's daughter, had grown up playing finger games and tag with her Aunt Mei Xing, running between her home in the village and the courtyard in the Huang family compound a hundred metres away.

During their childhood, Ah-Ging had spent many hours telling stories to Mei Xing, repeating her favourites without tiring. Mei Xing could recount *Xi xiang ji* and *Liang-Zhu* by the time she entered school, prompting her teacher to inquire how she had come upon love stories at the age of six. At lunchtime on certain days, her classmates would gather under the eaves and listen to Mei Xing tell of scholar Zhang's trials in *Xi xiang ji* (West Chamber Romance) as he strove to finally win the hand of the beautiful Oriole. On other days, the children would be transfixed by the famous legend of *Liang-Zhu* in which the impoverished scholar Liang Shanbo died of a broken heart after being thwarted from marrying Zhu Yingtai, the daughter of a wealthy nobleman. In the story, Zhu Yingtai visited her lover's grave one last time on the day she was to be married to a rich man. While she was crying bitterly at the tombstone, a clap of thunder suddenly split the tomb open, and the girl leaped into the exposed grave. The lovers, united, turned into butterflies, never to part again. At this point, Mei Xing would act out Zhu Yingtai's fatal leap by jumping off the lowest branch of the banyan tree in the schoolyard amid loud clapping from her friends.

Since Ah-Ging entered National Taiwan University four years ago (the occasion for a banquet that had cost her beaming father a week's earnings), aunt and niece had been able to see each other only during vacations, when Ah-Ging would come home from Taipei. She had returned this time for the April tomb-sweeping ceremonies.

"Here, give me your load. You can rest for a bit. I know you're still tired from your train ride."

Mei Xing dragged both baskets to the water's edge and emptied Ah-Ging's hamper into her own. Dresses, pants, shirts, blouses, and underwear cascaded down. A pile of bloodstained menstrual pads crested the heap of clothing.

"I see we're still on the same cycle. Regular as drumbeats," she remarked.

Tying her braids together, she squatted by a flat boulder. After soaking the pads, she lathered then scrubbed their cotton folds with a stone until no traces of red remained. Throwing the pads into Ah-Ging's basket, she tackled the rest of the load, careful to keep her footing on the bank; a woman had once drowned while doing her washing.

"His name is Wang Gaoliang and he speaks of such wonderful ideas. Things we can't even imagine here. Camelot. Civil rights. I didn't know what any of it was. I asked him, 'Is it like the Three Principles of the People?' He told me, 'Yes, but it's actually practised.' He worships the new American president: 'Ask not what your country can do for you; ask what you can do for your country.' Wang Gaoliang says our generation will change the way things are done in Taiwan. We're going to bring democracy to this country. We only need to find the courage. And I'm going to be with him every step of the way." Ah-Ging drew her legs up to her chest and hugged them.

Mei Xing dropped the shirt in her hand and hurried to Ah-Ging's side. "Shh . . . be careful! Lower your voice. You don't know who might be listening. People have been reported for saying far less. Only last month, a fisherman was arrested as a Communist spy, just because he said he could see the Mainland from where he was fishing and his boat could probably make it there in an hour."

She sat beside Ah-Ging and looked around. There was no one on the path that connected the family compound to the village. Mei Xing had never known Ah-Ging to be so indiscreet. Didn't she remember that her Fifth Uncle was in prison, on Green Island? Had she forgotten that there was still martial law in Taiwan, and there were government spies everywhere?

Mei Xing leaned forward and asked, "Do you speak so openly at school?"

"Only among friends. And of course when I'm alone with Wang Gaoliang," Ah-Ging paused, then flushed and lowered her eyes, but quickly collected herself.

"Oh, Ah Yi, you really have to get into the University. Study hard and pass the exam. I know you can do it. If I can get in as a literature major you will surely pass with your gift in math and science. Taipei is a different world. It'll open your eyes."

Ah-Ging hugged her aunt. "And who knows, maybe you'll meet your future husband there too."

"Are you really getting married? Have your parents consented?"

A frown crossed Ah-Ging's face. "Wang Gaoliang will ask them when they come to Taipei next month."

She suddenly brightened. "We're fated to be paired. We went to three fortune-tellers in Shi Lin night market a few weeks ago. The first performed Ba Zi. Our birthdates are well matched. Then we did the turtle divination. I asked if we were destined to be linked for life and the answer was 'inextricably.' The last was with the fortune-telling bird. It picked three cards and the reader said there was water in our futures. Maybe it means we'll go overseas later."

"Hey, didn't you scoff at this just a few months ago? A modern, educated woman like you doesn't believe in such superstitions. Isn't that what you said?"

Ah-Ging reddened and attempted a light-hearted laugh. "Well, it's all in fun, isn't it? Sometimes it's just comforting to know everything is preordained and will turn out for the best."

"You don't foresee any objections from your parents, do you?"

"Well . . . he's . . . *guah seung lung.*"

A Mainlander! Mei Xing gasped, her eyes widened.

"But don't worry. Wang Gaoliang will persuade them. It'll be just like *Xi xiang ji.*"

"I hope so, for your sake. As long as it's not like Liang-Zhu."

"Wang Gaoliang says we have to be optimistic. 'Amor vincit omnia,' he says. That's Latin. 'Love conquers all.'"

She fell silent for an instant then said, smiling, "Hey, did you know there's a Western version of Liang-Zhu? It's called Romeo and Juliet."

"Did those lovers turn into butterflies too?"

"No . . . they died."

Mei Xing wanted to believe that the couple would be able to overcome the hatred that Ah-Ging's parents bore against the Kuomintang government and, by association, all Mainlanders. She had always looked up to Ah-Ging. But when did her niece lose her common sense? How could she think that any Huang villager would be able to accept, let alone welcome, a *guah seung lung* into their family? The Huang clan would never forgive the government's so-called purchase of their farmland and Fifth Brother's arrest. Ah-Ging was foolish beyond belief. Did love really change people that much?

Mei Xing walked over to the pond's edge. Ah-Ging rolled up her pants and followed. A chorus of cicada song rose from a banana grove, signalling the hottest hours of the day. The young women worked without speaking.

"Well, I suppose we are all Chinese in the end. Our ancestors followed Koxinga from China centuries ago, didn't they? Maybe your parents will see that we are all from the same stock and be open-minded," Mei Xing said after a while, without much conviction.

"Yes! Maybe they will." Ah-Ging nodded in gratitude.

Just then, she caught sight of someone coming up the path from the village. "Oh, it's Didi."

Mei Xing looked up and saw Ah-Ging's seventeen-year-old brother swaggering towards them. The streaks of grey in his pomaded hair were so incongruous with his face that strangers often looked twice to determine whether he was a middle-aged man or a schoolboy. His hands were stuffed in his trousers and a sweaty T-shirt clung to his bony chest.

"Elder Sister, working hard as usual? Making me look bad again, heh?"

He stopped by the baskets and stood over them, a cigarette dangling from disdainful lips.

"You're not going to see Ah Mah again, are you?" Ah-Ging asked.

"Who's going to stop me if I am?"

Stepping back onto the path, he tramped up the short distance toward the red-tiled roofs of the family compound.

"Aiyah . . . I wish he would stop begging from Ah Mah," Ah-Ging said. "Everyone knows that he just spends the money on cigarettes, liquor, and gambling. I don't know why she keeps indulging him. Your mother is too generous."

"It's her money, I suppose. You know Okasan only does what she pleases. Maybe he'll improve when he turns eighteen and the government conscripts him. Three years of military service should mould him into a responsible man."

"I hope you're right. He's a good kid at heart . . . "

⌒

Mei Xing sat on a long bench at the kitchen table shaping two bamboo leaves into a cone, the first step in making *bah-zan,* Taiwanese rice dumplings. Okasan had charged her with preparing batches for their clan. The previous day, Ah-Ging had arrived for the Dragon Boat Festival, her first trip home in two months. She had promised to help Mei Xing wrap eighty *bah-zan.* Mei Xing glanced at her watch. Ah-Ging had been in the living room with her brother and Okasan for a quarter of an hour already. Sixty-four more dumplings still needed to be wrapped and each had to cook for three hours. If Ah-Ging didn't come back soon, they would be having dinner at midnight.

Mei Xing spooned some sticky rice with peanuts and dried shrimp into the cone, added a piece of stewed pork and a Shiitaki mushroom, then topped the dumpling with another layer of the rice blend. She carefully wrapped the ends of the bamboo leaves tight to close the *bah-zan,* shaping it to form a pyramid. She straightened herself and searched behind her through the cluster of dumplings that hung from a nail. The *bah-zan* were tied to string ends which emerged from a centre like the arms of an octopus. Picking up the last loose string, she attached to it the *bah-zan* in her hand, then dropped the bunch of eight dumplings into a vat which sat on top of the stove. Flames shot up as she threw in scraps of wood through the arched front of the brick stove.

She scooped five salted duck eggs out of a pot with a slotted ladle, removed the yolks, then dropped them into a bowl on the table for the next batch of *bah-zan.* Yolk-filled dumplings were a treat. If she and Ah-Ging had their way, all dumplings would have yolk fillings . . . maybe in the future, when their world changed and they were their own mistresses!

Mei Xing wiped her face on her sleeve and stretched her body. Stepping over the kitchen threshold, she stood in the courtyard looking up at the forbidding clouds looming over the hills; there had been typhoon warnings on the radio this morning, storms moving south from Taipei. A light wind played over the tops of the banana and mango trees that lined the path to the village. She shivered and turned back into the smoky haze of the kitchen.

Mei Xing unrolled a ball of string and cut eight long strands with a knife. She dipped the strands in a bucket of water to soften them, then gathered the eight ends together into a single knot. As she hung the bunch of cut strings over the nail, she thought about living in Taipei. She wanted to browse in the city shops, maybe even try on a miniskirt (though she would never buy one, of course). With luck, she might be able to catch a glimpse of the foreigners at the American military compound or the University campus. Her niece's descriptions of the "golden-haired" had made her curious to see the freckled, pointy-nosed people for herself. Failing that, movies featuring Marilyn Monroe or Elizabeth Taylor, in a theatre or on television, would do. Mei Xing imagined sitting in a late-night coffee shop with her classmates, passionately debating, free from parental scrutiny; she looked forward to tasting café au lait for the first time.

Last week, she had stolen away to the night market in the town and found a fortune-teller. The man had asked her to sprinkle grains of rice into three bowls and assured her that the patterns spelled out an illustrious future in higher education. Nevertheless, Mei Xing resolved to study even harder for the university entrance exam.

But she told herself she would not be as foolish as Ah-Ging was in Taipei. She would remember the lessons learned at home: circumspection in all dealings and respect for tradition. She would honour her parents' wishes when it came to marriage. And when she had children, she would teach them folk legends such as the story about the origin of rice dumplings. "Gather close, children, and let me tell you about the noble poet Qu Yuan, a great patriot, who once lived in the kingdom of Chu, a part of China long, long ago. Banished from court, thanks to jealous and corrupt rivals, he travelled the land and was much loved by the people. Upon learning that enemy troops had taken the capital, he jumped into the Milou River in despair. The grieving peasants got into their dragon boats, beating their drums, and threw *bah-zan* into the river to prevent the fish from nibbling at his body." And her children would take pride in their heritage. And she would pass on Okasan's family recipe for *bah-zan* to her daughters. Mei Xing returned to the table and picked up two more leaves.

She wondered what was keeping Ah-Ging and Didi. In the past, whenever Didi came to the compound, he would speak with Okasan for a few minutes before leaving with a bulge in his pocket and a whistle on his lips, satisfied that he would be able to finance his indulgences for a few more weeks. Ah-Ging, though quietly disapproving of her brother's habits, had never gotten involved before. But then, she hadn't been herself all day.

Earlier in the afternoon, as they had often done, aunt and niece were washing clothes at the pond. As they squatted on the bank, one on each side of their boulder, vigorously soaping and scrubbing, Mei Xing had sensed a tension in her niece but didn't know what to make of it. Their conversation was superficial and awkward. At one point, Mei Xing said, "Ah-Ging, you don't have pads to wash today? Is your cycle different from mine now?"

Her niece looked up, dropped a clean shirt in the laundry basket, then covered her face and sobbed. Alarmed, Mei Xing eased her into the shade of the willow and rocked Ah-Ging in her arms. "Tell me what's wrong!"

The words came tumbling out then. Her parents had refused permission for her to marry Wang Gaoliang. They had selected a native Taiwanese from a nearby village who was "more suitable" and were encouraging her to consider her future carefully. "You can never trust a Mainlander. Don't know when they might turn on you," they'd said. "Look at how many Taiwanese have died at their hands. Betrayed after placing their trust in a *guah seung lung*. No, it's better to stick to our own kind. People we can count on."

Mei Xing retrieved a wet handkerchief from one of the baskets and wiped her niece's face, feeling helpless in the face of such distress.

Ah-Ging said huskily, "But that's not the worst part. Last month, Wang Gaoliang was arrested and sent to Green Island. He's been sentenced to twenty years."

"Oh no!"

"Yes. Charged with sedition. The government slogan, 'Better to kill ten thousand in error than let one go by mistake' strikes again." She laughed bitterly. "Oh, why do I have such a cursed fate?"

Mei Xing held her until the heaving subsided.

⌒

Ah-Ging sat back in the pedicab and wished for a toothbrush. Though she had rinsed her mouth with water from her canteen, the acrid taste lingered. Having successfully fended off several attacks of nausea over the last weeks, she had thought she would be able to escape motion sickness during the hour-long ride to Green Island; but the boat had pitched and rolled, and she had expelled her breakfast over the sides.

When she climbed into the cab, the driver had carried on a cheerful banter as he pedalled away from the dock to the heart of the island. Did you know, Miss, our hot springs are one of only three salt-water springs in the world? You should see our reefs and cliffs too while you're here. And look at those houses there—made of coral, the whole length of them. Oh, to the prison, Miss? Oh, I'm sorry. Then, mercifully, he had fallen silent.

Peering over the shoulders of the wiry man, she could see the spiky tops of screw pines scattered over the lush green of the craggy hills. Mulberry bushes and white lilies colonized what appeared at first glance to be infertile volcanic rocks by the roadside. Acacias and macarangas filled the spaces in between to provide resting places for butterflies and moths. A water buffalo raised its head from a muddy bath as they passed, while his mate placidly continued grazing in the fields. Ah-Ging breathed in the sharp, salt-tinged air and stilled her trembling hands, determined to present a picture of calm upon arrival.

As they neared the prison gates, the pounding of the ocean waves upon the shores became louder and she could make out gigantic rock formations along the coastline. Shaped like oxen and ancient warriors they jutted out from the white sands and turquoise waters. A battery of square buildings came into view. She pulled a mirror from her purse and nervously patted her hair in place.

Alighting from the pedicab, Ah-Ging asked the driver to wait outside the gates. A guard checked her identity papers and granted her entry. She looked up at the high walls topped by coils of barbed wire. The first political prisoners had built the fortifications to enclose their own cells, each rock carried up from Kungkuan Beach by the barefoot men. She shuddered and pulled her light sweater close about her dress and plodded across the scorching yard into the visitors' room.

A mother with two young boys stood at the glass barrier separating visitors from the inmates. The man behind the glass was speaking to them in a strained voice; a guard stood next to him. The woman held back tears and the children looked frightened and confused.

Ah-Ging chose a spot out of earshot of the family and waited for Wang Gaoliang. She didn't know how she was going to tell him, but she must. Shadows of passing clouds drifted through the high windows on the inmate side of the barrier and skittered across the dingy walls of the room.

When he shuffled through the far door, accompanied by a guard, Ah-Ging wasn't certain who he was. For a few moments, she thought they had brought in the wrong inmate. Then she realized what was amiss. Dressed in prison attire, the pale-looking man now approaching her was not wearing his horn-rimmed glasses. His hair had grown past his chin and he wore a scraggly beard. She longed to touch him through the glass.

"Gaoliang . . . " She couldn't think of what to say.

"Ah-Ging, thank you for coming but I'm sorry you came." He cast his eyes down. The guard clicked on a tape recorder and checked his watch.

"Please don't say that. I'll wait for you."

"No, don't. Marry someone else. You're still a young woman. Don't squander your life on a hopeless case like me."

"Please. Is there something I can do for you? Something I can bring you? New glasses, perhaps?"

"No. My family is taking care of that. I don't want you to come back. Do you understand?"

"Gaoliang, wait a moment!"

"Go now. Forget me." He nodded at the guard, then turned and walked to the door.

⌒

Mei Xing rose and tied up a dumpling. She stepped into the courtyard with a wooden bucket and crossed over to the well in the centre of the compound. Moving the cover aside, she lowered a tin pail into the water. Ah-Ging's revelations had brought back memories of Fifth Brother's arrest. The police had drawn water from this same well to quench their thirst the night they took him. There were three of them, in uniform, their features indistinct in the waning moonlight. The tall one with the rifle did the talking while the other two held a bellicose Fifth Brother between them. When Fifth Brother denied involvement in the Luku incident, the tall one threw the water in his face.

"My son would not rise up against the government. He's only a seventeen-year-old boy. Please have mercy," Okasan pleaded, plucking on the man's sleeve, sobbing.

"We have witnesses. Now get out of my way." He pushed her aside.

Fifth Brother was sentenced to fifteen years. Every month, Okasan would take the train and then the ferry eastward to Green Island. The one time Mei Xing had accompanied her was her last. She had only been allowed to go when she turned thirteen, a year into Fifth Brother's sentence, but the sight of her proud brother reduced to a limping skeleton in prison garb had so disturbed her that Mei Xing couldn't make herself return no matter how much she loved him. She didn't know how Okasan could go back repeatedly to "Oasis Villas." Even the name of the prison stuck in her throat. And now Ah-Ging had made the same trip. Mei Xing shrugged off the thought and returned to the kitchen.

She carefully emptied the bucket into the steaming vat. How many times had Okasan stood here and prepared chickens for the offerings . . . to ask her gods to protect her loved ones? And her incessant search for unblemished fruits—peaches, pears, wax apples, mangoes, lichees, strawberries—so she could keep taking her four-fruit offerings to temple, to implore the gods to guard her fifth son. Wouldn't it have been more practical to save the money to bribe some government official instead, perhaps to get a reduced sentence for Fifth Brother? Instead she prayed to her deities, resigned to her son's fate, believing that Heaven's will would prevail and her interference in what was pre-destined would alter little; but she held out hope that her appeals to the gods might afford her son safety. Mei Xing sat down and spooned rice mix into a leaf cone.

There came a clatter from the living room, followed by Okasan's yelling. Dashing to the threshold, she saw her nephew tromping past the kitchen, a frown on his face, Ah-Ging at his heels.

"Standing up for that good-for-nothing brat! Nobody from your family will ever cross my threshold again. Do you hear me?" Okasan shouted after Ah-Ging from the doorway.

Ah-Ging marched toward the path, retorting, "My brother is not a thief! And I'll tell you something else. If you think your son is coming back alive from Green Island, you're a fool! You'll be lucky if you see his burnt bones. You won't even see a speck of his ashes, I tell you!"

Tears streamed down Okasan's face as she went across the courtyard to her bedroom, her tall frame bent, black hair flying out of her bun.

Mei Xing stood open-mouthed, rice trickling through her fingers, and watched Ah-Ging and her brother run along the path into the village. A clamorous wind whipped Ah-Ging's dress and Didi's shirt tight against their bodies. The leaves on the banana and mango trees shuddered as a sloping drizzle struck, the tree trunks standing firm against the rising wind.

⌒

Ah-Ging went back to the University the following day. Okasan forbade any mention of the Chen family in her presence and Mei Xing from further contact with them. Despite her mother's edict, Mei Xing wrote an explanatory letter to her niece but received no reply.

⌒

Years later, at an age when Mei Xing found herself chronically astonished by the naiveté of youth, she would hang tangles of cut strings on wooden coat pegs as she had done years ago and drop clusters of *bah-zan* into a stainless steel pot in her Vancouver kitchen. Sometimes, she would recall words from Bo Yang's "Cries on Green Island" and hope that the survivors from the thousands of political prisoners incarcerated from 1951 to the late 1980s, had found some consolation in the government's construction of the Human Rights Monument on Green Island. That the expressions of regret and promises to "correct the mistakes of the past" from a democratically elected government would help diminish the rage and anguish of the former prisoners. Then she would shake her head and reproach herself for thinking that wounds so deep could ever heal. At other times, she would wonder if Ah-Ging had ever received her letter and, if she had, if she had decided not to respond; or if Okasan had somehow, despite being illiterate, intercepted Ah-Ging's reply—perhaps recognizing her feminine script on an envelope drawn from the green mailbox on the family compound while Mei Xing was at school. On those occasions, Mei Xing would fill all the *bah-zan* with salted duck yolks.

⌒

Almost three months after Ah-Ging's falling-out with Okasan, Mei Xing heard that her niece had returned to Huang village for the Autumn Moon Festival. The village gossips said Ah-Ging was shut up in her parents' house; no one had seen her since she disembarked from the train in a loose, paisley dress. Rumour further had it that she had quit university and was home for good. And that Wang Gaoliang had been shot dead while attempting to escape from Green Island. Okasan rejected her daughter's request to see Ah-Ging, and Mei Xing dared not disobey.

As she squatted beside the flat boulder with the day's washing by her side and the sun on her back, Mei Xing wished Ah-Ging was on the other side of the rock. A pair of grebes splashed loudly when they landed near their nest in the reeds a few metres from shore. Mei Xing looked up and sighted what appeared to be paisley cloth among the reeds. The cloth, caught in the tangled grasses, bobbed up and down. Mei Xing craned her neck and squinted but the grebes obstructed her view. She gathered up her skirt and waded carefully into the pond, frightening the grebes into sudden flight. Before she had taken two steps, she saw the swollen hand next to the cloth. Mei Xing screamed. A sound full of horror, despair, and limitless anger.

The Colonel and Mrs Wang

"DID YOU HEAR?" Mrs Chang whispered in alarm, leaning closer to me as we walked from her house towards Roosevelt Road, "Mrs Tang's husband 'disappeared' last night."

I hoped that my face did not betray my fear.

Mrs Chang looked at me intently but continued after a short pause, "They came in the middle of the night, as usual. I knew it would just be a matter of time. Tang always had a big mouth."

The lane was quiet except for the rhythmic squishing of our rain shoes in the mud and the warning peals of bicycle bells from pedicabs as they passed us. The thundershower had lasted two hours and the air smelled fresh—as it always did afterwards, despite occasional whiffs from the open sewers. Though I had been in Taiwan province since 1949, I still couldn't get used to weather that fluctuated between sudden rain and fierce sunshine. I had not seen snow in the thirteen years since I left Peking and would often dream of it during sleepless summer nights in Taipei. I looked around cautiously, just in case, but saw only wet azalea bushes next to concrete walls topped with fragments of coloured glass glinting in the late afternoon sun—protective barriers for the Japanese-style one-story homes behind them. There was no threat of being overheard so I looked encouragingly at my companion.

"Mrs Tang is beside herself. She's gone to the police station but they say they have no knowledge of his arrest. That's a bad sign. If they were going to try him, they would have put him on record. She's afraid they've already killed him," Mrs Chang said. She shifted the bundle of clothing on her back and tsked, shaking her head. "It's too sad. Such a bad fate."

I reassured myself that Gaoliang would be safe; my son had not spent enough time with Mr Tang to be considered an associate. Holding tight to my umbrella, I asked casually, "Do you know if he has implicated anyone else?"

"Heaven only knows. We'll find out how much they tortured out of him when we see who gets arrested next."

We made our way to the end of the lane in silence. Coming out onto the main road, we walked in the mud next to the gutters, keeping out of the way of bicycles and the odd private car. At Gongguan market, the street vendors were already setting up their stalls for the evening—steam rising up from the noodle-sellers' metal vats, oil sizzling on hot griddles. Aromas of fried chicken and roasted nuts mingled with the smells of scallion pancakes and grilled squid. We turned into an alleyway towards Mrs Chang's shop.

Mrs Chang unlocked the metal door and went and dropped her bundle on the table at the back of the narrow room. I wheeled a rusty clothes rack of dresses out the door, parking it under the awning. We were so used to our routines that neither of us spoke; there would be plenty of time for chatter during the lulls between customers. Mrs Chang unwrapped the bundle and handed a silk qipao to me.

"Some sequins and seed pearls should do it, I think, Fen-Fen. And your special embroidery of course."

Mrs Chang had managed to make a lean living from her clothing shop for the last decade—altering second-hand clothes and reselling them to bargain-hunters in the night market. The store provided her with enough to live on and school fees for her son but not much more. After Major Chang died of a heart attack when the boy was only three, the daluren (Mainlander) community had taken up a collection for her and she had used it to set up the shop. Mrs Chang couldn't afford help in the store but I offered my services as a friend, though she pressed the occasional cash "gift" into my hand.

I took my work basket from a shelf and sat down at the table. While Mrs Chang sorted the rest of the clothes we'd brought, I chalked out a lotus blossom design on the pink silk of the qipao. My mother had instructed me in all the womanly arts since girlhood—grooming me to be the wife of a wealthy man—never imagining that the lessons in music and fine embroidery at our home in Peking would be put to use in this way. At my father's insistence, she had reluctantly agreed to my marriage to an up-and-coming officer, Wang Aiguo, a graduate of the prestigious Whampoa military academy headed by Generalissimo Chiang.

My father had said of Captain Wang at the time of my betrothal, "As an officer in the ruling party, he'll protect you in these uncertain times. And be a shield for the rest of our family as well."

My father had proven to be prescient: Wang had risen in the army ranks and, as a newly promoted colonel, used his connections to make it possible for us to escape Peking with my parents and two sisters, ahead of the Communist hordes, and go south to Nanking before crossing the Strait to Taipei—each of us with a single suitcase, weighed down by gold bars and jewellery sewn into the linings of our clothing. Unlike so many of the military and civilian daluren, we were fortunate to leave before travel between Taiwan province and the Mainland became prohibited for four decades, leaving families on both sides of the Strait wondering if they would ever see their loved ones again.

Seated next to the tall, muscular captain, sipping wine from silver cups at our wedding banquet, I had been convinced of the wisdom of my father's choice. During the ceremonies, three "wishes" were chanted by my matron of honour: may the couple grow old together; may the bridegroom sing and the bride harmonize; and may the newlyweds be blessed with many children. I resolved then to be a wife even Confucius would approve of and threw myself into making a home for my husband where he was Heaven to my Earth. According to the great Confucian thinker, Mencius, the greatest unfilial act is the failure to produce a son to continue a family's line. With Gaoliang's birth, I helped Aiguo escape that dreaded fate. I only regretted that we were unable to have more children.

Mrs Chang shook out a dress from the bundle and said, "Fen-Fen, nobody can compete with you when it comes to embroidery. The woman who bought your last creation came back to thank me yesterday; she was so pleased. When we get back to Peking, you should start an embroidery school."

"No, Hua-Ling, when we go home, my husband will be given a fat commission with loads of benefits and I will be a lady of leisure. And I will find a good husband for you too, just you wait and see."

Mrs Chang laughed and sat down beside me to rip open the hem of the dress in her hands. "I'm too old for such foolishness. Not everyone can have your good fate and be so lucky in the choice of a husband. I'll be happy when my son finds a good job and gets married. Then I can rest."

As the threads started breaking, she said, "Do you remember how we used to shop for dress materials at Ruifuxiang Silk Store?"

"Oh yes, I certainly do. Who can forget how we made our mothers take one rickshaw while we piled into another? Our sisters were always so much fun. I can't believe the five of us all fit into one rickshaw. And the way our mothers bargained with the shopkeepers! I learned a lot from watching them. And do you remember we would walk down to Wuyutai teashop and drink peach-blossom tea afterwards?"

I can never forget the paved streets of Peking, crowded with rickshaws, bicycles, trolleys, horse-drawn carts, and sometimes even a laden camel. I can still picture the bustling markets and shops in my mind. The imposing buildings of all the international banks: Banque de l'Indochine, Chartered Bank of England, National Bank of New York, and the Hong Kong and Shanghai Banking Corporation where my father was a senior manager in the days before the fighting started, first during the war against Japan, then our civil war.

My favourite outings back then were to a park just west of Tiananmen. Although it was renamed Zhongshan Park in 1928 after Sun

Yat-Sen, I'll always think of my old haunt as the "Altar to Soil and Grain" no matter what new name has been given to it. The peonies, pine trees, cypresses, and wisterias will always seem to me a more fitting tribute to the gods of nature than to a politician, even one as revered as Dr Sun. Of course, I would never voice such thoughts; even a woman understands that.

I yearned for the home that I had not seen for over a decade. When Generalissimo Chiang led us to Taiwan province in 1949, none of us thought we would stay for long. Who could have foreseen that America would interfere and "neutralize the Straits of Formosa?" We should have been back in Peking long ago. I asked Aiguo why our troops had not attacked yet. He told me the issues involved were too complex for women to understand, the men would act when the time was right. He said we would "retake the Mainland" soon and our suffering on this island would be over—no more resentful looks from the locals, no more feelings of displacement—we would be home at last.

~

"You may well look sceptical at my recollections, Amy, but I assure you that they are accurate even though the events took place almost forty years ago," I said to my foreign-born niece, daughter of my younger sister, Chu-Hua.

We were seated outside my shack, shucking corn for dinner, taking refuge from the blistering late afternoon sun. She had been my guest for nearly three days, but I was still reeling from astonishment. Not only because she had managed to find me in Li-Shan village but that she had taken the trouble to search at all. Overseas Chinese do not often return to ferret out lost members of their extended families, especially ones who left no forwarding addresses with their relatives in Taipei. Amy had said that she was working on an oral history of our family for a university thesis. "The record would not be complete without your story, Auntie," she said. "It wasn't easy finding you but thankfully there are very few practitioners of Peking embroidery in Taiwan these days. It's fortunate that Mrs Chang keeps a record of specialty seamstresses. It was a stroke of luck to find her in Taipei." I'd smiled uneasily, unsure whether her success was good fortune or bad. At the mention of my old friend, a surge of surprise and annoyance had arisen; Chang Hua-Ling should have asked my permission before divulging my whereabouts, or at least warned me about her intentions. But upon reflection I am grateful that Hua-Ling kept my secret for so long despite my silence.

Many daluren fled to the West soon after landing in Taiwan. It seemed, for the most part, only the less wealthy or the poorly connected stayed behind. I am glad that my sister found the means to escape to a better life in New York. Her children can count on peaceful lives where they are.

"It's just hard for me to imagine what sort of restrictions you must have been under as women," Amy said, shifting her weight on the low stool beside me. She had left off typing on her laptop when she saw me come home with the corn and jumped to help.

"We didn't see them as restrictions. They were a normal part of life. All our friends were treated the same way by their families. Men were segregated from women: we didn't eat together or sit in the same room for idle talk. Even our laundry was separated from the men's and boys'. The only virtuous woman, before the reforms were introduced, was an untalented one. Women were kept illiterate. It may be hard for you to understand our ways back then but they were quite common."

Amy shook her head in wonder, placing a bare ear of corn into the basket at my feet. She swatted at a fly buzzing near her ear.

"Your mother and I were lucky to be born after the Republic was established. We were sent to school and taught to read and write. But even in our time, the better class of Peking families still found it hard to give up the old Confucian ways. Centuries-old customs do not die easily. Our parents demanded absolute obedience from their daughters. You know when the Republic was formed, don't you?"

"Yes, of course. 1912," Amy said with a note of impatience. "And I know all about Sun Yat-Sen, the father of the Republic of China, too. And how Chiang Kai-Shek took over the leadership of the Nationalist party and then retreated to Taiwan after the civil war. And how the Kuomintang has ruled the island as a military dictatorship since then. It's not the story of modern China that I'm interested in. It's your story. And that of your husband and son too, of course."

"I'll do my best by you, Niece."

But even with the best intentions, I knew that there were incidents—out of loyalty to my husband—that I could never reveal. It was no one else's business to know about his flare-ups—the times when the pressures of life overwhelmed him. The moments that cannot bear remembering.

"My husband has had a hard life. He came from a poor family and pulled himself up the ranks solely on the strength of character and ability. Life in the military is not easy, you know. And coming to a foreign province. He suffered greatly from homesickness at the beginning. It was a harsh blow when the borders closed and he never saw his parents or other relatives again. But he was very good to my parents and your mother. We were his family after that."

It all seemed so long ago, more than a lifetime, surely. The young girl who married Captain Wang is no more; replaced by this old woman cognizant of the contrasts between her former, conservative life and her modern existence, but who is also aware that vestiges of her old values remain. I hoped that Amy would ask her fill and return to her alien life across the waters very soon, for I was weary.

"Auntie, my mother told me all about you shortly before she died. In fact, part of the reason that I came here was because she has always been worried about you. It made her sad that she left Taiwan without saying goodbye to you. She always meant to come back and look for you. In the end, she sent me instead. I didn't find you in time though. It's too bad; she would have been glad to know that you were happy."

Amy took the full basket and brought it into my shack. She returned and sat on the stool, taking my hands between hers.

"Auntie, I know you didn't have an easy life with the Colonel. My mother told me about her suspicions."

I jerked my hands from her grasp. "You won't write about it, will you? Family business should stay within the family."

"No, I promise you. Your part in my thesis will be very general. I'm just going to list bare facts. Only tell me what you feel comfortable divulging. I won't embarrass you. My mother has taught me that much. I would never shame the family."

I looked at my niece, one of my few claims to kinship now. Perhaps, after all these years, it was time for someone else to know.

My son pushed open the wooden gate and we walked into the courtyard, past the camphor and osmanthus trees to the low-slung cottage. Unlocking the door, we shook off raindrops from our umbrellas and plastic raincoats, politely making way for each other on the wooden floor of the passageway. I rooted out some slippers for him from the row of footwear by the raised entryway of the Japanese bungalow. He set down the bag of fruits and vegetables from the market. It felt strange that he was not living with me, preferring instead to occupy a rented room in a house next to Taida (National Taiwan University) where he was an associate professor. When Mrs Chang asked why our son was not living at home like the other children of the military personnel in our neighbourhood, I told her, "Oh, you know these modern young people. They want their independence," rather than tell her about my son's relationship with his father.

I walked down the passageway and slid open the door into the sitting room. Usually the wide windows in the passage provided ample light for the entire house but this evening the windows were covered by rain boards, so I switched on a desk lamp before bringing in a pot of tea. We sat on the squat couch in front of a low tea table and spoke of his classes and the state of my flower garden. Then my son matter-of-factly announced his intention to marry a university student with the family name of Chen, a girl from a village in the south, near Tainan.

"Gaoliang, I don't want to tell you what to do with your life. But are you sure? A native Taiwanese?"

He folded his arms. His jaws were set in the way that I knew so well. He had looked this way the day he told his father that he was going to study abroad. At that time, he hadn't even gotten word of his acceptance at Stanford. When his father asked him where the money was coming from, Gaoliang didn't have an answer. Luckily, he had gotten a scholarship and earned his PhD in American Literature. He'd lived up to his name: High Bright Light. Everyone was amazed at his masterful command of English. Even Aiguo joined in the bragging when we got word of Gaoliang's successful doctoral defence. That was one time when the Colonel had "face" in front of his cronies.

Gaoliang pushed up his horn-rimmed glasses and looked me in the eyes. "Yes, I love her. I'm going to ask her parents for consent when they come to Taipei next week."

I shuffled my slippered feet on the tatami mat and trusted Heaven to direct my son on his path. When it came to major decisions in the family, I subscribed to old-fashioned Confucian values: a woman ruler is like a hen crowing. I poured more tea for us and set the pot, its cracks mended with staples, down on the table.

"I'll leave it to you and your father."

The lamp flickered and I looked up, then my eyes rested on the two familiar photographs that stood on the shelf above the old wooden desk. The first was Aiguo's most treasured possession: a faded black and white picture of the stern-looking Generalissimo Chiang next to my young husband, both uniformed men standing proud in the days before their retreat to Taiwan province. The photo, taken in Nanking, showed a nervous Aiguo saluting his hero for the first time—the dark stain under his arm visible if one knows where to look. The second frame held a family photograph. In the ten-year-old picture, Aiguo and I sit smiling in the foreground while Gaoliang stands behind, his right hand on my shoulder and his left in his pocket.

A sudden fear gripped me and I knew I had to speak.

"Gaoliang, there is something that concerns me greatly. I'm sure you've heard Mr Tang has been taken. Well . . . I'm really worried about you."

"Don't worry, Ma. I may be outspoken but I'm not careless. I only speak my mind when it's safe."

"But all your talk about democracy. These are dangerous times."

"The time is coming for a change. Democracy will come to Taiwan and I'm going to be a part of it."

At this point, a baritone boomed from the doorway. "Stay out of things you know nothing about!"

The Colonel marched barefoot onto the tatami mat, wearing the undershirt and comfortable slacks that he reserved for off-work hours. He always changed from his uniform upon his return from the army offices each day in order to maintain the stiffness in the collar and the creases in the pants between cleanings.

Gaoliang stood and faced his father, standing half a head taller than the grey-haired man. "Baba, good evening."

"I don't ever want you talking like that again in my house, do you hear?"

My husband strode past him to the desk, unlocked a drawer and, with his back toward us, withdrew a wad of cash. Aiguo only came back for money in the middle of a mahjong game when he was losing. Though we could ill afford the losses, my husband continued his weekly games, preferring to scrimp elsewhere rather than to lose face in front of other officers. From his agitated manner, I was certain he was faring particularly badly. I turned to Gaoliang, put a finger to my lips, and shook my head. He moved closer to his father.

My son said, "Like what? Like the Three Principles of the People? Nationalism, democracy, socialism. Isn't that what the Kuomintang stands for?"

Aiguo turned and sputtered, "Don't you ever talk against the government!"

"I'm not talking against the government. I'm just repeating what the government supposedly believes. Of course, nobody ever said anything about years of martial law being part of the Principles."

Aiguo put his red face up to Gaoliang's.

"Don't you get smart with me. Generalissimo Chiang is doing what needs to be done to control the Taiwanese rabble."

"Sure. Putting people in prison on trumped-up charges. There's a real leader for you."

"Gaoliang, please don't talk to your father like that."

"You stay out of this. This is men's business." My husband glared at me.

"Yeah, a real man. Do you know the Americans laugh at your government's ambitions? Do you really think that your puny Kuomintang forces will be able to overcome the Communists?"

"We will! We will take back the Mainland and liberate our compatriots!"

"Empty slogans, old man. Wake up. The only reason the Maoists haven't overrun this island is because of American protection. Let go of your pipe dream."

"Don't you dare talk to me like that, you . . . you traitor!"

Aiguo raised his hand as if to strike Gaoliang.

I couldn't keep quiet any longer. "Please, please, stop!"

When I regained consciousness, Gaoliang was leaning over me, dabbing at the corner of my mouth with a bloodied face cloth, the anger in his eyes still undiminished. "The bastard's gone back to the Lees to get drunk and lose more money."

He helped me up onto the couch and said, "Why don't you leave him, Ma? I'll support you. I've got a job now. It's time I do my filial duty."

I pitied my son for his lack of understanding. "Gaoliang, this is my fate. Anyway, he's not so bad. There are husbands who are far worse. You didn't know him when we first got married. He telegraphed me from every town where the army stopped. He counted the days until he could come home on leave. And the atrocities that he saved us from. The suffering of those poor people in Nanking at the hands of the Japanese! Your father kept us from all that. He had foresight. We're lucky to be alive. How can I leave him after all he's done? Besides, your father would never be able to accept the loss of face. He would never let me leave."

Gaoliang allowed me to caress his face.

"Try and understand his position. He became a revolutionary because he wanted a united China. A modern China free from Western and Japanese imperialism. A country without warlords and secret societies. Generalissimo Chiang delivered that. He unified China. Your father is as loyal to the Generalissimo as the Generalissimo was to Dr Sun. Try and understand your father's impotence while he's waiting for military action . . . These days, his favourite poet is Lu You. Do you remember who he is?"

Gaoliang shook his head.

"One of the patriotic poets from the Song dynasty. He wrote, 'My wish to become the Great Wall in the frontier has yet to be fulfilled/ While my hair has already turned to grey in the mirror.' No, Gaoliang. I cannot leave him."

My son looked at me with frustration and sadness then turned away without another word. Despite my exhortations to him to stay for dinner, Gaoliang said he wasn't hungry and left abruptly, leaving a lonely silence behind.

I paced the passageway and ended in front of the only room in the house that I could call my own. Sliding open the door to reveal the small altar in the corner of the storage room, I knelt in front of the Buddha and bowed my head. I prayed to be a good Buddhist: one who does not complain, one who is not angry. I thanked the Good Buddha for giving me a home, a husband, a son. I prayed to be worthy of Heaven's blessings. I prayed until I could no longer sustain coherent thoughts.

Early morning found me curled in front of the altar, my tear-stained face marked with tatami mat indentations, my body stiff. I lit an incense stick and chanted mantras with my mala between two hands, comforted by the familiar feel of the wooden beads, finishing only when starling and thrush songs urged me to rise and start a coal fire in preparation for Aiguo's return.

⌒‿

My husband and I walked hand-in-hand past the gates of Taida, at the southern edge of Taipei. Gaoliang took his undergraduate degree here, carrying his bookbag daily from our home a few blocks away. Beyond the gates, I caught a glimpse of the red brick buildings where my son would never again enter.

The funeral rites had been performed the day before. I had gazed upon his still face before they nailed the coffin shut. We had been unable to replace his glasses prior to his death and Gaoliang's face had seemed as vulnerable as when he slept in his cradle. The navy suit and white shirt hid his bullet-ridden body and he looked like the young professor that he had been.

When I visited him at the holding prison while he was awaiting trial, Gaoliang had told me of the night sounds he could hear from his cell: squealing jeep brakes bringing new prisoners; inhuman cries from tormented men and women; names of stellar Taida students being called, followed by gunshots outside. I'd stopped my ears and begged him not to tell me any more. It was a relief to know that he would be imprisoned for twenty years on Green Island—and he would live. I never dreamed he would try to escape.

Aiguo and I walked along the dirt-paved road beside the university and saw children frolicking near the grassy banks of the canal that ran alongside the road, parents and grandparents keeping vigilant watch over their charges. Beyond the canal, carefully tended rice paddies boasted rows of stalks ready for harvest. We sauntered past a store advertising goods for the Mid-Autumn Moon Festival—lanterns, incense, pomeloes. A poster with the moon goddess, Chang'e, was prominently displayed over a glistening array of mooncakes in the store window. Mooncakes were Gaoliang's favourite treats when he was young; I used to set aside the ones with egg-filled centres, allowing him to have more than a quarter portion at a time, unperturbed by what other mothers thought of my coddling. As we entered the alley leading to our home, I imagined the families gathering in the houses behind the concrete walls, with sons and daughters who had returned home for the Festival, from cities around the island, or even from overseas, sharing the joy of family reunion that

I would never again know.

In our sitting room, Aiguo rested on a rattan chair, his arms hanging at his sides, his head drooping. I bent over him and hugged his head to my chest, blinking back tears. After a week of frantic funeral activities, the full realization of our loss finally descended on me in this hour alone with my husband.

I smoothed his grizzled head and moaned, "I always thought our son would take care of us in our old age. What is to become of us? Why did he have to get involved with men like Tang? Men like that can't be trusted. Couldn't he see that? Oh . . . that Tang! Why did he have to denounce our son? Curses on his next life!"

Aiguo pressed his head against me and croaked, "It wasn't Tang . . . "

"Then who else could it be?" I cried, stepping back to look into his face.

Aiguo looked startled. He hesitated then said, "Uh . . . I don't know. It must have been Tang. Who else could it have been?"

Then he turned his face away, biting his lower lip. Tears trickled down his face as he stroked my forearms.

I dropped my arms. My feet backed off of their own accord over the tatami mats. I could not breathe, a tight band encircled my chest, mercilessly squeezing my heart. Try as I might, I could not look at Aiguo as I closed the door on his piteous sobbing.

⌒

It has been many years since Peking was renamed Beijing by the Communists, and I no longer think about returning to my ancestral home. Taiwan remains an island unto itself and none of the Kuomintang followers harbour illusions about "retaking the Mainland." Though the government now allows travel to the Mainland, I do not have the means to do so.

I have not had contact with the Taipei daluren since the day I took all that belonged to me—my clothes, the gold bracelets and pearl earrings from my trousseau, the money I saved from my labours at the clothing shop, my workbasket—and came to this farming village where no other daluren ever visit. Even my parents and sisters do not know where I am. The only exception was Chang Hua-Ling—she had helped me start my embroidery business in the early years but I thought Hua-Ling would have lost my address by now. For years, I did not care that my husband had lost face through my abandonment; I desired only to escape from the tyranny of expectations—my husband's, my parents', and those of the other daluren. But, with the passage of time, I suppose secrecy is no longer necessary.

In my shack, an altar with a statue of the Buddha sits on a wooden platform beside an incense burner. Every morning and evening, I light incense sticks and pray. Some days I pray for wisdom. Other days, I pray for forgiveness. Having stymied fate in departing from my preordained path, I can only ask for mercy from the gods when they choose my next incarnation. I am prepared to suffer for my wrongdoings in this lifetime: for not honouring my husband, for choosing my own fate. I chant mantras with a fearful heart, my fingers clicking over the wooden beads, knowing I am an unworthy novice, but still feeling soothed by the familiar words and the smoothness of the worn beads.

On days when I feel more audacious, when my thoughts stray toward Aiguo, I try and understand what had prompted his actions and wonder how he is, but I invariably fall into confusion and have to retreat into the comforting routines that I have fashioned over the last forty years. Once, when I was very daring, I thought perhaps I was on my destined path, but then I quickly realized that fate would not be so cruel as to deprive my husband of both a son and a wife, only my wilfulness could cause him such pain, and I turned again to my prayer beads and incense sticks.

On nights when the rice stalks are heavy with the golden grain and the moon shines in cloudless skies, I walk through the sleeping village, remembering the paddies near the house in Taipei and the stores with trays of mooncakes. I pretend that two lifetimes have been granted to me in my present incarnation, the first ending with the happy return of my son from abroad and the second beginning with my arrival in this village. I have carved out a place here among the rural folk of southern Taiwan, in a valley where the villagers indulge my peculiar habit of sequestering myself before the Autumn Moon Festival.

"The old seamstress is in her mourning clothes again. Let us pray to the Goddess of Mercy to grant her peace, for she is one to be pitied."

I hear them and images of my son and husband play in my mind's eye, and I think, "No, you are mistaken, for I am the fortunate one."

The Patriot

THE INTERROGATORS POURED WATER *on his face. Huang Bing-Yi, tell us who you're working for. When he remained silent, they tightened the cord around his neck until he lost consciousness again—men who acted against the government were not to be handled gently.*

Seven-year-old Ah-Bing arranged the wooden soldiers in battle formation, his back hunched in the dark recess under the rosewood desk in his father's study, his chin resting on one knee. He dreamed of one day serving in the Imperial Army, as a true Japanese should. He had once seen a troop of Japanese soldiers marching through the village—green khaki arms and legs in brown boots pumping in unison, swords and rifles in place, eyes looking forward, tenor and bass voices raised in a patriotic song—it was the most glorious sight.

When five rows of wooden soldiers had been satisfactorily arranged on the dirt floor, Ah-Bing took his tin samurai from a breast pocket and set him at the head of the troops. The tin warrior, legs planted wide in combat position, wore Tokugawa armour and seemed ready to pounce at any moment. Ah-Bing thought the warrior's strong body and scary expression was just what a samurai should look like. But what Ah-Bing loved most about the wind-up toy were the movements: when he turned the key at the back, the samurai would spin around and raise and lower his katana sword.

Tick-tick-tick-tick. The samurai spun around before the soldiers.

Ah-Bing had been given the tin samurai that spring by his mother, Ah-Hong, when his sister, Mei Xing, was born; his mother was afraid he would feel neglected with a new baby in the family.

Of course, in 1944, nobody pronounced the baby's name in Mandarin or Taiwanese. The Japanese authorities frowned upon the use of Chinese names, in either dialect. Japanese was the official language and the Taiwanese locals, as loyal subjects of the Japanese Empire, were expected to speak it at all times; speaking Taiwanese within hearing of the Japanese was inviting trouble. It was only after Taiwan was returned to China, and Mandarin became the official language, that the family started calling the girl Mei Xing—the first Mandarin-pronounced name in the Huang family after generations of Taiwanese monikers. Eventually, all of Ah-Hong's five boys and four step-daughters adopted their Mandarin appellations for official use but they still called each other by their Taiwanese sobriquets at home. Not that the Chinese characters were different in either dialect; but the familiarity of Ah coupled with one of the characters from their Mandarin names seemed more intimate. And the clan persisted in this traditional practice; calling the baby Ah-Xing as an endearment and Mei Xing the rest of the time.

Ah-Bing wound the toy up and watched the warrior throw up dust as it spun around once again.

He practised field maneuvers with his brothers' wooden soldiers but would not allow any of his siblings to touch his tin samurai unless he was there to supervise. His older brothers respected Ah-Bing's claim to the toy and only rarely stole the warrior for their own amusement. His mother warned him to keep the toy at home lest it tempt others but Ah-Bing would not be parted from the samurai and carried it everywhere, keeping the toy hidden in his uniform pocket at school, surreptitiously showing it to his closest friends when the Japanese schoolmasters weren't looking.

Ah-Bing's favourite spot for field exercises was under the writing desk in his father's study. As a landowner and village elder, his father dealt with the affairs of the village and the administration of his huge tracts of sugar cane fields and rice paddies behind the closed door of his study, oblivious of his son's frequent presence.

Ah-Bing was too young to remember the incident but it was purportedly in this study that Mr Lu, a neighbouring landowner, had rushed in and proclaimed, "Tojo is a fool! He has attacked the United States! This will be the end of us!" His father said it had taken him an hour to calm the man down by reminding him of the consequences if the Japanese police overheard his remarks. His father laughed when he recalled the incident one evening while out on a stroll with Ah-Hong, forgetting that Ah-Bing was walking beside his mother.

Ah-Bing wiped his nose on the sleeve of his shirt, leaving a green streak. Had it been earlier in the day, he would have worried about staining his school uniform but it being Saturday afternoon, Ah-Bing relished the freedom to play without worries. His mother would be doing the morning wash at the pond with the other village women, and he would have an immaculate uniform come Monday. Mr Sakaki, the schoolmaster, would be pleased; there would be no need for blows to the head. Ah-Bing would be able to stand with his classmates and sing the national anthem before the Emperor's photograph at the front of the schoolroom, his head held high. He would be a clean Japanese, not a dirty Taiwanese.

Ah-Bing coughed and swallowed the phlegm, hoping his mother had not heard. She would probably make him drink more of that horrid Chinese soup. Mr Sakaki said Chinese medicines should be outlawed in favour of modern cures. Ah-Bing hoped Mr Sakaki would never find out about his mother's hoard of Chinese herbs.

"I am your samurai commander. You shall obey me with honour," Ah-Bing said haughtily in perfect Japanese, parading the samurai in front of the soldiers.

Just then, he heard his mother calling for his oldest brother, ten-year-old Ah-Shiong. "Come and help me put these away! Quickly!" she said in Taiwanese.

Ah-Bing crawled out from under the desk and ran to the doorway, the samurai in his hand. Beyond the study was the living room where his mother, carrying his infant sister strapped to her back, was hurriedly removing all the ancestral tablets that she had left on the table in front of the kamidana. She had forgotten to clear the table after the incense burning ceremony the night before. Chinese ancestor worship had been outlawed in favour of Shinto rites a few years earlier. Ah-Bing wondered what was occasioning his mother's fear; she had never been anxious about hiding the tablets before. Just as his mother was straightening the water jar in the shinki set, the village policeman and his son appeared at the living room threshold.

Ah-Bing had often seen the Japanese policeman walking through the village in his black uniform enforcing the edicts of the Emperor. When the erect, moustachioed man stalked by, Ah-Bing knew better than to make noise or spit. The villagers said even babies dared not cry when the Japanese were near. Fortunately, Constable Yamada made his annual appearance in the Huang family compound only to check that the wooden family name plate was properly hung and to ask for census information. Ah-Bing drew back and stayed hidden in the shadows.

The policeman's son, Ah-Bing's classmate, was a pudgy boy with close-cropped hair whose aggressive air made the Taiwanese boys wary; the entire school kept a wide berth from him. The Taiwanese girls envied his black leather shoes and whispered behind their hands when he walked by. Even for a policeman's son, leather shoes were a luxurious departure from canvas running shoes or bare feet, especially during wartime.

That afternoon, Taban Yamada was wearing his school uniform and carrying a burlap bag. Ah-Hong called for Ah-Shiong to translate when she spied the Yamadas at the threshold.

"In the interests of the war effort, I command you to surrender all your metal objects," the policeman said. Taban Yamada stood obediently by his father's side.

"My father's not home. Could the honoured officer please return later?" Ah-Shiong said on his mother's behalf.

"This business can be concluded without men. Start bringing

everything here so we can fill the bags." He shook out a bag from the front of his uniform.

Ah-Hong, being only the concubine, sent her eldest son to his step-mother's chamber to inform the bedridden mistress of the news and scurried all over the family compound to gather all the metallic articles that she could see: iron woks, door handles, shovels, copper vases, zinc plates, a gong, finely-crafted gold and silver jewelry—no item was too small or mean for the war effort. When the two bags had been filled, she bowed to the policeman and asked Ah-Shiong to convey her respects to the officer. As father and son turned to leave, the Yamada boy caught sight of Ah-Bing by the doorway and pointed excitedly at him while pulling on his father's tunic.

Ah-Shiong turned pale when he heard the policeman's request but he turned to Ah-Bing and said, "Give him your samurai."

Ah-Bing's eyes widened and a cry escaped, "No! I won't!"

He held tight the tin toy.

"You have to. Don't get us in trouble."

Ah-Shiong reached for the samurai but his brother jumped back.

"Okasan!" Ah-Bing appealed to his mother.

Ah-Hong, her upper lip trembling, gently took Ah-Bing's hand and pried the toy loose despite the rising squall from her son. She handed the toy to the policeman with downcast eyes. Taban Yamada watched quietly with a triumphant look on his face.

In the evening, after he had returned from his inspection of the sugar cane and rice fields, Ah-Bing's father cloistered himself in the study with Mr Lu, whose family had suffered a similar fate while he was absent that day, unaware that Ah-Bing was bemoaning his loss under the rosewood desk.

Mr Lu began in Taiwanese, "Those Japanese dogs will stop at nothing to win this war. What do they think a little bit of iron will do for them? How many bullets can they scrape together from a child's toy?"

At this, Ah-Bing bit his lip to stifle a sob.

"Listen, old Lu. It will only be a matter of time before the war is over. The Allies are too strong for them. I just hope it's over before more of our Taiwanese boys lose their lives fighting their own people. I'm glad I'm too old to be drafted to fight on the Mainland. Chinese killing Chinese in the name of Japanese imperialists. Tsk . . . the Taiwanese fate is too sad."

Ah-Bing heard his father swishing water in teacups and saw the splash on the floor when the rinsing water was discarded.

"Half a century of being treated like second-class citizens. What makes the Japanese so special that they deserve three times the meat rations of us Chinese? Who do they think they are fooling with this Kominka! Trying to make us believe we are full-fledged Japanese citizens. Assimilation without the privileges of true citizenship. Do they think we are so ignorant that we can't see through their ruse?" Mr Lu said.

Ah-Bing jumped when he heard the bang on the desk.

"I tell you, old Huang, we are better off with anybody else but these cold-blooded dogs. If the Japanese lose this war, maybe we'll be returned to China. The dogs won't be able to *kee hoo* us anymore."

Ah-Bing's father said, "Let's not get our hopes up. In the meantime, we need to act like Japanese patriots. To the Empire!"

Ah-Bing saw globules of spit land on the dirt as the teacups clinked.

⌒

That night, Ah-Bing threw back his cotton quilt, knocking his elbow against the head of the platform bed. He sat on the tatami mats until he got used to the darkness, then climbed over the sharp elbows and complaining feet of his four sleeping brothers to the outer edge of the bed and jumped off. He stooped down and found his getas in the jumble under the bed. Ah-Shiong woke and said, "Where are you going, little brother?"

"Outhouse."

"Well, be quick about it and don't bother us when you get back in."

Ah-Bing stepped over the threshold and clomped his way into the main courtyard but instead of walking on the paving stones to the edge of the compound, he veered towards his mother's bedchamber next door. He could see lamplight seeping through the cracks between door and frame and hoped that his father was in his own bedchamber tonight. Ah-Bing pushed on the door and found it unlocked. Relief spread through him. These times alone with his mother always made him feel better.

His mother looked up from suckling the baby when he climbed under the mosquito netting onto the tatami mat of her bed. Ah-Hong buttoned up her tunic, put the baby to her shoulder, and started rubbing the girl's back. The sated baby closed her eyes. Ah-Hong laid the baby down on the far side of the bed and moved over to make room for her son.

"How are you, baby?"

"Okay," Ah-Bing said, taking gentle hold of his mother's plait. He liked her better with her night-time hair instead of the bun that suited her daytime businesslike manner. Her face looked softer in the lamplight too.

"I'm sorry about the samurai, Ah-Bing. Mama will try and find something else for you."

"It's okay. It's just a piece of metal. Ah-Shiong says we can make better toys."

Ah-Hong took a handkerchief from her tunic and wiped the boy's tears before ordering him to blow his nose. She rose and retrieved a headscarf from a nail on the wall. Ah-Bing had often seen her tying the scarf under her chin as she headed towards the hills to gather firewood.

She knotted one corner of the scarf and, putting her hand under the cloth, danced her improvised puppet toward Ah-Bing, tickling him when she got close to his chin. He let out a reluctant giggle.

"Do you know who this is?"

Ah-Bing shook his head.

"Why it's Zhuge Liang, Chancellor of Shu Han," said Ah-Hong, making the puppet puff out its chest and strut.

Ah-Bing giggled again. Ah-Bing vaguely remembered hearing about the Chancellor during one of the weekly Chinese lessons that his father conducted with the boys. He thought the Chancellor was a learned scholar from the time of the Three Kingdoms but couldn't be sure—the battles held his attention more than the titles of dead men.

"He was a great military leader in olden times." Ah-Hong held up three fingers and wriggled them at the foot of the puppet.

"Now, these are three tanners." One hand chased the other in an exaggerated cat-and-mouse routine until Ah-Bing was openly laughing and the tanners had brought down the great Chancellor.

"Remember, my son. The saying goes, 'Three reeking tanners will overcome one great Zhuge Liang.' Although the Japanese are great now, if we work together, even we common people will be able to defeat them. Let's just bide our time."

With that, she blew out the lamp and pulled the quilt over her son.

Ah-Bing tucked his head between his shoulders and tightened his right hand around the handle of the wooden bucket. Water trickled down his bamboo hat into the bucket of slimy snails. He had spent nearly an hour that morning gathering the brown-shelled mollusks from the shrubs surrounding the family compound in order to fulfill his war duties—schoolchildren were expected to present buckets of the gastropods each day to feed the troops—Taiwanese snails being prized for their size. The snails would be canned and shipped to the front—to the places that Mr Sakaki marked with red ink on the big map of the world at the front of the schoolroom. Perhaps this batch would end up in Malaya, the Philippines, Thailand, Guam, China, or even Singapore.

In the pocket of his short pants, Ah-Bing had the ball that the Japanese schoolmasters had distributed the day Singapore fell—a red ball like the sun in the Imperial flag, marked with the year 1942. "Remember the might of the Japanese, children. Keep this memento to remind yourselves of that." The ball usually sat in the box that he kept hidden under the rosewood desk along with his prize marble and an old-time coin that his father had given him several years ago. Now, since the loss of his samurai two days ago, Ah-Bing had started to carry the ball around with him. It comforted him to squeeze the ball whenever he remembered the lost toy.

Ah-Bing wiped his nose on the sleeve of his raincoat. He raised his chin so the rain could fall on his face. Maybe he would pass the hygiene inspection if the rain washed away all the dirt and snot. He didn't want to have his ears boxed again; the schoolmasters were very particular about clean faces and fingernails.

Ah-Bing shifted the bucket to his left hand and called to his four brothers to slow down but even Ah-Shiong, who normally watched out for him, couldn't hear him through the roar of the rain. Ah-Bing could barely make out their backs as they ducked into the sugar cane fields to take the shortcut to school.

The brothers' customary route to school was north, toward Tainan. The Huang family compound was situated on the periphery of the village, by the side of a pond where the village women did their washing. Past the compound, where the dirt and gravel road led to the train station, the Huang family fields lined the sides of the road. The fields closest to the compound were rice paddies; two jias away were the sugarcane fields. When the men were not tending the cane, Ah-Bing and his brothers, like many of the village children, cut through the fields where the road curved.

Ah-Bing resigned himself to a solitary trek and tramped on the mud towards the curve in the road. He had seen his mother put sweet buns into his bento box this morning and he felt the weight of his lunch at the bottom of his schoolbag, his mouth watering in anticipation. The mud felt pleasantly cool as it squished between his toes and even though his schoolbag hung heavy on his small frame, Ah-Bing sucked in the muggy air as he ran towards the canefields.

He swam through the pampas grass at the edge of the fields and found a narrow path between the rows of cane. Under a canopy of green leaves, where the rain came down less heavily, Ah-Bing blinked a few drops of water out of his eyes and set his bucket down, breathing heavily. The four-metre-high cane towered over him and the purple stalks glistened. Ah-Bing blew his nose into his hands and wiped them on the front of his raincoat. Picking up the bucket with both hands, Ah-Bing wended his way through the cane stalks.

Before long, he heard a sound. At first he thought he must have been mistaken. But then he heard it again. *Tick-tick-tick-tick.* It was getting closer. Ah-Bing set his bucket down again and waited.

Taban Yamada rustled past a stand of cane, the spinning samurai cupped in the palms of his hands, his oversized, yellow rain hat bent over the toy. He jerked to a stop when he found his way blocked by Ah-Bing.

"That's mine! Give it back!"

The policeman's son quickly stowed the samurai into the pocket of his rain slicker. *Tick-tick-tick-tick.* The pocket pulsed. He stood with his hands on his hips, his shiny black boots sturdy in the mud, a defiant smirk on his face.

Ah-Bing's head started pounding and his breathing accelerated. He thought of his brothers' warnings about crossing the policeman's son. He thought of the lot of the Taiwanese: the need to appear submissive at all costs to avoid trouble. But he could not bear the injustice.

"Give it back!"

Ah-Bing lunged, kicking over his bucket in the process.

Bakaro! Yamada, you go straight home and change. Don't disgrace the Japanese this way again!" Mr Sakaki pushed the mud-covered boy out of the schoolroom.

"As for you, Huang. Take off your raincoat and kneel in the corner."

Ah-Bing put his bucket and schoolbag by the door and threw his raincoat and hat on top of them. He shambled past his desk, avoiding the sympathetic glances of his Taiwanese classmates and the gloating looks of the Japanese students. He swiped the back of his hand against his nose and smeared the gooey residue on the front of his school uniform, heedless now of the consequences.

Ah-Bing shuffled to the front of the classroom next to the teacher's desk. Mr Sakaki kept his bamboo stick in the corner. Ah-Bing knelt. The concrete floor felt gritty and cold. Ah-Bing shivered and bowed his head, his hand squeezing the red ball in his pocket tightly. He could feel the class staring at his back and knew it would just be a matter of time before Mr Sakaki picked up the stick. He heard the whispers cease as the schoolmaster made his way to the front of the room. As the air above him swished, Ah-Bing could smell Mr Sakaki's clean soap fragrance.

"*Ichi!* That's for not bringing snails!"

Ah-Bing bit his lip and squeezed the ball tightly. He could feel the welt on his back starting to rise. Ah-Bing scrunched his shoulders together and waited.

"*Ni!* That's for having a dirty uniform!"

Ah-Bing blinked madly. He could feel bits of rubber flaking off the red ball where his fingernails dug in.

"*San!* That's for being late! Now, stay there until break time!"

Ah-Bing heard the cane slamming against the teacher's desk.

"Class, take your math books out!"

Ah-Bing ducked his head and closed his eyes, thankful that he had gotten off so lightly. The punishment paled next to the knowledge that he had not been able to wrest the samurai from the policeman's son. Ah-Bing squeezed the ball again. When he got home, he would tear the ball apart.

⌒

"What happened? Ah-Bing, why are you covered in mud?" his mother cried out when she looked up from frying yams and saw Ah-Bing in his soiled uniform. "Did your brothers *kee hoo* you? Tell me what happened!"

Ah-Bing stood at the threshold and shook his head, looking at his toes.

"Then you fought with someone? I hope it wasn't someone smaller. I've told you not to *kee hoo* the little ones in the village. You didn't, did you?" She gave him a piercing glance as she deftly stirred the yams in the wok.

Again, Ah-Bing shook his head. Ah-Hong removed the wok from the stove and knelt down, first helping her son out of his raincoat then holding tight to his arms. "Tell me what happened."

Silence.

Ah-Hong waited. Finally, she stood up and returned to her cooking, tucking loose strands of hair back into her bun. "Suit yourself, little man. Get Ah-Shiong to help you clean up. Dinner's almost ready."

On August 15, 1945, Mr Lu's dream came true. The people of Taiwan huddled around their radios to listen to Emperor Hirohito deliver his speech of unconditional surrender, urging his subjects to "bear the unbearable." Taiwan was returned to China after fifty years of Japanese colonization.

The Japanese officials prepared for a peaceful handover to the Kuomintang government. Constable Yamada and his family had only a month left in Taiwan. Though the villagers were uncertain about their future under the Kuomintang, at least the Nationalists were Chinese—they were brothers.

The Chinese troops arrived in Huang village just before the sugar cane was to be harvested. The villagers were discomfited by the ragged appearance of the soldiers: dirty blue cotton uniforms and straw sandals on illiterate, uncouth youths. The villagers' initial welcome for their Chinese brethren rapidly vanished as they watched the undisciplined troops take over the village with arrogance. The villagers started to speak of the "good old days" when the Japanese had kept the peace on the land. Epithets about dogs were replaced with curses about pigs.

Still, daily life continued: water buffalo carried cartloads of people and goods to town, farmers worked their fields, mothers nursed their babies, and the Huang boys studied the Classics under the tutelage of Taiwanese teachers while waiting for the new government to assign Mandarin-speaking teachers. Taban Yamada no longer attended school. Scattered reports of hated Japanese policemen being attacked by resentful mobs in neighbouring villages drifted in but Huang village remained peaceful.

One September afternoon, Ah-Bing returned home to find an auntie in the kitchen and his mother locked inside her bedchamber. "Your mother's not well" was the sole explanation given. His father, busy with the farm hands during the harvest, sat at the head of a grim table, then retreated to his bedchamber directly after dinner. His brothers, unbalanced by their father's serious mood, also retired early, dragging Ah-Bing with them. One by one, his brothers fell into easy slumber while Ah-Bing thrashed on the tatami mats. Through the latticed window, he could see dark clouds obscuring a part of the full moon. Ah-Bing wanted his mother but was afraid to disturb her. He tried to will himself to sleep but gave up after a time. Climbing over the inert forms on the tatami mats, Ah-Bing crept barefoot out of the chamber and stopped at his mother's door. A lamp was glowing but before he could push open the door, Ah-Bing heard his parents' voices. Indistinct mumbling with the occasional recognizable word: food, rice, sugar, two men. Then his mother's wail: they *kee-hooed* me. His father saying "Sh . . . sh . . ."

Ah-Bing stood and imagined that his father had his arm around her in loving comfort. He wanted to do the same. He pushed on the door but it would not yield. Ah-Bing considered pounding on the wooden barrier but suddenly felt shy. He stood undecided for a long time. Long enough for his father to open the door and start upon seeing him.

"Ah-Bing. Get back to bed," he said in a jagged voice.

"I want to see Mama," Ah-Bing whined.

"She's asleep. See her in the morning," his father said tiredly. His hair seemed to glow whiter in the semi-darkness.

"I want to sleep in her bed!"

Whack! "I said go to bed!"

Through his tears, Ah-Bing saw his father's rage. A coiled, living, barely-controlled force. He had looked like this the day of the metal collection. Ah-Bing scampered to his room and fell into a restless sleep.

Ah-Hong was not up to make the fire in the morning. One of Ah-Bing's step-sisters cooked breakfast and sent the boys off to school before going to her factory job in town. Ah-Bing knocked on his mother's door before leaving but there was no answer.

That afternoon, Ah-Bing, walking through the sugar cane fields on the way home from school, heard grappling noises nearby. He froze and looked around for the source of the sounds. Then he saw it. Black leather shoes flailing under blue cotton legs and straw sandals. Grunting and huffing. A boy with his tear-stained face turned sideways in the dirt, mouth open in a soundless scream. A metal object glinted on the ground. After a few minutes, Ah-Bing heard muffled sobs rapidly receding through the stalks of sugar cane. The two men emerged from behind the columns of ripe sugar cane with satisfied grins, knotting the drawstrings of their cotton pants. Ah-Bing gasped and ran towards the family compound as quickly as he could.

His mother was drawing water from the well when he rushed into the courtyard. She dropped the bucket and hugged him to her when she saw his face. Ah-Bing sobbed into her shoulder as if the image of what he had seen could be erased with his tears.

In the evening, Ah-Bing heard his father tell his mother that the Yamadas were leaving Huang village immediately. The villagers suspected something had happened to the family. Maybe someone had even *kee-hooed* the son, though that was total speculation.

"The poor boy!" Ah-Hong exclaimed, then dissolved into uncontrollable weeping.

Ah-Bing wrapped his thin arms around his mother and attempted to quiet the terror coursing through his body. He tried not to remember Taban Yamada's face in the dirt. He clung to his mother and cried, briskly dismissing incipient associations between Taban's and his mother's tears; the thought of his mother with those men was unimaginable. When their weeping ceased, mother and son parted with embarrassment, aware that their bond had been irrevocably altered. Ah-Hong quickly rose and attended to the feed for the hogs without looking at her son. From that day on, Ah-Bing never again entered his mother's bed.

Early the following morning, Ah-Bing returned to the sugarcane field. He looked up at the tough, water-rich stalks now ready for harvest. The men would start cutting them down soon with their machetes. He found the spot where he had stood before and eyed the ground carefully. Seeing only dead cane leaves and dirt, he knelt and frantically scrabbled through the layers of decomposing leaves. Finally, he found it half-trampled into the dirt. The tin toy was dented in the front but seemed undamaged otherwise. Ah-Bing wound the key. *Tick-tick-tick-tick.*

His mother was frying eggs in the kitchen when he entered the family compound and his brothers were playing tag in the courtyard. She looked up and smiled weakly at him when he stepped into the kitchen. Pouring some water from the wooden bucket by the threshold onto his shirt tail, Ah-Bing carefully wiped the samurai clean. He stepped back into the courtyard and announced, to the enthusiastic shouts of his brothers, that the toy was now common property.

One of the Kuomintang interrogators prodded him with his boot. Ah-Bing opened his eyes. The man repeated the question: Tell us who you belong to. Are you a Japanese sympathizer? Are you a Communist spy? Ah-Bing replied, "I do not belong to the Japanese. I do not belong to the Chinese. I am a Taiwanese who answers only to truth and liberty." When the man slapped him for his impertinence, Ah-Bing said no more—patriots in limbo had no recourse other than silence.

Departure

Twenty-third day of the seventh month, Year of the Pig
September 4, 2007

Stray afternoon sunlight stealthily pushed through the slats in the
bamboo blinds but failed to illuminate the dim interior of the bedchamber. Ah-Hong dropped the rusty hook of the door into its ring
on the wooden frame; she pulled on the door handle just to be sure
the hook would hold. Her breathing ragged from the exertion, she
rested on her cane for a minute. She could barely make out the outline
of her bed even though it was less than two metres away but dared not
pull the cord of the naked light bulb next to the door. No one knew
she was in here, and she preferred to keep it that way.

Ah-Hong straightened up and tightened her grip on the cane;
though she had shrunk with age, at five-foot-six and ninety-two, she
continued to stand at least half a head taller than most women she
knew. Ah-Hong hobbled over to the bed and rested her cane beside
it. She leaned her weight against the wall next to it and, taking a firm
stance on the dirt floor, gripped a panel above the bed's carved dragon
design. She pried the panel loose with her fingers to reveal a small
pigeonhole beneath the tatami mats. Cobwebs and powdery grit
clung to her damp palms as she removed a black lacquer box from
the hole. She blew a layer of dust off the box and started coughing. A

shiver of excitement ran through her. She hadn't opened the box in seventy years.

Ah-Hong fumbled through the opening of the tangled mosquito netting hanging over her bed. She laid the box upon the cotton-filled quilt. After wiping her hands on her drawstring pants and slipping off her cloth shoes, she climbed onto the high bed with the aid of a step stool. She drew the netting closed and sat on the tatami mat, her legs stretched out in front of her, her back against the headboard, and breathed unevenly. Ah-Hong tilted her head back and closed her eyes until the dizziness passed. Then she drew the box onto her lap and lifted the ornately carved lid. A faint cloud of jasmine scent emerged. From the red felt interior of the box, she pulled out a jewelled hairpin.

She held the hair ornament close to her eyes and squinted. It didn't look like much. A person could even be forgiven for thinking that it was a cheap trinket. They sold so many imitations like it in the night markets these days. But if a person polished the silver filigree and cleaned the jade and ruby inserts, she would see that the pin was shaped like a dragonfly; she would know this was a hairpin worn by noblewomen in the past. Like the ones they showed in TV melodramas about the emperors and empresses of ancient China. Ah-Hong used to watch them before her eyes got bad. She missed seeing the costumes and hairdos. She missed a lot of things. But old age demanded courage. Ah-Hong sighed and sat up straighter.

She gently shook the hair ornament to hear the clacking of the three strings of jade beads and remembered the last time she had heard that sound. It was in this very room; only, it was Tao-Gey-Nioh's room then. Ah-Hong was eighteen.

⌒‿

Clack, clack, clack. The beads of Tao-Gey-Nioh's hair ornament clacked as she shook her head. Her gaze drilled into Ah-Hong. The lines on her face seemed more deeply etched and the grey in her hair looked more metallic than usual. Her wide, deep-set eyes were like caverns in her implacable face.

"There will be no further discussion about it. He will call you Ah Yi and he will call me Mama."

My son will call her Mama and me auntie? How was a person supposed to answer that? If she could get out of this stuffy bedchamber
she might be able to think straight. She turned around and busied
herself with the basket of clean clothes she had brought in so that
Tao-Gey-Nioh wouldn't be able to see her expression; Ah-Hong
wouldn't give her the satisfaction. After she had folded the silk robes,
Ah-Hong turned and faced Tao-Gey-Nioh's haughty scrutiny. Ah-
Hong lowered her eyes and nodded. "Yes, Elder Sister."

She left a tray with gingered chicken and rice on the bed beside the
older woman. And she rearranged Tao-Gey-Nioh's quilt to cover the
invalid's bound feet, remarking once again the difference between
the daintiness of the older woman's three-inch "golden lotuses" and
her own broad appendages. Ah-Hong could see the grease stains on
the satin cover of the quilt and resigned herself to another load of
heavy washing at the pond later in the week. She stifled a sigh and
closed the mosquito netting. Then she turned down the oil lamp on
the bedside table and stepped over the wooden threshold, closing the
door behind her.

The instant she was outside, Ah-Hong gulped the brisk evening
air and exhaled deeply, releasing some of her anger and frustration.
How dare she! Whose son was he anyway! But Ah-Hong knew she
would have to obey. Unless . . . did she have the courage?

It was six weeks since her son's birth. Ah-Hong's mother had
returned to her home village after the lying-in month and the Huang
family had resumed their normal routines: Ah-Hong was back to
cooking, cleaning, and washing; Tao-Gey-Nioh had wanted Ah-
Hong to wait on her again; and Tao-Gey, the head of the family, had
recommenced his visits to Ah-Hong's bedchamber.

All the field hands and tenant farmers called Tao-Gey-Nioh's husband Tao-Gey, or boss, including Tao-Gey-Nioh, so Ah-Hong had
done likewise when she joined the household a year ago. They called
the lady of the house, Tao-Gey-Nioh, or the boss's wife, as a sign
of respect but Ah-Hong was just Ah-Hong. There was no title of

deference for a concubine.

On the day Ah-Hong first arrived in the village, Tao-Gey-Nioh, dressed in silk robes, had swayed across the rectangular courtyard of the family compound with her "lotus gait," taken one look at the young concubine, uttered a faint cry, and collapsed in front of her husband's bedchamber. Tao-Gey had carried Tao-Gey-Nioh to her bed and she had not risen since, except to use the chamber pot. Physicians had been summoned and herbal powders prescribed, but to no avail; Tao-Gey-Nioh's headaches and fainting spells continued.

Tao-Gey-Nioh directed Ah-Hong and the servant girl from her bed: the dishes to cook for the field hands, the clothes to be cleaned and mended, the care to be given to her four children. Merchants hawking knives, fish, meat, vegetables, perfumes, and other goods were made to stand outside the threshold to her bedchamber, while Ah-Hong conveyed the wares to the platform bed for Tao-Gey-Nioh's perusal.

Tao-Gey-Nioh's four girls, ranging from sixteen to ten, were brought in for inspection each morning and evening and Tao-Gey stopped in for a visit every night. Ah-Hong knew that he would be stepping into Tao-Gey-Nioh's chamber just about now. That left only ten minutes for her to prepare before he knocked on her door.

She ran across the paving stones of the courtyard to her bedchamber and threw open the door. The servant girl was sitting on Ah-Hong's bed, crooning a lullaby to the baby. "Quickly, take Ah-Shiong to your chamber. Tao-Gey will be here soon."

As soon as the girl left, Ah-Hong poured water from the bucket by the door into a washbasin. Tearing off her tunic and pants, she hastily sponged and dried herself before donning a pink, form-fitting silk qipao, one of many brocaded and embroidered pieces of clothing stored in the bamboo hamper. Tao-Gey-Nioh had given Ah-Hong the hamper as a welcome gift, and Ah-Hong wore the clothes for Tao-Gey's pleasure, but never in public. Ah-Hong would not give her mistress the satisfaction of showing the villagers how well she treated her.

Ah-Hong unpinned her ebony hair and deftly caught the hairnet as it fell from the bun at the nape of her neck. She had always worn her hair as simply as possible. Two plaits hanging down her back when she was a girl and then the bun when she entered Huang village. Not like Tao-Gey-Nioh, who always had her hair oiled and dressed in complicated styles, coils of hair decorated with fancy hair ornaments.

Tao-Gey opened the door as Ah-Hong was brushing out her waist-length hair. He stood silhouetted against the full moon, his silver head reaching the top of the doorframe, his soft body enclosed in a blue changpao and mandarin jacket. Ah-Hong stood and the lustful look on Tao-Gey's face told her that, even after childbirth, she still held the same power over him as she had done on the day they met.

Tao-Gey had been visiting his friend, a farmer in the next village. Ah-Hong's mother had hired her out to the farmer as a cook during harvest season. Every day, Ah-Hong made barrels of steamed rice, pots of soups, and wokfuls of stir-fried meats and vegetables for the labourers who came in from the fields at sundown. They would sit on long benches at makeshift tables in the courtyard. The men ate first, then the women and children. She'd serve the field hands, with their sun-browned faces and lean bodies, constantly aware that their eyes hungered for her while they filled their stomachs. Tao-Gey had taken her home with him the following week.

Ah-Hong lowered her eyes. Tao-Gey stepped into the bedchamber, which at three pings was half the size of Tao-Gey-Nioh's bedchamber. He steered Ah-Hong towards the bed and they reached the tatami mats in a few short strides. Ah-Hong made sure her laughs and shrieks rang out as loudly as possible during the lovemaking, hoping the sounds would carry clearly across the courtyard to Tao-Gey-Nioh, whose heart would contort in pain.

After Tao-Gey had taken his pleasure and they were both resting their heads on the rectangular, wooden pillows, Ah-Hong pulled the quilt over their naked bodies and asked, "Are you pleased with our son?"

Tao-Gey ran his fingers through her long hair and murmured, "Of course. You've done well. Ah-Shiong is perfect."

Ah-Hong sat up and looked down at him. "What do you think Ah-

Shiong should call Elder Sister and me when he's old enough?"

Tao-Gey stiffened, then sat up to face Ah-Hong. He gently ran one hand down her left arm and tilted her head with the other so she could look into his eyes. "Elder Sister already spoke to me about this. Ah-Shiong will call you Ah Yi, and Elder Sister, Mama."

Ah-Hong emphatically twisted her face out of his grip and turned her body away. "But I'm the mother! Why should he call her mother and me auntie? It's not right!"

"Right or not. That's the way it has to be. Elder Sister has suffered enough humiliation. I took away her right to choose a concubine for me. I took away her chance to please me with that gift. This is the least we can do."

They had abided by Tao-Gey-Nioh's wishes until Ah-Shiong started school. He'd learned from his Japanese schoolmasters to call his mother Okasan and Tao-Gey-Nioh had retreated so far into her "illness" by then that she didn't bother to object. And as Tao-Gey-Nioh withdrew, Ah-Hong gradually assumed the household responsibilities until she was Tao-Gey-Nioh in all but name.

But hardly anyone called Ah-Hong anything but Ah Mah now. After Ah-Shiong's first son was born, everyone started addressing her as grandmother and Ah-Hong proudly wore the label. Now her offspring all referred to the family compound as grandmother's home, Ah Mah dao.

A few days after Tao-Gey-Nioh claimed Ah-Hong's son as her own, her dragonfly hairpin went missing. She questioned Ah-Hong and the servants several times and was finally persuaded that the pin had merely been misplaced. Ah-Hong and the girl servant searched each ping of Tao-Gey-Nioh's room for days but could not find it.

Every couple of months, until she died a decade later, Tao-Gey-Nioh would again remember her lost heirloom and another round of fruitless hunting would begin.

"Ah-Hong, look harder. It must be here somewhere. We have to find it. I can't have my ancestors count this as a demerit. Oh, I shouldn't have worn it so much. It's all my fault."

Ah-Hong would conceal her look of satisfaction even as she said, "Don't worry, Elder Sister. We're sure to find it this time."

⌒

Ah-Hong put the ornament back inside the black lacquer box. If a person looked closely, she would see that the engraved design on the lid resembled Guan Yin's lotus blossom and willow branch. Ah-Hong sighed. So long ago. So much passion on all sides. And what was it all for? All the duplicity. All the tears. What is left now? Tao-Gey and Tao-Gey-Nioh's names are already on ancestral tablets. Their descendants light joss sticks and bow to them regularly in the worship area of the family's living room. Soon it would be Ah-Hong's turn to have her name added to a tablet.

She looked up. Someone was walking towards her chamber. Her eyes darted to the door and her hand froze over the box. The sounds receded. Ah-Hong let out her breath. Probably just Ah-Shiong's wife on her way to the kitchen, wearing those ridiculous flip-flops. Ah-Hong maneuvered herself down from the mat, returned the box to the pigeonhole at the side of the bed, and replaced the dusty panel.

In her haste she knocked over the wooden bucket which had been protruding halfway out from under the bed. A trickle of yellow liquid streamed from the bucket, filling the air with the acrid smell of urine. Ah-Hong righted the bucket and carefully stepped over the puddle. Wheezing slightly, she bent over her cane and peered at the dark patch. No harm done. She had emptied most of the bucket that morning into her vegetable garden.

She started making her way to the door but was forced to sit down heavily on the mahogany stool at the dressing table. She squinted at the mirror and tucked thin strands of loose grey hair back into her hairnet. A wavering image of her face was all she could see now, but she still had the prominent cheekbones which had made her handsome in her day. The world had closed in all too quickly. She sighed, then heaved herself up with the cane. It was time to prepare her evening meal.

Ah-Hong slowly walked outside into the wooden enclosure that served as her kitchen and stood blinking and shivering in the dusk. When her son renovated the family home fifteen years ago, Ah-Hong had insisted that he not alter her sleeping quarters or cooking arrangements and Ah-Shiong, a dutiful son, had obliged and even built an addition to her wing to house the wood stove. He had stood firm regarding the plumbing for her personal kitchen, though, and since he would fill in the courtyard well, Ah-Hong saw no help for it but to allow the tap and piping to be fitted. It had taken her weeks to remember that she could run water into her bucket instead of carrying the bucket to the well, but once she got used to it, she liked the convenience of running water, although she would never admit that to anyone. Exposing weaknesses and declaring errors were rash acts reserved for fools. Ah-Hong was no fool.

Standing under the soot-blackened eaves of her open kitchen, Ah-Hong could smell meat cooking two rooms away in the main wing, animal parts roasting in the modern kitchen that Ah-Shiong had built for his wife. It turned her stomach. Ah-Hong couldn't understand people who ate breathing creatures. How did these people know that they wouldn't return as animals in their next lives? How would the gods look upon them come judgment day? The only times that Ah-Hong set foot in that kitchen was to retrieve her vegetables from the white refrigerator. At least Ah-Shiong had kept the outer frame of the house intact and only renovated the interior. Ah-Hong was glad. It would not do to tear down everything from the past. Ah-Shiong should always remember his family roots.

Ah-Hong shambled over to the stove and looked for the pile of firewood that she normally used, but she could not locate it. She crouched down and felt the ground beside the stove just to make sure her eyes were not deceiving her. Only one stick. Her grandson had forgotten again. Ah-Hong slumped. She didn't want to make another request of Ah-Shiong or that busybody wife of his. Lately she had gotten the feeling that she was becoming more and more of a burden to them. Perhaps tonight would be a good time to fast. She pulled herself up with her cane.

Ah-Hong leaned on her cane and listened to the rumble of cars driving past in the back lane as darkness crept over the red brick walls of the courtyard. Teenagers strolling home from school cram sessions joked and yelled obscenities at each other. Ah Hong cringed. Motor scooters sped by carrying office workers rushing to their evening meals, or housewives dashing back to their kitchens with last minute purchases.

She recalled a time when shrubs bearing purple bougainvillea, yellow clematis, and white honeysuckle flowers choked the lane; when she could clearly see Tao-Gey's sixty or seventy jias of land stretching beyond the hills, before the Kuomintang pigs came and took it all away. A lifetime gone by, so fast. She had bent to Heaven's will, followed her fate. But that didn't protect a person from her feelings of sadness and loss. A person needed the heady scents of flowers and the chirping of cicadas, the tender touch of husbands and the high-pitched squeals of toddlers.

"Aiyah, Mah. What are you doing? It's dinnertime. You didn't come for your vegetables so I've brought you some soup and rice gruel. Here, let me put this tray down. Then I'll help you inside. Standing outside in the dark. What next?" Ah-Feng, Ah-Shiong's wife, bustled past, her stout thighs and thick arms jiggling under a sleeveless print dress.

"I'm fasting today."

"Well, let me help you inside anyway. I'll leave the tray, just in case you change your mind."

Ah-Feng lit a white candle and set it in a bronze holder. "I'll leave the candle on your tray too. It's on your bed. Be careful with it. Do you need anything else?"

"Just to be left alone."

Ah-Shiong's wife muttered to herself as she stepped back into the courtyard. "Ingrate. I don't know why I bother. Cantankerous old woman."

Ah-Hong relieved herself in the chamber pot. Another concession from Ah-Shiong. He would have preferred that she use the Western-style toilet in the main family wing. But Ah-Hong was secretly afraid of encountering ghosts in the dark as she groped her way across the courtyard. Besides, she needed the urine as fertilizer for her garden.

Parting the soiled mosquito netting, Ah-Hong panted as she climbed onto her bed. Ah-Feng had left the tray an arm's length away on the tatami mat. A pungent aroma steamed up from the soup bowl and Ah-Hong's mouth watered. Perhaps she would fast another day. No sense in letting good food go to waste. She had lived through too many wars to refuse Heaven's blessings.

As Ah-Hong spooned the rice porridge, seasoned with seaweed flakes, into her sparsely toothed mouth, she considered the state of her preparations. So many details to think about; so many tasks still undone.

The preparations had started on her ninetieth birthday. Ah-Shiong had driven her to Tainan to have a suit fitted—a brown Western-style one with three buttons down the front and a skirt with a zipper up the back. Brown pumps to match. Not that a person would be able to tell the colour of anything in the black and white photograph she had commissioned. They had tried to sell her coloured pictures at the studio, but Ah-Hong preferred the old look. The photograph would serve as her ancestral image and hang in the worship area of the living room when the time came.

Ah-Hong had not been ashamed to send a copy to her only daughter, Mei Xing, in Canada. Mei Xing was the one who left, the adventurous one. Left her family to be with a white man an ocean away. Ah-Hong felt the loss keenly. But then, she had lost Mei Xing even before that; when she converted to her one-god religion. Ah-Hong would never understand that. How could one god take care of all a person's needs? Even with all the different gods in Taiwan, sometimes a person's requests were not granted no matter how many times she went to temple or how many offerings she made to the right gods.

But then, Mei Xing had a gentler life than she'd had. Mei Xing could afford to believe in the ideas that her church preached. Innocent ideals like if a person treated others well and was forgiving, then she would be rewarded in kind. And hadn't Ah-Hong encouraged that? Hadn't she taught her daughter adages such as "wang shi yi yi," what's done is done? Forgiveness was a luxury given to the fortunate ones that Heaven smiled upon, the ones born with good fates like her daughter.

Ah-Hong set the empty rice bowl down and picked up the warm bowl of soup. She peered at the contents and saw that Ah-Shiong's wife had taken the time to slice the bamboo shoots and black mushrooms finely for her. Perhaps she was too hard on her daughter-in-law. The absence of a mother-in-law was a blessing that Ah-Hong had not counted on when she entered the Huang household; Tao-Gey's mother had died years before. But Tao-Gey-Nioh had made up for that.

Ah-Hong didn't know what she had done to Tao-Gey-Nioh in her previous life but Tao-Gey-Nioh had certainly settled the tally in this lifetime. On top of the drudgery and sickbed attentions that Tao-Gey-Nioh demanded, and in spite of the insistence that Ah-Hong's five sons and one daughter be claimed as her own, Tao-Gey-Nioh had displayed a fierce antagonism towards them. Ah-Hong still burned when she remembered the lashings she had had to dispense to her children at Tao-Gey-Nioh's whim. If it weren't for Tao-Gey, Tao-Gey-Nioh would have limited Ah-Hong's children to rudimentary education, six years of schooling. But Tao-Gey had insisted that all his offspring receive as much formal instruction as they could handle. Heaven must have had a hand in that and Ah-Hong was grateful.

Ah-Hong wiped her mouth with the sleeve of her tunic. She watched the flickering candle melt down slowly. Her earthly suffering in this lifetime was nearly over. Only the final preparations remained. She hoped that she had performed enough good works to earn credit with the ancestors and the gods.

It was time to rest. Ah-Hong inserted one of her favourite folk tapes into her thirty-year-old tape recorder and pressed a button. Plaintive strains of moon guitar music trilled. Ah-Hong had been to only one concert in her life, decades ago, but she could still see the dextrous fingers of the musician plucking the yueqin strings. A baritone launched into the first verse of "Thinking of Which." Ancient Confucian saws about honouring one's parents and doing good deeds, sweetened by the seductive tune, lulled her into sleepy submission. Her breathing became deep and even just as the singer concluded the melody with the line "a tiger leaves skin and fur behind, a person leaves only his name."

The next morning, after some hesitation about imposing on Ah-Shiong, Ah-Hong took a piece of thin blue paper to him. She found Ah-Shiong in his study across the compound, next to her old bed-chamber. He was sitting on a rattan chair, rubbing a black inkstick onto a ceramic inkstone, calligraphy brushes and rice paper at the ready on the rosewood desk in front of him, the sleeves of his shirt rolled up, grey head bowed in concentration.

He looked up, startled. "Okasan, have you eaten?"

"Can you write something for me?" Ah-Hong laid the sheet of blue paper on the desk.

"Of course, what would you like to write?" He took out a black ballpoint pen from a desk drawer and uncapped it.

"I would like you to address it to Tao-Gey-Nioh's oldest daughter."

Ah-Shiong looked up in surprise. "Mei Lu? Why? You haven't spoken to her in years."

"That's none of your concern. Just write."

Ah-Hong had borne the shame of her illiteracy her entire life. And even though her fifth son, the one she lost too soon to the Resistance movement, had always praised her intelligence and even taught her proverbs in Taiwanese and Mandarin, Ah-Hong had never managed the time to learn to read or write. Perhaps it was just as well; the other villagers might have thought she was overstepping her station in life.

Ah-Shiong finished the short note:

Mei Lu,

This belonged to your mother and now rightfully belongs to you.
You should pass it on to your eldest daughter in time.

"And how would you like to sign it?" Ah-Shiong inquired, his pen poised to start the next line.

"No signature."

"No signature?"

"That's what I said."

Ah-Hong snatched the paper off the desk and folded it in half.

"Ah-Shiong, many thanks."

She limped over the threshold, leaving her son gaping in bewilderment.

Less than a year later, on a day when the sun shone bright and hot, Ah-Shiong had his mother's name added to an ancestral tablet. For several months before her death, Ah-Hong had repeatedly told him to look for a black box should anything happen to her. Earlier that week, he had found a carved lacquer box on top of a pile of embroidered and brocaded clothes in Ah-Hong's bamboo hamper. Inside the box were an old-fashioned hair ornament and a cassette tape. When he played the tape in his mother's old recorder, Ah-Hong's strong, rural accent recited what seemed to be a poem in Taiwanese, but not any poem that Ah-Shiong recognized, and he could not make sense of it:

Bitter wind descends.
Lone leaf trembles,
Clings, regrets, clings.
Hoarfrost soars. Crystallizes all
Fear. Melts.

The poem was followed by Ah-Hong's wishes for her funeral arrangements—the people to notify of her death, the style of the tomb, the geomancer to engage, the shop from which to order the flowers. Ah-Hong then detailed the dispersal of her estate down to instructions for the disposal of the clothes in the bamboo hamper and even the hamper itself. But there was no mention of a dragonfly hairpin.

Ah-Shiong presented the hair ornament to his wife as a curiosity.

She found the old bauble not to her taste and gave it away to the village drunkard's wife thinking she was earning credit with the ancestors.

White Skin

IT IS SEPTEMBER, 1983, and Ah-Hong is sixty-eight. Her only daughter, Mei Xing, moved to Canada with a white man eight years before, the same year Ah-Hong lost her youngest son. She still lives in the Huang family compound with her eldest son, Ah-Shiong, and his family; her three other sons having found jobs in the more populous cities of Taiwan, one in Taipei and the other two in Tainan. She has worked hard all her life and now she is retiring to Vancouver.

Midmorning, she rides the crowded bus to Da-San, the closest market town, instead of walking on the hot and dusty road; she can splurge a little now. When the bus stops near the day market, Ah-Hong gets off in front of the oldest jewellery shop in town, coughing as the bus rumbles off in a cloud of dust and exhaust. The weather-worn sign reads Tan's Jewellers. She remembers the old man who made the baby rings for her children and grandchildren. His son, Ming, owns Tan's Jewellers now. Ming, a stocky middle-aged man, looks up from his abacas as Ah-Hong walks in. He was a frequent customer when Ah-Hong had her market stall and still raves about her rice dumplings and baked goods. She gave up her stall after her youngest son died; there was no one to save money for any more.

"Welcome! Welcome! Long time no see," Ming says. "I miss those mantous you used to make."

Ah-Hong beams. She used to make trays of the Chinese breads; sometimes she would fill them with meats but most often not—plain

72

is best. She knows that her mantous are incomparable: white, shiny firm skins enclosing soft, squishy interiors with just a hint of sweetness; they were one of her bestsellers.

Ah-Hong draws a silk pouch from her tunic pocket and sets it on the glass counter. She unties the pouch to reveal several gold rings. "I would like you to melt these down and make two adult-sized bracelets. If you need more gold, I'll pay the difference."

Ming examines the rings then unlocks the sliding door behind the counter and withdraws a velvet-lined tray of bracelets, handing one to Ah-Hong for examination. The bracelet depicts a coiled dragon with a pearl in its mouth. Ah-Hong turns it all the way around and sees that the dragon pattern is repeated eight times and the spaces in between are filled with embossed sea waves. She smiles.

"This is our best design. Will it be satisfactory?"

"Excellent. It's for my daughter and granddaughter so make sure you do a good job, old friend . . . I am going to be emigrating to Canada and will take the bracelets as presents," Ah-Hong says proudly.

"Canada?" he says quizzically.

"Yes. It's next to America."

"Ahh . . . America. Congratulations! Congratulations! To live with your daughter?"

Ah-Hong nods. "Yes, I leave in two weeks. I will return next week to pick up the bracelets. Will they be ready?"

"Yes, yes, certainly . . . America . . . you have a good fate. I am envious."

Ah-Hong tries unsuccessfully to act indifferent.

And so it goes for the rest of the day.

"I am emigrating to Canada," Ah-Hong boasts to everyone she knows in town.

"Waah . . . so lucky!" says the woman who has taken over Ah-Hong's stall in the market, her red face dripping with sweat as she picks pork buns with tongs from a metal steamer.

"My daughter has a big house in Canada," Ah-Hong says at the bank.

"When you get there, send for me," jokes the man who is closing out her bank account. "My coworker emigrated ten years ago and when he came back to visit, I didn't recognize him. His skin was so white and tender. Just like a woman's."

To the dressmaker, Ah-Hong says, "I haven't seen my granddaughter in eight years."

"She will have to be extra good to make up for the lost years then," says the woman as she hands Ah-Hong a package containing her new tunic and pants. "Ah-Hong ah, do you think you can help my son get to America?"

"I will see what my daughter can do," Ah-Hong says importantly. Though she has grown accustomed to being highly regarded by the village women, she still glows when the townsfolk show her enough respect to ask a favour. It has been many years since anyone has treated her as a lowly concubine. As an elder among the village women, she is often consulted on matters large and small. "Let's see what Ah-Hong has to say about this" is a common conclusion to many female arguments and sometimes even the occasional male disagreement.

As the departure date draws near, the farewells begin. Her sons and their families return from Tainan and Taipei bearing gifts. Ah-Hong adds the photographs that she had requested from them to her album. Her friends and neighbours pause from their clothes-washing by the pond and their vegetable-scrubbing by the well to inquire about the state of her preparations and to wish her a safe journey. Ah-Hong herself makes a final offering at the local temple to ensure a safe passage.

The day before departure, Ah-Hong takes one last walk to the hills. She sweeps her husband's and fifth son's tombs, burns incense and paper money, and leaves a final feast of meats, wine, and oranges. She prays for her husband's blessings. On her way down the hill, she gathers a bundle of firewood in readiness for the last dinner she will cook on the brick stove that has fed the Huangs for generations. That evening she tends her vegetable garden one last time and tells Ah-Shiong's wife, Ah-Feng, not to let the patch go to seed.

On departure day, Ah-Shiong takes the early morning train with her north to Taipei airport. Ah-Shiong has stowed the suitcase, filled with her clothes, gifts, and photo albums, on an overhead rack. Mother and son munch on mantous and rice dumplings and sip the mango juice that Ah-Hong prepared the day before. Ah-Shiong dozes to the rhythm of the train while Ah-Hong drinks in last images of paddy fields and sugar cane stands, barefoot children playing by run-down shacks, colourful laundry fluttering on lines, and long stretches of green hills. She looks at Ah-Shiong's tired face and knows that, though he has performed his duties as the eldest son diligently, he is secretly relieved he no longer has to provide for her. Ah-Hong has no ill feelings towards him; she knows Ah-Shiong has enough trouble trying to eke out a living from the farm to feed his wife and two sons. Her old resentment against the Mainlander government's annexation of the Huang farmlands revives but she is determined not to let the past blight this day. Her cheerful exterior lasts through Ah-Shiong's last minute fussing at the airport until she is seated on the plane. Only then does she feel the full force of her decision to emigrate, but the momentary pang of homesickness and uncertainty is quickly buried amid the novelty of air travel.

As the plane lifts off, Ah-Hong feels herself flying away not only from the oppression that she suffered under the Japanese and the Mainlanders but also from the constraints of male-dominated village life. Her heart exults at the first glimpse of blue skies above grey clouds as the plane climbs higher. A life of liberty and luxury awaits her. Mei Xing has promised her no more outhouses, no more wood-burning stoves, and no more worries. Ah-Hong sleeps peacefully on the long flight; she is flying towards her heaven on earth. Such a good fate.

When Ah-Hong arrives in Vancouver, Tracy is almost fourteen. Tracy's mother, Nancy, says as she pulls into the airport parking lot, "You remember what to call grandmother?"

"Ah Mah," Tracy says curtly from the back seat. Does her mother think her an idiot?

"I want you take care of Ah Mah. She speak only Taiwanese and little Mandarin. You help her. Specially when Daddy and Mama are at work."

Tracy is silent. When did she volunteer to be a babysitter? Besides, from what she can remember, Ah Mah is quite capable of taking care of herself. The last time she saw her grandmother was at Taipei airport when she was departing for Canada. Ah Mah helped her put on a winter coat with a "made by grandma" label beneath the rabbit-fur trimmed collar, and gave her a lingering hug. Ah Mah stood at the airport gate with an armful of snacks and a face wet with tears. Even then, she seemed strong and invincible. Tracy does not expect her grandmother to need help.

Tracy's father, David, jumps out of the front passenger seat as soon as Nancy parks. He sprints towards the Arrivals lounge. "Meet me inside. I'll look for Okasan. I hope she hasn't been waiting long," he shouts over his shoulder. Tracy has never heard either of her parents refer to her grandmother as anything other than Okasan, Japanese for mother. She wonders if Ah Mah minds being addressed like that by David.

When she sees Ah Mah exiting the customs area, Tracy is surprised that her grandmother is no longer the brown bear of her memory: fierce and terrifying during moments of ire, calm and cuddly when the day's work was done. Instead, Tracy finds herself staring into a pair of startled eyes in a lined, darkly tanned face; the top of Ah Mah's headscarf is no higher than the crown of Tracy's "The Farrah" hairdo.

"Waah…Ah-Ying, you've grown so much. I would never have recognized you. Come help your Ah Mah with her luggage."

It takes a second for Tracy to realize that her grandmother is speaking to her; no one except her mother has called her by her Chinese name since she was five. It's even stranger to hear her mother addressed as Mei Xing instead of Nancy. Though Tracy finds her grandmother easy enough to understand, she strains to remember Taiwanese phrases when she tries to answer; her mother speaks to her in the old dialect only sporadically now, English being a more efficient means of communication with her father in the house.

They pile into the Toyota Corolla and David drops the women off at their three-bedroom West Point Grey bungalow before going back to his United Church office to attend to ministerial duties. Tracy carries the suitcase from the garage, through the laundry room and into the guest bedroom, now her grandmother's room. She throws her purse onto her own bed, in the room across from her grandmother's, before strolling past the bathroom that she would have to share with Ah Mah, and into the kitchen. Taking a bag of chips and a glass of water through the dining room, ignoring the breakfast dishes still on the table and hoping that her mother will not order her to clear them, Tracy settles on the couch in the family room and switches on the television.

"Tracy, help Ah Mah unpack!" Nancy snaps as she clears the table. "I say before. Make her comfortable."

Tracy groans. "Just a minute, I'm hungry."

Nancy stacks the dishes together louder than she usually does. Tracy channel-hops for a few moments, finishes her chips, then saunters down the hall.

"Ah Mah, may I help you?"

Ah-Hong is sitting on the bed next to an open suitcase. "Yes . . . you can put my clothes away."

As Tracy shakes out tunics, pants, sweaters, and vests from the suitcase, she tries not to gag; the smell of mothballs and some unidentifiable Chinese odour rises even from the old-fashioned button-up cotton undergarments. Tracy hopes her mother will take Ah Mah on a shopping trip soon; she doesn't know how she'll face her friends if they catch her with an old woman wearing cloth shoes and an obviously home-sewn rabbit fur overcoat.

Ah-Hong takes three large photo albums from the suitcase and stacks them neatly on her night table. From her handbag, she extracts two silk-covered jewellery boxes. With a proud smile, she gives one to Tracy.

"Ah-Ying. This is for you. Open it."

Inside the box, Tracy finds the ugliest gold bracelet she has ever seen. She wonders if her mother will ever make her wear it. Maybe for one of those stupid family dinners that Nancy's planning for Ah Mah. At least the chances of her meeting a friend in a Chinese restaurant are low. Tracy puts on a smile. "Thank you!"

Ah-Hong smiles broadly and takes the bracelet out of the case. "Try it on."

She helps Tracy with the clasp then settles on a rocking chair beside the window while Tracy pretends to admire the bracelet. Ah-Hong glows. "I'm so glad you like the bracelet. It's the best design in Taiwan."

Tracy tries to keep her face expressionless.

"You finish with the clothes then you show Ah Mah where to take a bath."

Tracy is glad to hear her mother calling her to set the table for dinner. She hurries out of the bedroom, pointing out the door to the bathroom for her grandmother. As she is setting out the last of the cutlery, Tracy hears "Ah-Ying!" coming from the bathroom.

"Do I have to?" Tracy asks Nancy, who is peeling carrots in the kitchen.

"Yes, of course. What kind of granddaughter you are?"

"She's your mother!" Tracy spits as she rushes past the kitchen quickly enough not to hear her mother's gasp of incredulity.

Tracy finds her grandmother on her knees next to the bathtub, pulling on the chrome faucet handle.

"Ah Mah, what is it?" Tracy asks.

"I can't find the wash basin. And I can't find water."

Tracy recalls the plastic wash basins in the bathhouse at her grandmother's farm. They were big enough for her to lie down in and she remembers how her grandmother would fill them with pails of cold well water and pots of boiling hot water carried from the brick stove in the kitchen. Tracy shows her grandmother how to turn on the tap and retreats, feeling demoralized. She can see the signs of things to come.

Over the next weeks, Tracy shows her grandmother how to flush the toilet, turn on the electric stove, control the thermostat in her room, raise and lower venetian blinds, operate the washing machine, and use the microwave, among other things. She is responsible for filling her grandmother's nightly hot-water bottle; Ah Mah isn't used to the cold rains of Vancouver. When she comes home from school each day, Tracy takes her grandmother out into the neighbourhood for short strolls. After a month, Tracy, knowing that appeals to her mother would be fraught and fruitless, begs her father to be relieved of her caretaking duties.

"Be patient, honey. Your grandmother will get used to things in time," her father urges. "You remember how kind she has always been to you. Now is your chance to show how much you care about her."

Tracy remembers the treats her grandmother used to give her when she and her mother lived on her grandmother's farm that year before they came to Canada, when she was five. She always looked forward to the honey balls that her grandmother made with puffed rice. Weightless, white, melt-in-your-mouth delicacies. And her grandmother's special mantous: white breads filled with sweet potatoes and cane sugar; her grandmother had invented them especially for her. Tracy is impatient for her grandmother to become comfortable in their kitchen so she can taste those treats again.

In November, Nancy convinces Ah-Hong to take English classes at David's church. "You'll make new friends. Tracy can help you with the lessons."

Tracy glares at her mother behind her grandmother's back but Nancy ignores her.

When Ah-Hong brings her first English assignment home, Tracy pretends that she has to do homework in her room. She turns up the volume on her tape deck and hums along to "Ebony and Ivory." Later, as Tracy is watching *Three's Company* in the family room and wondering how she can get her mother to allow her to buy a T-shirt like the dizzy blonde's on the show, Ah-Hong sits down beside her with a piece of paper.

"Ah-Ying ah, can you help me?"

Not taking her eyes off the TV, Tracy says, "Sure, Ah Mah. What do you need?"

"I can't learn the words. Can you read them to me?"

"Just a minute, okay?"

Ah-Hong stares at the two women bouncing around in clingy T-shirts and shorts on the television screen and waits. Tracy reluctantly takes the paper when a commercial comes on. She reads a list of words: Hello, Good-bye, Thank you, Please. Tracy points to the first word and says, "'Hello' means *Li-he*." Ah-Hong repeats the word. They make their way down a list of twenty words but when Tracy starts at "Hello" again, Ah-Hong can't remember it.

"Here, let me write it down for you . . . Oh, I forgot, I can't. I'll have to ask Ma to write it in Chinese for you."

"No," Ah-Hong says.

"It's okay. She wants to help. She'll be happy to do it."

"No. No use," Ah-Hong repeats, vigorously shaking her head. A lock of hair falls out of her bun. A flush creeps over her face as Tracy scrutinizes her.

Thinking that perhaps she has been unclear, Tracy tries again. "If Mama writes the characters beside the English words, you'll be able to remember the meanings more easily. You'll be able to study them on your own. Maybe she can even write the sounds in Chinese to remind you." Tracy hopes her Taiwanese pronunciation has been clear enough for her grandmother to understand.

"No. It won't help. I won't understand the characters." Ah-Hong bows her head. Her face is bright red under the fading tan.

Tracy is so shocked that she doesn't notice when the TV program resumes.

Oddly, it is Tracy who feels ashamed. Shame for her grandmother's illiteracy, shame for failing to know that her grandmother had come by her state naturally, that poor women of that era were rarely taught to read and write. She feels particularly ashamed at being the cause of her grandmother's embarrassment. She speaks to her father and he says, "Don't worry, honey. Your grandmother's been illiterate all her life. She's used to it. Don't feel bad."

Tracy is also bothered by the stiff relations between Ah Mah and her father. Although Tracy is annoyed by the forced politeness with which her grandmother treats her father, she does not speak to him about it, suspecting that he would be just as blasé on that score as well. She admires her father's restraint. But then, perhaps he doesn't see the way Ah Mah stiffens when her father addresses her in his pidgin Taiwanese. Even beyond the language barrier, Ah Mah and her father do not seem to have anything to say to each other. Though it has only been hinted at by her grandmother and never mentioned by her parents, Tracy senses her parents' marriage likely met with resistance from the Huang family in Taiwan. Tracy wishes her grandmother would give her father a chance; he's helping to support her after all.

Ah-Hong refuses to attend any more English classes after the first. Nancy says it's just as well. Most of the Chinese students speak Cantonese anyway. There's no one who would be able to speak Taiwanese with Ah-Hong, so there'd be little likelihood of her finding a friend in those classes. What about the seniors' centre? The YWCA? The community centre? Ah-Hong nixes all suggestions.

Later, in midlife, when Tracy is a United Church minister herself, she will look back at her mother's attempt to be a dutiful daughter and wonder how her intelligent mother could have overlooked her grandmother's language difficulties when planning Ah-Hong's immigration to Canada. Her grandmother's experiences will give Tracy greater understanding when she's working with immigrant women, but they will also make Tracy less than enthusiastic to sponsor older immigrants who do not know English and are set in their ways.

Ah-Hong becomes house-bound. Her skin becomes lighter and she begins to gain weight. When she asks Nancy if she can plant a vegetable garden in the backyard, she is told that it would ruin the landscaping, besides, the yard is in shade and it's difficult enough to get shrubs to grow, let alone vegetables. Nancy buys fresh produce from the supermarket each week so she can prepare vegetarian dishes for her mother. She also provides material for Ah-Hong to make new clothes for herself but Ah-Hong says her eyes are too bad to sew now. Skeins of yarn purchased by Nancy sit untouched on the shelf in Ah-Hong's closet. When Ah-Hong asks to cook for the family, Nancy tells her there will be no more drudge work for her; she is supposed to be enjoying her retirement now. Tracy believes that Nancy, whom she has secretly nicknamed "Geiger Counter for Imperfection," just doesn't want anyone to sully her immaculate kitchen. Tracy can't figure out what her grandmother does all day.

In late November, David parks the family car on the street in front of the house and takes a broom to the garage. He moves the lawn mower, storage boxes, and sports equipment to one side of the garage and sets up a shrine on the other. Nancy had taken Ah-Hong to the Buddhist temple in Strathcona, a half-hour drive away, but when Ah-Hong discovered that most of the worshippers were of Japanese descent, she'd refused to return. Her opinions of the Japanese are indelible and she can't stomach the thought of spending hours with her former oppressors.

"They're not the same Japanese. So many of these people weren't even born in Japan," Nancy says in frustration.

"No. I can't," Ah-Hong says. The terror and anger in her eyes are unmistakable.

"Oh well . . . it's a long drive anyway," Nancy says.

Tracy is amazed that her mother does not put up a long series of arguments as she does on the few occasions when her parents disagree. But then, her grandmother has brought out a different side of her mother, which surfaced not too long after her arrival, when the subject of Tracy's wardrobe arose.

Tracy's clothing became a volatile topic between Tracy and her mother as soon as she entered her teens. Instead of the tidy dresses that Nancy favoured for her, Tracy started to prefer more casual attire. The matter came to a head in October when, following the trend started by *Flashdance* in the spring, Tracy began wearing ripped sweatshirts and leggings like many of the girls at school. Nancy threw out the ripped clothes and purchased new ones, which

Tracy doctored to her tastes.

"I spent good money on the clothes!" Nancy yelled.

"Yeah, and I'm wearing them. You didn't waste your money. I'm still wearing them. If you think about it, you're the one who wasted money. The other sweatshirts were just fine before you threw them out!"

"You pay for new clothes!"

"No. Not until you pay for the ones that you threw out!"

Nancy shook the sweatshirt at Tracy. "Disrepectful girl!"

Although Ah-Hong couldn't understand English, she had somehow figured out the situation. She walked into Tracy's bedroom, stood between her daughter and granddaughter, and said to Nancy, "Do you remember when you were a teenager?"

Nancy walked away to the bed and sat down. "Okasan, what are you talking about?"

"I'm talking about when you wanted to start going to church instead of temple. And when you wanted to marry a white man," Ah-Hong said quietly.

Nancy flushed. "That's different!"

"Is it?"

"I was older and . . . Look, she's my child and I'll raise her the way I see fit!"

Ah-Hong stood over her daughter. "I remember when you used to value my opinion. When you didn't dare to disobey me."

"Those days are long gone, Okasan." Nancy's set face left no doubt of the veracity of her statement.

Though Ah-Hong had left the room without another word, Nancy never raised the subject of the ripped sweatshirts again. Tracy later wondered if her grandmother would be able to convince Nancy to allow her to watch *Fast Times at Ridgemont High* with her friends, or even just to stay out after nine PM, but decided not to cause more trouble, for her grandmother's sake.

Try as she might, Tracy's imagination cannot stretch to the point of conjuring up images of a youthful Nancy obedient to her mother; the gap between the mother she has always known and the girl that she was supposed to have been is simply too wide. Even when her grandmother shows her black and white photographs of a young woman in a poodle skirt, all Tracy can see is her mother's all-too-familiar flashing eyes accustomed to giving "the look" when she is displeased. Still, Tracy can see that her mother's devotion to Ah Mah is real.

After some time, Tracy begins to think of her grandmother as she would a dog that she has to take out for daily walks. Most days they stroll down tree-lined streets to West Point Grey Park, pausing at times to admire particularly striking window frames or chimney spires on heritage houses, and at other times to examine the hydrangeas and holly bushes bordering the well-groomed lawns, or to smell the climbing roses on arched gateways. Ah-Hong asks Tracy about the history of the houses and owners only to be met with blank looks. To Tracy's dismay, her grandmother promises that she will pass on all she knows of their family history so that Tracy will not have shallow roots in this sterile city. Ah-Hong likes the view of English Bay from the park and will contentedly sit on a bench while Tracy jogs around the fields with her Sony Walkman blasting "Billie Jean" or "Do You Really Want to Hurt Me?" into her ears. On days when Tracy has little homework, they will trek down Trimble Street to Locarno Park or even to the west end of Spanish Banks. Tracy is constantly on edge during these walks; she plans to introduce Ah-Hong as a Third World refugee seeking temporary shelter at her house, should they run into one of her friends.

Two weeks before Christmas break, Ah-Hong asks to walk to Spanish Banks when Tracy arrives home from school. The afternoon dusk is rapidly turning to darkness but Ah-Hong insists on the outing despite the chilly air. "It's not raining. Let's go." She puts on her rabbit-fur overcoat and winter boots, then waits for Tracy at the door. Tracy reluctantly agrees but says, "We can't stay long, I have a science project to do." She is annoyed with herself for having put off the research essay until now and she doesn't know if she will be able to do the term project in two days.

They walk in silence, Tracy leading the way with quick, angry steps and Ah-Hong silently trailing behind. By the time they reach the deserted beach, Tracy's hands and feet are cold. She fists her hands deeper into her ski jacket and thumps down on a log, sullenly waiting for her grandmother to be done so they can turn back.

Ah-Hong ambles down to the water's edge and stares out at the waves. To the east, the lights of downtown Vancouver glimmer on the far side of the dark waters of English Bay. She stands unmoving for what seems to Tracy to be hours, then dawdles along the shoreline for what seems to be hours more. Finally, she bends down and picks up something from the sand. Tracy breathes a sigh of relief when she sees Ah-Hong strolling towards her. Ah-Hong sits down heavily on the log and turns over the white object in her hand.

"What do you have there, Ah Mah?"

"A shell. See?" She hands it to Tracy.

Tracy examines the shell: a worthless piece of broken clam, covered with grey-white barnacles, like so many pieces of debris on the beach. Most people would step on it as they would rock and sand. She can't understand why her grandmother would bother to pick it up.

Ah-Hong points to the barnacles. "Do you know they are alive?"

"Naah . . . no way!"

"It's true. The barnacles will live again if they are in the right waters."

"Right. Can we go now?"

Ah-Hong takes the shell back and says, "Just a bit longer, Ah-Ying."

Tracy sighs and huddles into her jacket. She wishes she had worn snow pants and boots instead of jeans and sneakers. She draws circles in the sand with the toe of her shoe. A man with a dog on a leash walks by and waves at them but does not stop.

"Ah-Ying. What is out there?" Ah-Hong points west.

"I think it's Burrard Inlet?" Geography isn't Tracy's strongest subject.

"And if you keep moving past the water, would you eventually reach Taiwan?" There is a wistful look on Ah-Hong's face.

"I think so. I'm not sure. You'll have to ask my parents." Tracy can't keep the note of impatience out of her voice. She huddles further into her jacket.

"I have lived a long life. I have suffered and I still do," Ah-Hong says.

Tracy suddenly notices the tears on her grandmother's cheeks but pretends she hasn't seen them. How can her grandmother say that she is suffering in Canada? As far as she can see, Ah Mah has a pretty good life. Tracy says nothing.

"I have lost many people and many things," Ah-Hong continues. "Property, friends, children, husband, family. And your mother, she has lost a child as well."

Tracy thinks of the photographs of a baby with dark curls that her mother still keeps in her bedroom, the brother who died when she was in elementary school. She doesn't understand why her grandmother is dredging up old sorrows.

"A mother's bond with her children is never broken but sometimes a mother has to look out for herself. Sometimes, a mother has to save herself. Some losses are too much to bear."

It will not be until she becomes a mother herself that Tracy will understand what her grandmother meant about a mother's unbreakable bond with her children, and even later before she understands what her grandmother meant about saving herself. But on that dark evening by the sea, all Tracy can think about is getting out of the cold and into the warmth of her home.

Ah-Hong walks back to the water's edge and throws the shell into the waves.

When they get home, Tracy begins her science project. She receives an "A" on her research project about rock barnacles. With the project out of the way and other school commitments easing in the last days before break, Tracy is able to take her grandmother to the beach many more times before school lets out. Each time, her grandmother picks up a barnacle-encrusted shell and throws it into the water.

When winter break starts, Tracy goes shopping with her friends for presents and makes plans for movie dates. At home, she helps her mother start the Christmas baking. She also catches her mother hiding her grandmother's presents in the lower drawers of the dining room hutch: a cashmere sweater with matching scarf and mitts, expensive-looking Chinese medicines, and a set of pearl earrings.

"I hope you'll be as good to me when I'm old," Nancy says.

Tracy can't imagine Nancy living with her when she retires.

A few days before Christmas, David excitedly tells the family that they are to expect a visit from the General Secretary of the United Church, an honour bestowed only on select ministers. Nancy launches into a whirlwind of activity, cleaning and cooking nonstop for three days. She looks up new recipes for lunch menus; David is deputized to search out the best Noble Fir in the neighbourhood Christmas tree lot; and Tracy is told to make a new wreath for the door, under Nancy's strict supervision. Nancy gets her hair cut and plucks her eyebrows the day before the lunch.

At 11 AM on the appointed day, Ah-Hong comes into the kitchen in her best tunic and jacket while Nancy is putting the icing on a chocolate cake and Tracy is sprinkling icing sugar on dessert plates. Nancy looks up and inspects her mother, noting the cloth shoes and the neat bun in a hairnet. She says, "Okasan, you look tired. Maybe it would be better for you to rest while the General Secretary is here. The visit will surely tire you out more. I'll bring some food to you in your room."

Ah-Hong's eyes flare. She turns and walks out of the kitchen without a word.

After the General Secretary leaves, Nancy goes into Ah-Hong's room and closes the door. Tracy stands outside the door and deciphers as many Taiwanese phrases as she can in the torrent streaming from her grandmother: "Ashamed of me!" "What kind of a daughter are you?" "You used to respect my wishes!" Tracy can hear her grandmother's sobbing even after Nancy opens the door in a rage and, discovering Tracy outside, banishes her to the family room.

Nancy and Ah-Hong will be tight-lipped and tense during the ride to the airport but there will be tears on both sides at the departure point. Ah-Hong will never return to Vancouver.

Twenty-five years later, on the day after her grandmother's funeral in Taiwan, her First Uncle's wife, Ah-Feng, in a rare moment of confidence, will say to Tracy, "We don't understand why she didn't stay in Canada. She would never say why. When she came back, the whole village was surprised. She looked so healthy and plump and her skin was so white!"

Tracy will think of rock barnacles and remember that the barnacle's protective plates cover cirri which are only exposed when the tide rises and the barnacle senses favourable currents. That in the winter, the barnacle subsists on its stored food reserves and the hardy greyish-white shell prevents desiccation of its fragile interior. Then she will imagine a thoroughly white barnacle setting down her antennae and making fast to her homeland, a sessile creature with feathery cirri waving in friendly waters, contentedly gathering nourishment for subsistence.

Shu

IN HER YOUTH, when she was known as Mei Xing, Nancy had believed in forgiveness. "Mei Xing, wang shi yi yi." Beautiful Star, what's done is done, her mother used to say. But that was before Ah-Ging and Fifth Brother's deaths, before she came to Canada, and before she met her mother-in-law, Beryl. Now, as she closed in on sixty, she believed in carrying on her life without hindrance from bothersome notions born of childish naiveté.

Nancy found it hard not to sink into bitterness when Beryl died—leaving her to guess eternally at the truth about her son's death; harder still when Beryl's sister, Margaret, invited herself to Vancouver for the funeral—eight days in the house of someone she'd never met, the nerve of the woman! When she first met Margaret at the airport, Nancy thought Beryl had performed a miraculous regression and come back to life. There she was: the straight nose; the tall, upright carriage; the white bouffant hair; the clipped accent; and, it seemed, the same air of British entitlement. That is, until Margaret mouthed more than banalities to Nancy's husband, David, at the dinner table.

Margaret had spent almost her entire life as an Anglican missionary in India, making her the perfect dinner guest at the Andersons'—David being a United Church minister. He would have been a gracious host regardless of his aunt's vocation, but having common interests with his guests, especially religious ones, invariably brought out the raconteur in him. He gesticulated over the glasses of red wine, his liver-spotted hands leaping up and down between forkfuls of roast beef, punctuating key points with impassioned looks, while Margaret nodded and smiled. He and Margaret traded anecdotes about his stints in Asia (first as an English teacher in Taiwan and later as a minister in Singapore) and her work in India, of which she spoke with genuine enthusiasm, displaying a sympathetic understanding of Indians, with no trace of condescension or superiority.

"Margaret, what was the biggest change that you noticed during your years in India?" David asked.

"Aside from the rise of the Indian middle class and the advent of technology?" She paused. "Actually, it's not India that's changed. I'd say the biggest change has been my attitude towards ministry. When I set off for the Lahore mission in the late '40s, I thought I was going to bring salvation to the heathens. Well, the natives have taught me otherwise. Nowadays, I bring what help I can to the poor but have no thoughts about converting anyone. Basic education—giving people the means to escape from crushing poverty. That is my work."

"You don't teach the Indians about the Word of the Lord?" David said incredulously.

Nancy stopped topping up water glasses and sat down, gaping at Margaret.

"Only as an incidental matter, should any interest arise during my daily travels. I gave up evangelizing ages ago."

"But isn't that what the Church wants you to do?"

"At my age, David, I define my own ministry. The Indian people have religions that have served them perfectly well for thousands of years. My beliefs are not to be imposed on unwilling audiences. If I see a soul in need of comfort, I share my beliefs, but I never force my views on anyone."

Nancy made a mental note to check for scented soaps and fresh flowers in the guest bathroom. She resolved to find other services to perform for this unusual woman during her brief stay with them.

"And how have you been received by the Indians over the years?" David asked.

"Once I got over the idea that I was somehow 'saving' them, we got along splendidly. I've learned to appreciate curries and they've learned to tolerate and, perhaps even *like* the well-meaning memsahib."

Nancy concluded that Beryl must have inherited a rogue gene; for Margaret felt more like family to Nancy in one evening than Beryl ever had during the nearly four decades that she had known her.

Nancy recalled her first dinner at Beryl's house. She had thought she was being helpful by setting the table. She'd even researched place settings in *The Joy of Cooking* in advance. Beryl had taken one look and said, "I don't know who set the table but that person really needs to learn some basics," then went around and turned all the knife blades to face the plates. They'd both pretended nothing had happened when they sat down to eat.

But that was just the beginning. Whether out of ignorance or sheer malice, Beryl would come out with the most offensive remarks that would nowadays be called racist. "Now, Nancy. Have you ever had pork loin before? I hear you people mostly eat dogs." And, "You'll have to send Tracy over here so I can teach her some proper table manners. I want my granddaughter to grow up civilized." "David only likes his potatoes cooked a certain way. I'll bring some over for him tomorrow. At least he'll have two decent dinners this week."

Poor David. "Mother, please," he would say but she just pretended she didn't understand what he meant, and maybe she really didn't. Oh well, he made an effort at any rate. Some husbands would have feigned ignorance. Nancy couldn't have expected him to be disrespectful to his mother. It would have been wrong for her to incite discord between mother and son—only bad daughters-in-law were malicious enough to sever filial ties. Incurring Beryl's wrath by marrying her was rebellion enough for David. Enough for an entire lifetime.

Nancy had blazed with shame at that dinner. Nancy, the perfect student who never lacked for friends or regard, whose father was a respected village elder and landowner. Nancy, with her MSc in chemistry, descended from a long line of scholars, looked down upon by a woman with God knows how little education, who thought she was superior simply because of the colour of her skin. How vulnerable the young can be!

Nancy dished out more peas and carrots for David. She refilled Margaret's and David's wine glasses while they continued their discussion about evangelical ministry. Nancy recalled that Beryl—proud of the British who had "converted a lot of heathens when they were in China"—used to give generously to the Anglican mission fund at her church. Once, Nancy had heard Beryl telling a woman from her church choir, or maybe it was her gardening society, that she'd just returned from the mall and "seen a group of Orientals there. They all looked clean and well-fed. I gave them a nod and a smile." And the woman had replied, "And you're always so kind to your daughter-in-law too, aren't you?"

David laid down his knife and fork and asked, "Margaret, what do you think is the highlight of your work in India?"

Margaret sipped her wine and closed her eyes, a contemplative look on her face. "I suppose I would have to say it's the work that I do with the children. I love going to see the new mothers and offering them my help. And when the children get older, teaching them at our mission. I give the parents hope for the future. Sometimes, they'll let me care for the newborns. As a sign of trust, you see." Margaret wore a proud look on her face.

Dripping honey into a cup of tea, Nancy thought of the time directly after her son's birth, so long ago, when she had been in Canada barely a year and commanded only rudimentary English. It was the first time that Beryl had visited alone since Nancy's return from the hospital with Luke.

Nancy had just come home from dropping her daughter, Tracy, off to her Grade One classroom. She had two hours before Luke's next feeding and had put the time to good use: started a stew in the crock pot, put Luke down for his nap, soaked in a sitz bath, and now had time for a leisurely shower. She closed her eyes and her shoulders relaxed as the warm spray washed over her, reminding her of languid childhood swims in temperate seas. She turned off the tap, slid the shower door open, and stepped onto the bath mat.

Beryl was standing at the ensuite door with a mewling Luke in her arms. Nancy hastily grabbed her robe and wrapped it around her dripping, pregnancy-slack body, barely concealing her surprise and anger.

"I let myself in with the emergency key. Hope you don't mind," Beryl said and carried Luke out of the master bedroom and into his. Nancy followed, leaving a water trail behind.

"I think he needs a diaper change." Beryl laid him down on the change table and started to undo the lower snaps of his jumper.

"Baby just changed. Need sleep." Nancy hoped she didn't sound shrill.

"No. Trust me. I know babies. He needs to be changed." She continued to undress Luke and he started flailing, knocking his clenched fists against a silver tin at the head of the change table.

"What's this?" Beryl lifted the tin, lowered her glasses, and squinted at the "Dahua" label on it.

"Baby powder. My mother shopped it. Send from Taiwan."

"Humph. Remind me to bring you some Johnson and Johnson next time. And I don't know why you buy these new-fangled disposable diapers. Cloth was good enough for David. What a waste of money. Oh, I'm sorry, I hope you don't mind my directness. But you must admit, I do have a bit more experience than you."

Nancy gritted her teeth and willed herself to keep her mouth shut. And then, as Beryl exposed Luke, a stream of yellow liquid made a parabolic arc from his erect penis to her nose. Beryl turned her face away and held the diaper up to shield herself from the spray, drops trickling down her chin onto her newly pressed lavender pantsuit. "Nancy, can't you teach your son better manners?"

Nancy blew on her tea and smiled faintly.

Perhaps it was jetlag or else a bent for sentimentality that only surfaced with alcohol, but as they lingered over coffee, Margaret's voice gradually took on a melancholic tone.

"I can't believe Beryl's gone. It seems just yesterday we were building snowmen in our front yard. I remember that day distinctly . . . it was 1938."

The Andersons stirred in their seats and waited, politely attentive. Margaret toyed with a napkin ring then set it beside her plate, as if she had come to a decision. Her eyes fixed on the neat stacks of china in the cabinet behind David, she said, "Beryl had just left school. She was fourteen. Mum had her doing most of the housework by then. But there was a terrific snowstorm. Hadn't seen anything like it before in London. We had great fun. Until Dad came home. He was in a right temper. Seemed some bloke had made a remark about his origins at work. Wasn't the first time. We saw the back of his hand for no reason. I remember what Beryl said afterwards: 'I hate being working class. Always somebody who thinks they're a blue blood compared to us. Blue-arsed fly, more like. Just you wait. I'll make something of myself yet.' Always a fighter, that Beryl."

Margaret rolled the napkin ring back and forth over the tablecloth and looked at her hostess.

Nancy nearly spilled her tea. No wonder Beryl never talked about her background; constantly made out like she was an empress or something. Just yesterday, when Nancy was preparing for the estate sale, she'd found those antique Tiffany pickle forks and asparagus tongs in Beryl's mahogany hutch; every piece of silverware still polished. She had asked David what they were. Beryl was never one to stint when it came to heirlooms. Thought she would start her own Anglo-Canadian pedigree. Too bad David spoiled the purity of the lineage. In Taiwan, they would have called him an unfilial son for disregarding her wishes.

Margaret continued her reminiscences, as if she were unable to stopper the memories now she had uncorked them. "Mum was broken-hearted when Beryl left with Arthur. She cried for days. But Beryl was set on going with her dashing Canadian soldier." Then, glancing at Nancy, she added, "I imagine it's difficult for all parents when a son or daughter emigrates, though, no matter what the circumstances . . . "

Nancy looked up from her tea and thought of the day she had left Taiwan to join David in Vancouver. She saw her mother standing at the airport gate, her arms full of bags of crackers and dried seaweed, part of the care package for which Nancy and Tracy had had no luggage room, smiling through her uncontrollable tears, saying in a mixture of Mandarin and Taiwanese, "Mei Xing, um men huan luh. Yao xiao xin." Beautiful Star, don't worry about us. Take good care. Mother and daughter both knew what she really wanted to say was, "Will I ever see you again?" But that wasn't the Taiwanese way. She didn't want to burden her daughter with sadness on her departure for a better life, though Nancy had heard her mother's weeping earlier in the day when she thought no one was near. It would have been a curse to admit the possibility of permanent separation.

As it turned out, Nancy had only been able to see her mother three times since then—when her mother visited Vancouver for a few months in the early 1980s, and when Nancy returned to Taiwan for the funerals of Fourth Brother and her step-sister Mei Lu. Her last visit home had been to her mother's funeral. Nancy pushed the sad thought away and busied herself with serving a piece of apple pie to her guest.

Margaret spooned a dollop of whipped cream on top of the slice and went on, "Mum always regretted that we didn't have enough coupons to get Beryl a proper wedding dress. But then it was a rare war bride who had a white dress. With the Blitz and rationing, we were lucky to have food at all. My mouth used to water when Beryl wrote home about fresh bread and bananas at her in-laws here. She never got along with her mother-in-law, though. Always thought the in-laws had wanted Arthur to marry a Canadian girl instead."

She looked pointedly at Nancy and seemed on the verge of adding more but refrained, perhaps not wanting to reveal anything delicate. Nancy gave her a probing glance and wondered how close the two sisters had been and how frank were the contents of Beryl's letters. She realized how little she had known Beryl despite their long history together. Did Margaret know about what happened the night Luke died? And would she tell if she knew?

When the grandfather clock struck nine, David rose and retired to his study—a sermon to prepare, he said, difficult to find a fresh angle on Matthew 18:21 but such was the life of a minister. Margaret offered to help with clearing the table but was ushered to her room and urged to finish unpacking by a scandalized hostess.

Nancy returned to the kitchen and rearranged the dishwasher so all the plates were lined up in tight rows, like her hairdresser did with the curlers. It gave her pleasure to set things in order—a contentment that kept the uncertainties of life at bay. She felt powerful when she stacked Tupperware containers one inside the other with their array of matching lids; when she aligned the bottles of chemicals in the storage room at work, separating organic from inorganic compounds, flammables from incombustibles, ensuring alkali metals were well distanced from chlorinated hydrocarbons lest they ignited spontaneously. She swept a satisfied look around the kitchen: counters wiped clean, tea towels tidily hung, spice racks filled with topped-up jars—cassia, cumin, parsley, peppercorns, star anise—and pasta tubes ranged in descending order from perciatelli to penne in glass containers.

Fifth Brother was the same way, with his Chinese classics and calligraphy brushes all lined up and arranged by size on his immaculate rosewood desk, unforgiving in his meticulousness. Nancy pushed the thought aside. Ah-Ging and Fifth Brother belonged to a part of her life that she had long put away. What had happened to them was unforgivable but no amount of scrutiny would alter the past, and she saw no point in futile efforts.

Later, as David sat on the four-poster bed that dominated their room, scribbling on a yellow legal pad, Nancy picked up a brass frame from the dresser and wiped the glass clean with the sleeve of her pyjamas, as she did every night. Nancy stroked the glass. The memory of Luke's toothless grin and brown curls turned her heart even now. They took her baby and cut him open and they still couldn't figure out why he died. Sudden Infant Death Syndrome. Happened to thousands of babies every year. They wouldn't let her hold her baby one last time at the funeral home, didn't keep a single lock of his hair or make hand and foot imprints. She had nothing of him other than a few baby photos, his receiving blankets, and his clothing. It was one of her biggest regrets—her failure to preserve more of the ephemeral spark of life that had passed all too briefly through her own. But she had not let his death affect Tracy's or David's lives—of that she was certain.

Nancy set the picture back on top of the leather case containing a golden baby bracelet sent from Taiwan. She rearranged the dying marigolds and baby's breath in the vase next to the photograph then switched off the overhead lights, leaving the bedside lamps on. David's blond-turned-white head was still bent over his pad. Under the droopy skin, he remained the handsome man who had brought her to this foreign land so many years ago. Nancy's hair was probably the same colour under the black dye. They'd had a good marriage, even with the heartaches. She had no regrets about marrying him.

Nancy settled beside him with a pair of reading glasses and opened her Chinese-English Bible. David had given it to her when they were courting and it still served the dual purpose of improving her English and providing her comfort. The Holy Book fell open to the story of Ruth and Naomi. As Nancy read, David turned off his lamp and placed his pillow flat on the bed.

"David . . . what was your mother like when she young?"

David, prone, turned his face towards her. "Well, she was a good mother. Always waiting for me with a healthy snack after school. Never asked too much of me or my father. She worked hard to be a good housewife. Hao tai tai."

"How she act with Chinese?"

"I wouldn't know. We hardly ever saw any in our neighbourhood and she didn't go too far from home. I don't think she encountered too many when she was in England either. In fact, you may have been the first Asian that she ever knew well."

"You think I was good daughter-in-law?"

He paused for a lengthy second. "I think you both tried your best. Are you going to be ready to turn off your light soon? I'd better get some sleep if I'm going to go to work tomorrow."

As Nancy lay in the dark, she wondered if she could have done anything differently to smooth her relationship with Beryl. Should she have been more tolerant? More solicitous? More accommodating? Perhaps she should have tried to become a gardener. Joined Beryl's choir. Learned about antique furniture and silverware. Perhaps . . . perhaps she should have been more forgiving. She closed her eyes and tried not to think of wide-open spaces and infinite, untapped, lost opportunities. She wandered through ruthless desert storms of thought before finally reaching a merciful oasis of fitful sleep.

The following day, after David closed the front door on lingering odours of sausages and toast, Nancy sat on the patio with a cup of green tea. The house was quiet again—a bungalow in West Point Grey, first lived in by Beryl and Arthur, then given to David as an early inheritance thirty years ago, a fact Beryl never let them forget. The dwarf hemlock that Beryl planted in the garden had grown how many feet since then? She said the hydrangeas changed seven shades from pink to blue the first year she planted them though Nancy had only ever seen cobalt blue. The ferns, variegated butcher's broom, and wild ginger with mottled silver leaves beside the rock garden were flourishing. As was the cherry tree, dropping snowy petals, that took over a decade to bear fruit. Who would have thought a full shade garden could have turned out so nicely? But then she was a master gardener. Coaxed life out of shrivelled, collapsed plants when anyone else would have given up.

Nancy started when the screen door screeched open behind her.

"Oh, Margaret. Have good sleep? Please sit down. I make toast."

"No. Don't bother, dear. I won't take breakfast this early. System still out of sorts from the flight."

She seated herself in a chair across from Nancy's and watched the iridescent hummingbirds cluster around the red basin-shaped feeders on the edge of the patio. Nancy poured a cup of green tea and set it on the round, steel-rimmed table.

"It's nice here, isn't it, Nancy? Beryl did a brilliant job with the garden. She's been kind to you?"

"Yes. Beryl been very generous."

"Unconscious racists are the worst, aren't they?"

"Excuse me?!"

"I'm very good at reading between the lines, my dear. Beryl kept up a faithful correspondence with me. I'm sorry for the way she's treated you."

"No need. Beryl been very good to me."

"Alright, dear, have it your way."

Nancy considered the soft, wrinkled face looking at her with such honest concern, the features so familiar and yet so foreign, and was struck by the unmistakable kindness. "Something Beryl did. Don't know if she told you. About night Luke died . . ."

Margaret interrupted, "Yes, I gathered she never told you. It was awfully clear from the letters. She found blood on the sheets, you know. Carried the guilt to her grave."

"Blood on Luke's bed? But it was SIDS. No cause of death. And why did she not tell me?"

"I know the autopsy results were inconclusive but she believed she might have done something dodgy. She put the baby to sleep on his side, you see. That's why she tried to stop the autopsy. I know you asked her repeatedly if Luke was on his back when she put him down. She would never tell you, right? Some people just can't bear challenges to their ideas of themselves. She was accustomed to being competent in everything, you see."

Does that excuse her secrecy? Her lack of concern for David and me? When she knew we were searching for answers in our grief. Am I to feel sorry for her? To forgive her? Nancy watched cherry blossoms pirouette through the air to join the growing blanket in the backyard, her heart learning new rhythms in true syncopation as it arced and swooped with the moribund petals. The sight quickly blurred. Margaret reached across the table and took her hand.

"My dear, if I may be so presumptuous, as the Good Book says, 'They know not what they do.'"

"Please excuse," Nancy rose from the table and walked through the kitchen to her bedroom. She closed the door and pulled the shades, craving escape from excessive illumination, preferring umbral refuge.

She sat on the edge of the bed and stared at the vase on the dresser, which overflowed with sprays of cherry blossoms snipped earlier that morning, the slash on her thumb from a careless movement of the shears now bandaged over. She had not cried out and not a single drop of blood remained from the trail which she had left on her way to the kitchen. The cut had seemed trifling then, but her thumb throbbed now.

Memories of forgotten slights returned to her. The incidents seemed clearer and more comprehensible now. Beryl's complaints about the gifts Nancy had purchased for her at David's request for Christmases and birthdays. Her interminable doubts about Nancy's ability to provide David with a clean home, a good diet, and well-behaved children—never once reflecting on how she was interfering with their happiness.

Even after three decades, the pain had not diminished; and the knowledge that Beryl was the last person to see Luke alive was still insufferable. But Beryl had insisted on babysitting and Nancy was not brought up to counter her elders' wishes. Good daughters-in-law did not extend their chopsticks until all the zhangbei had selected the choicest morsels from the dishes in the middle of the dinner table; they knew their place.

The sow! Nancy fell on the bed and pounded her fists against the pillows. She sobbed and sobbed . . . for her dead son, her unanswered questions, her pent-up grief and anger, and yes, even lost opportunities . . . after a time, when her tears were spent, she sat up and assumed the sukhasana pose, breathing deeply, wishing for some respite from her tumultuous feelings. Catching sight of the cherry blooms, she stepped to the dresser.

She pinched a handful of blossoms and inhaled, then frowned, disappointed at the lack of scent. In the Chinese poems she had learned in her youth, she recalled, cherry blossoms were always symbolic of feminine beauty and sexuality, and of female dominance and power. But cherry blossoms also symbolized the fleeting nature of life. A brief birth in spring followed by death and decay. There was a cherry blossom poem with the line "my tears will flow together with your tears." She couldn't remember any more. Ah-Ging or Fifth Brother would have known. Nancy had never felt the weight of her age as heavily as she did at that moment.

She crushed the petals between her fingers, the softness reminding her of her mother's touch. Nancy imagined her mother saying, as she had on so many occasions, "Mei Xing, guai kee ah. Suan le." Beautiful Star, it's in the past. Let it go. In her mind's eye, Nancy saw the Chinese character for forgiveness, "shu" in Mandarin. Why hadn't she noticed before that "shu" was made up of two characters: "Lu," same as, sat on top of "xin," heart. When hearts were the same. Or as her mother would have said, "jiang xin bi xin" David would have concurred: "walk a mile in their shoes."

All these years, Nancy had never been able to forgive Beryl her racism, her attempts to exclude her from the family, her interfering; and, most of all, Beryl's refusal to tell her the truth about that night. But would it have eased her grief if Beryl had told her? Perhaps the anger towards her mother-in-law might even have helped propel her through that terrible period in their lives. And if she were in Beryl's position, would she have told? After all, Nancy's motto was "no need to tell" when it came to the unhappy past.

When Mei Xing was young, an astrologer had told her mother that she had a good life awaiting her. She was at an age when she could forgive easily. It was child's play to excuse a friend's hurtful words or absolve a brother's thoughtless pranks. When she became a woman and gained understanding, she left those ways behind. But then...perhaps she shouldn't have rushed to put away childish things.

She picked up Luke's photograph and the leather case from the dresser. Moving aside the sweaters on the top shelf of her closet, Nancy pushed the case and frame towards the rear, as far back as she could, then closed the door firmly behind her. She stepped back, slightly out of breath, and contemplated the sprigs in the vase. Then she slowly sat down on the bed, her hands clenched together in her lap.

The Good Lord had blessed her with a daughter and a grandson. She lived in a country free from the danger of disfigurement by acid baths, from threats of death by stoning, and from the shame of being sent back to her mother by an unhappy husband. She had never cowered at the approaching steps of Japanese colonizers like a Taiwanese peasant, nor had languished in an internment camp like the Japanese-Canadians. She didn't have to pay a head tax to enter this country. Racial slurs were seldom hurled at her and most of the time she felt safe from physical threats, knowing that the law protected her. Apartheid, ethnic cleansing, and race riots were events in distant parts of the world. Her mother would have said Mei Xing had fulfilled her destiny.

Nancy looked down at her clasped hands and wondered what it would take to forgive for all time, annoyed that untidy thoughts still dared to intrude upon her life.

Face

MY MOTHER SLIDES THE CLOSET DOOR closed and suddenly it is dark but I am not afraid because I have my new watch. My grandparents gave it to me when they came from Taiwan last week. It's a waterproof watch and works even when it is deep under water. The face lights up with a green glow when I push the button. But I don't push the button because I don't want to give myself away. I pretend I am a diver sitting at the bottom of the ocean. I puff out my cheeks and hold my breath. I count to ten in French like Miss Thompson taught us. When I reach eleven I forget the word so I let out my breath.

I like Mama's closet. It has her smell. Like soft flowers. Baba says women are soft and men are strong. He sends me to kendo classes so I can learn to be strong. He goes to kendo classes too so he can take his 4-dan exam. He says a man who cannot defend himself has no face. "The Wu family has a long tradition of courageous warriors, Stanley. You are part of an illustrious line. Hold your head up high." I pay attention at kendo class so I can make Baba smile when I practise my kiais at home. My sensei says when I meet an opponent face-to-face it is good to have a strong kiai so I can scare his spirit with my voice. Sometimes my throat hurts after I practise my kiais but I have to keep trying so I can make Baba proud.

I lie down on the hardwood floor and breathe in Mama's smell. Her closet is so big that four of me can lie down and still have room left over. Baba's clothes are in here too but they only take up one high rack and I can't smell them. Soon, I am cold lying alone. Mama didn't notice that I had taken my hoodie off when we got home. Usually, she would have said something like "It's raining. Put your sweatshirt back on or you'll catch a cold." I pull my arms out of my T-shirt and tug the shirt over my knees. I curl up into a ball and pretend I am inside a space capsule. The hairs on my arms stick up when I blast into deep space. I roll to the side of the closet and feel something brush my cheek. I put my arms back through the holes in the T-shirt and reach out in the dark. Mama's fur coats! They are so soft. I bury my nose in them.

Baba says Mama is the most beautiful woman on earth. He says she has perfectly balanced features in an oval face. I know it. I watch her sometimes when she "puts on her face." She always puts on powder, eye shadow, and lipstick. Sometimes when she has blue spots on her face she uses what she calls "concealer" before she puts on the powder. I bet she could teach a man with no face to make a new face with the bottles and jars on her dressing table. Like the clown face we had to make in art class today. We started with a big empty circle then we filled in the rest. Miss Thompson said my clown was the jolliest little man she had ever seen, just like me. The only jolly man I know is Santa Claus. I don't think I'm fat like him so I don't know why Miss Thompson said that. My tummy doesn't jiggle like jelly when I laugh. Aunt Helen, that's my mother's sister, says I'm losing my baby fat. Aunt Helen says my cousin Rose didn't lose her baby fat until she was ten but I'm growing much faster than either of her girls. It must be all those kendo classes, she says, though she doesn't know how I'm shooting up so fast with my picky food habits. She said that again at Grandma and Grandpa's "Welcome to Canada" dinner.

We went to a restaurant called Sun Sweewah. We had to drive a long time in the Lexus to get there because it was all the way across the city. Mama said it was in East Vancouver. Uncle Pete and Cousin Rose and Cousin Jasmine—I have to call them "big sisters" in Mandarin—were there too. They teased me.

"Try the eel, Stanley. You'll like it."

"Have some squab, Stanley. It's delicious."

I didn't like any of that weird, slimy stuff. Gooey duck, crab, and oysters. I told Mama I wanted chicken nuggets when we got home. She just sighed and ate my leftovers. Baba didn't even notice. He was too busy talking to Grandpa and Uncle Pete. Baba said they were going to have to close the business. Something about "tax evasion." I asked Mama what that was but she just shushed me. And what about the capital, Grandpa asked. Baba just shook his head and picked at the little bird on his plate. Nobody said anything. Mama and Aunt Helen looked at each other with big eyes. Grandma and Uncle Pete stopped eating too. Grandpa started talking in that funny, loud language that I can't understand. Mama says it's called Taiwanese. Then Baba slammed down his chopsticks and pushed his chair back. Uncle Pete got up and put his hand on Baba's arm and talked in that funny language too. Pretty soon Baba sat down but he didn't eat any more. He just ordered the beer with the dragon picture and was quiet for the rest of the meal. I asked him if I could try the dragon drink but he didn't answer.

At the end of the meal, Grandpa, Uncle Pete and Baba played the "grab the bill" game. Usually Baba wins the game but Grandpa spoke to him in Taiwanese and Baba turned around and walked outside for a cigarette. Grandpa said something else in Taiwanese and shook his head. I saw Uncle Pete give his plastic card to the restaurant man. We waited for Grandpa to finish talking to Uncle Pete before Grandma and Mama hustled me into the car. Baba was already in the driver's seat but he didn't say anything. I waved to Uncle Pete and his family as we drove away but they didn't wave back. Mama said, Stanley, they can't see you through the tinted glass. Nobody said anything else the whole way home.

When the five of us got home, we all went into the room with the white sofas and high ceilings that I'm not supposed to go into without asking. Baba, Grandma, and Grandpa started talking in Taiwanese and got so busy talking that they didn't notice me on one of the couches. But Mama did and took me upstairs. She ran a huge bubble bath and gave me a rubber book. She told me to take off my watch but I said no, it'll work under water. She just sighed and didn't say anything more. She seemed to be in a hurry to go back downstairs. She told me to be good in the bath, she would get a towel. Then she closed the door. I tried to read the book but it was a picture book of Peter Rabbit that I had read a million times already. I pretended I was an underwater explorer and lowered my whole body into the bath. I tried to count to twenty in Mandarin before I had to come up. I made it to twelve. I tried my watch's stopwatch under water. It worked! I played my diving game some more with the stopwatch. Mama was taking a long time coming back. I climbed out of the tub and decided to make myself a bubble bath kendo uniform with the bubbles that were left. When I was mostly covered in bubbles, I tried to open the door but my hands were slippery so it took a few tries. The banister was slick too but I made it down to the landing. I could hear my family talking in that loud language again. Sometimes one of them would say a few words in Mandarin but I couldn't make out what they were talking about. I crept down the stairs and stood by the door so I could see better.

Baba was standing next to the fireplace. There were two holes in the plaster next to the switch that makes the fire turn on and off. He didn't have a happy face. Grandpa was walking up and down next to the big windows with the closed blinds. Mama and Grandma were sitting on the smallest couch holding hands and their big eyes were moving back and forth between Grandpa and Baba. I could only understand the Mandarin words when they talked. I think the rest of the words were in Taiwanese.

" . . . [loud words that I didn't understand] . . . I will never agree," Baba said.

"No option if we take them with us," Grandpa said in Mandarin. He sounded like the principal when he talked to the big boys at school. The ones that set the garbage cans on fire.

"I can take care of them! I'll find work . . . [loud words] . . . " Baba replied.

Then there were no more words in Mandarin. Everything was in Taiwanese. I didn't think that funny language could get any louder but it did. By then my kendo uniform had dripped down to the carpet and I was getting cold. That was when Mama noticed me. She said something in Taiwanese and everyone turned to look at me. Aiyah, didn't I tell you to stay in the tub? Mama rushed over, took me by the arm, and we went upstairs to bed.

"I want chicken nuggets."

"I'll bring it later, Stanley. Try and sleep now."

I waited and waited but Mama didn't come and I was too sleepy to go downstairs again. Later on, I thought Mama and Grandma came into my room but I might have been dreaming. Grandma said, "I don't know how we'll manage without the money that you send us. I'll never be able to show my face at mahjong again." I thought I heard Mama crying but it was dark and I was half asleep. I remember thinking she had forgotten to give me my good night kisses. It's a game we have. She gives me little kisses all over my face and I give her one big kiss back. I was going to tell her but the next thing I knew Mama was shaking me awake and telling me to hurry so we wouldn't be late for school.

When Mama fetched me home from school, I peeked in the living room and saw the holes in the wall had been fixed. There was a nice fresh paint smell. I asked Mama who had made the holes and she said the room needed repainting and holes were something the workmen had to do to prep the room. She made chicken nuggets for my after-school snack before we went to kendo class. When we came home, Grandma and Grandpa said they would take us out for Chinese food but Mama said no, she would make some noodles at home. Baba was working late again so I didn't see him that night or the two nights after that.

On Sunday, Mama brought Grandma and Grandpa to church. Before we left, Mama told me not to talk about Baba's business to anyone, to say it was very good if someone asked. If anyone asked why Baba wasn't at church, I was to say he was not feeling well. I also promised to be good so she wouldn't be ashamed of me. Tracy was teaching Sunday school so it was fun. Patrick, that's Tracy's son, was there too. We learned about Adam and Eve and the apple. Tracy said Adam and Eve both tried to save face by blaming other people for their mistakes and that was wrong. We should always face the music when we make mistakes. Then Tracy showed us how to make caramel apples. So yummy! Patrick tried to take a bite of my apple after he had eaten all the caramel off his but Tracy made him stop and apologize. I don't like Patrick. Patrick's grandpa, Reverend Anderson, made funny faces to make me laugh when we were leaving. I like Reverend Anderson. When we got home, I saw Baba's Bentley in the garage but Mama said I wasn't to disturb him, he needed to sleep, so I didn't see him that day either.

Last night, Baba came into my room after I was in bed and sat beside me but he didn't turn on the light. I hadn't seen him since the welcome dinner. I jumped up and gave him a big hug. Baba hugged me back. It was a long hug and I could hardly breathe but I didn't say anything because I was so happy. Baba made me lie down, then he tucked me in. Only my nightlight was on so I could barely see his face. His eyes were very shiny. He sat beside me and looked at me for a long time. I was starting to fall asleep again when he said: Stanley, you know Baba loves you very much, don't you? I woke up quickly and nodded as hard as I could.

He ran a finger down my nose and said in Mandarin, "You have my nose. Straight, a round tip. We are destined for great wealth." Then he sighed.

I didn't know what to say so I said, "We're lucky, aren't we, Baba?"

"Yes, lucky." He felt my earlobes. "You have thick earlobes. Very auspicious."

I wrinkled my nose and looked blank.

"Means very lucky." Then he brushed my hair back from my forehead. "And a very smart forehead. A good face."

He kept stroking my hair. I began to close my eyes. Then he said, "I will always take care of you, Stanley. You and your mother. No matter what happens. Forever and ever. Don't forget that."

He began speaking in Taiwanese but it might not have been because it wasn't loud at all. I'd never heard anyone in my family speak Taiwanese quietly so maybe it was a different language. It sounded like the Huron Christmas carol they sang at church last Christmas, only without the music. I smiled and felt happy. Like when it's really cold and rainy outside and I'm wrapped inside a toasty blanket on my mama's lap with hot chocolate and chicken nuggets.

I don't know how long he sat on my bed but when I woke up this morning he was already at work so I went to school without saying goodbye to him. But now he's home and I'm so excited! I pull down one of Mama's fur coats and wrap it around me. I roll around on the floor and pretend I'm in a cocoon. I wait for Baba to find me.

It's not often that Baba has time to play with us. Mama says he's "it" and we are all to hide. Grandma and Grandpa and me. Mama is excited too. I can tell because she has her big-eye look. She is happy about Baba being home too. We are one big happy family. Baba says he'll take me to Disney World for my next birthday. I can go on the *20,000 Leagues Under the Sea* ride! Maybe Grandma and Grandpa will come too. I burrow deeper into my cocoon and shiver with excitement.

I hear Mama's voice outside. Then Grandpa's and Grandma's voices. They are speaking real Taiwanese. I hear heavy things being dragged across the hardwood. Bumping against the door. Then I hear Baba speaking loud, loud Taiwanese outside the bedroom. Loud banging. Grandpa speaking Taiwanese. Mama speaking English, "Please help. Please send police . . . " Sounds of heavy things falling. Screams. Grandpa and Baba speaking loud Taiwanese to each other. What sounds like a kiai, only this one is mixed with sobbing. Something falling. Grandma and Mama's screams. More sob-kiais. More sounds of things falling. Then there are no more sounds.

I feel hot all over. I crawl out of my cocoon and try to look out through the gap left by the sliding door but I see only black. I try to slide the door open but it's too heavy. My heart is beating hard and it's dark in here. "Mama! Mama!" I yell. The door slides open. I see bare feet. Then a black kendo uniform with wet splotches. A silver blade stained with red.

Baba!

⌒

I missed the funeral while I was in the hospital but Aunt Helen says it's just as well. Aunt Helen, with barely contained anger, refers to that day as the one when my parents and grandparents "passed." She arranged for my mother and grandparents to be buried at Ocean View Cemetery and we pay our respects there at the annual tomb-sweeping each spring. Aunt Helen had my father buried elsewhere but I've never been there. When you're older, she used to say, I'll take you there. I'm twenty now and have stopped asking for fear of incurring her wrath. "Best to forget, Stanley!" She prays for us to forgive my father's insanity.

She changed my last name to Shen when she brought me to live with Uncle Pete and my cousins in Coquitlam. "Nobody need ever know about your father," she said. "You can use our name from now on. You are a part of our family now." I spent my childhood as a Shen by name but a Wu at heart. My Shen cousin-sisters protected me at school and at home. None of my schoolmates guessed that I wasn't born into the Shen family; my Facebook albums only show images of me with the Shens. Now Rose and Jasmine have left home—Rose to study medicine in Calgary and Jasmine to be a scientist in Palo Alto. Uncle Pete has retired from his accounting firm and spends his time cultivating bonsai and koi. Aunt Helen hopes that I will follow Rose into medicine. I study biology so I don't seem ungrateful though my heart is not in it. I think archaeology or geology might suit me better.

On the surface, we are a happy family. We take ski trips to Whistler in the winter and road trips down the Oregon coast in the summer. Birthdays and holidays are marked with ten-course meals at Chinese restaurants. Rose and Jasmine continue to tease me whenever they are home. But the laughter masks a gentleness that crept into their teasing after the deaths, even when they talk about my "girlfriends," knowing full well that I have not let anyone, male or female, past the armour that I have built around myself. I grow impatient with their unspoken pity and sometimes feel an urge to repay their kindness with cruelty. But I know I have marred the Shen family's tranquillity with my presence in their midst and refrain from showing anything but gratitude. I feel that I am the flaw in the smooth face of a perfect diamond.

Except for a long scar near my heart, my body betrays no physical traces of that day. I have grown tall and muscular. Aunt Helen urged me to quit kendo when she first adopted me but, even at the age of six, I refused to deviate from the path that my father had set out for me. She relented but insisted that I take up bonsai and koi culture with Uncle Pete as a counter to the violence. She doesn't know that I am happy only when I don my kendo uniform, complete with face mask, and focus on striking enemies with my shinai. Or that my mind turns to dark thoughts in the bright sunshine while I prune miniature trees or toss fish meal into a pond hopping with golden carp. The avatar that I have chosen for my favourite video game is a kendo warrior with my father's lean build. It is as if my father's blood, staunched too early, now courses through me with renewed vigour. My youthful body encases age-old warrior genes. Depending on my mood, the gene expression ranges from silent obedient Terracotta warriors standing eternal guard for emperor and family to Warring States soldiers quaffing boiling soup from cauldrons brimming with the severed heads of their enemies. When I find myself in the latter state, I lock my door and keep the Shens at bay.

My recollections of the past alter with each passing year like glacial beds being transformed by sliding rivers of ice. Occasionally, glacial quakes occur. My discovery when I was thirteen of a scrapbook of newspaper clippings among Rose's boxes in the basement caused seismic waves. The perfection that my parents had presented to the world was shattered by my father's single act. The clippings sent me into a six-month-long depression, partly because I couldn't bear the unjust portrayals of the man I'd loved. A failed suicide attempt during that time, after years of seeming normalcy, prompted Aunt Helen to find me a psychiatrist. Though I went into shock from blood loss on the day of the stabbings, it's the aftershocks that have caused me the most pain. Unexpected glimpses of my mother's necklaces and earrings in Aunt Helen's jewellery box or worn by my cousins bring back forgotten images of my mother in diamonds and furs; I incorporate these images into my active memory, accompanied by renewed pain at losing her and anger at my father for causing the loss. At times I long for the glacial movement to stop, for my memories to remain static so the misery of fresh recollections will cease. But I know that under the masses of solid ice, even barring fresh movement, the glacier's pure weight causes deformation of the earth beneath and crushed rocks accrue. I must rebuild with the jagged rocks that have been left behind.

My memories of that day have morphed with age. I am no longer certain of the details. Was my father barefoot? How tall was he? What were my grandparents wearing that afternoon? Was my mother in a dress or jeans? Did she wear her hair up in a ponytail or flowing loosely down her back, her bangs held off her face with a black hairband? Rose, who is planning to specialize in psychiatry, says there are methods of altering painful memories so that they are less so. Apparently, there is a reconsolidation period during memory retrieval which allows for "re-learning" to make memories benign. I have told her I have no interest in messing with my mind. In truth, I wish to preserve what fragments I can. I have forgotten my parents' and grandparents' faces and can only visualize them now with the aid of old photographs and homemade videos. I am glad that the Shens do not speak of that day. I would hate for their recollections to contaminate my own. I guard my memories jealously; they are all I have left.

Aunt Helen says I mustn't dwell on the past. But the past is supposed to be permanent; history is forever. It's the present and the future that are meant to be fluid and changeable. I yearn for permanence, for solidity, and find it distressing when the past shifts in my memory. Despite my best efforts to preserve my memories in amber—like one of my mother's pendants, so I can lock them safely away and bring them out at will, turning the translucent jewel in sunshine, perhaps allowing the light to shine through the best inclusions beneath the smooth surface—the liquid does not set. I can only hope for my memories not to be lost as the past flows inexorably forward.

I have often speculated on what possessed my father that day. Was he overpowered by uncontrollable anger, goaded into rashness by my grandfather? Was it a desperate, irrational act born out of despair? Was it really momentary impulsiveness or had the seed of a plan germinated while he sat with me that last time? I cannot reconcile the sobbing kiais with the calm kendo warrior whom I had known since infancy always in control of his every movement. Each time I revisit the events, I feel a greater distance between my father and myself. I try not to think about my father's final act in order to keep him close. I dread the day when even my memories will be lost. The pain I felt in my chest that day will be nothing next to the devastation that I will feel if I lose my parents and grandparents completely.

At times I feel anger toward my father for his stupidity, his lack of inner fibre. That he had cared about what other people thought of him, about preserving face. That a kendo warrior had let external events disturb his inner core. That he embodied the stereotype of a violent Asian male instead of being a strong wise man of whom I could be proud. Though I have long strayed from the church and its prohibitions against suicide, and intellectually I know that "the son shall not bear the iniquity of the father," I feel deep down that slaughter is necessary so the children of iniquity will not rise to carry on the legacy and defile the earth. Only constant vigilance by my intellect prevents me from succumbing to the easy escape that would allow me to permanently remove my aunt and uncle's unwanted burden (though they would vehemently deny that I have been anything but a joy to them) and to end the continual fear and suppression of my shadow side. I am resigned to a future of unending vigilance but sometimes fear that I am too much my father's son to continue the battle indefinitely. My hatred for my father at these times overwhelms me and I long for him to appear—so I can shout at him or attack him in a kendo match, but at least for him to explain himself.

At other times, I feel guilt. Had my father not been burdened with a wife and child, he might not have felt the need to take the actions that he had. If my mother hadn't had such extravagant tastes or if I hadn't attended an expensive private school, would my father have been so thoroughly felled by his setbacks? I would have been happy without the ten-course meals and the kendo classes, Baba, I cry out at night when I find the loneliness and the frustration unbearable, well aware that there is nothing to be done and it's best for me to move forward, as my psychiatrist, Dr Gray, has repeatedly said.

Dr Gray says I must not idealize what might have been. When I think of the occasional marks on my mother's face and the holes in the living room wall, I see the sense in Dr Gray's words. I hear the bickering between Aunt Helen and Uncle Pete and know that even seemingly harmonious marriages have moments of discord. Even so, I would gladly trade an eternity of discord between my parents for the everlasting peace that now exists.

I have spent countless hours in therapy but have never told Dr Gray that I admire my father still. He did his best to take care of us. Had he not missed my aorta, he would have taken care of me as well. When I was a child, whenever I felt my mother's absence at night, I would cry into my pillow. But then I would lie in bed afterwards and think about my father resting underground. I would imagine a coffin inhabited by a man with no face, worms burrowing around the skeletal remains, shreds of flesh long dissolved. Then my father's face, noble and coura-geous, would fill the void in the skull. Baba would make his promise all over again and, despite the anger and pain, I would feel a deep love surround me and a passing peace would descend upon my face.

Lysander

A DIAMOND CANNOT BE POLISHED *without friction; a man cannot be perfected without trials.* Lysander's father was fond of Chinese proverbs; he had a quote for every occasion. *The man who resorts to violence shows he has no more arguments. Dig a well before you're thirsty. Slow in word, swift in deed.* The two that Lysander heard most often were: *Be resolved and the thing is done* and *Learning is a treasure no thief can steal.* That was what his father had said when Lysander begged to return to Taiwan last September. He had been in Canada for two months without friends and family, and food that he liked. "You'll get used to it. We're doing it for your future. Your job is to study hard and get good grades. Knowing English will give you a real advantage in the job market when you come back." At his father's request, Nancy, Lysander's Canadian guardian and his mother's only friend in North America, had found a suitable private school after an exhaustive search of Lower Mainland institutions. His parents chose to enroll him at St Thomas Aquinas, one of the few schools in Vancouver where the majority of the students weren't Asian, in the hopes that he would learn the language more quickly.

Now, four months later, Lysander sat in English class nodding knowingly as Mrs Hancock stood at the lectern reading from *Macbeth*— " … blood hath been shed ere now … "—hoping his pleasant demeanor would please the teacher, though he had little understanding of what she was reading even when she explained it. All he could make out was that there seemed to be a lot of killing. Blood everywhere. If only Mrs Hancock would focus on grammar lessons, then his marks would have been as decent as they were in English classes back home. When he was in Taiwan, his ambition in school had been to answer the teachers' questions correctly, now his goal was simply to understand the questions. He would have to intercept the report card again this term. It had worked the last time. He'd told his parents that the school only issued report cards at the end of the year. He'd have to figure out a way of dealing with the year-end report when the time came. Most of his marks were in the C-plus range except for the A in math, but his parents wouldn't have been satisfied. *If you do not scale the mountain, you will not see the plain.* Lysander simply couldn't show them the failing grades in English and Socials; he couldn't hurt them that way.

One of the two Chinese boys in the seats ahead of him passed a note to the other. They were the only two Asian students in his grade. Lysander had tried to make friends with them at the start of the school year but they were Canadian-born and spoke only a smattering of Cantonese—a dialect Lysander could not understand. The boys had been polite but he had little in common with them and he rarely spoke to them these days. Now that his English had improved, he was better able to understand them. Last week, he'd heard one of them groan when Mrs Hancock returned his essay. The other had laughed and teased, "Asian fail!" That meant any grade lower than an "A." Lysander no longer had illusions about reaching such lofty goals; a passing grade in English would more than suffice.

He checked the clock above the whiteboards at the front of the room. Still ten more minutes until the bell! "Gan!" he muttered. The blond boy in the seat next to him looked up from his book and frowned. Lysander reddened, suddenly conscious of the pimples on his face. He pushed his glasses up and brushed dandruff off his left shoulder. The boy flipped the page and turned his attention back to the teacher.

Mrs Hancock said something about Banquo's murder and then something else about Fleance. Lysander thought the only useful thing that had come out of English class was learning there were worse names than his. He considered himself lucky not to be Banquo, Fleance, or Donalbain. It was a narrow miss because his father had randomly chosen Lysander's name from a Shakespeare play. Too bad Baba hadn't checked if the name was actually still in use. When he was in Taiwan, Lysander used to think that his father knew everything about the world. How wrong he was! Lysander would like to see him try and figure out the Vancouver transit system or deal with homework assignments that made no sense. It was disheartening not to know what you were doing wrong when you were doing everything that you could think of.

Lysander had shortened his name to Sander after being teased in school. The teasing had gone on for a few days until the boys realized that he didn't speak enough English to rise to their baiting. He only found out what "lice" meant when they baited him with it, and was glad that he didn't know at the time; he would definitely have gotten himself into trouble.

Nowadays, everyone left him alone. Lysander felt invisible. He went to classes alone, sat in the lunchroom alone, and took the bus home alone. He had gotten used to it. Today was just like all the other days.

Mrs Hancock said something about a ghost. "Ooo . . . oooo," said a boy from the back of the room. Mrs Hancock gave the boy a stern look. The whole class laughed. Lysander laughed belatedly then flushed when he realized he was the only one still chuckling.

"Can anyone give us a summary of the action to this point?" Mrs Hancock waited.

Lysander looked around. Six hands were up. That should be safe, he thought. He put up his hand too. If she asks me, I'll just look around and pretend I was stretching. If she doesn't, maybe she'll think I knew the answer.

The blond boy began to answer. Midway through, he said, " . . . and the ghost . . . "

"Ooo . . . ooo," said the boy at the back of the room.

This time Mrs Hancock sent the boy out of the room. The class laughed uproariously. Lysander laughed too.

But are they making fun of ghosts? That's dangerous. We would never do that in Taiwan. Almost everybody believes in ghosts there. These white people better be careful or something bad might happen to them. Don't they know that you're supposed to keep ghosts happy? Show them respect? In Taiwan, during ghost month in July, nobody even dares to say the word ghost. Who wants to be on the bad side of ghosts that came up from hell? That's why we make so many offerings. I never go swimming in July, just in case the water ghosts decide to take a human hostage. Nobody rests easy until the ghosts go back to the underworld at the beginning of August. My favourite part of the month is when we release the water lanterns into the sea. I always hope that our family's lantern will go out the furthest. Good luck for the rest of the year.

Lysander wished he were back home. Or his family were living with him in Canada. Instead, his mother was an "astronaut parent," dropping in occasionally. She had been to Vancouver twice since his departure, staying for a week each time. Lysander understood that his father couldn't spare her at the factory—she was the only person he could trust to keep track of the accounts and run the office—and that Meimei and Didi were too young to be without their mother for long. Still, his parents should try harder to be with their favourite son. After all, he had been an only child for ten years before the arrival of his younger brother and sister. He and his mother had been inseparable until he started school. She had even composed a lullaby for him. Sometimes when he couldn't sleep during cold Canadian nights, he would croon the melody to himself.

Mrs Hancock was talking again. Lysander pushed his glasses up. His eyes were starting to glaze over. Oh good, the warning bell! What's the homework? I wish she would write it up on the board like Mr Leavenworth does in math class. So much easier when I can see it. I'll have to come back and ask her later. Don't want to look like a fool. Okay, what's next? PE. What a relief! I can play basketball and not have to think too much. I wish I could go back to Taiwan. Learning

English is just too hard.

⌒‿

At the end of the day, Lysander stuffed books and binders from his locker into his backpack. It had been another day where he had not spoken to a single person and nobody had noticed. If he had said something to the teachers, they would probably have answered; Ms Crawford or Mrs Hancock or even Mr Cartwright would have been nice to him. That old guy, Mr Lo, had told him not to run down the stairs on the way to his locker but that didn't count.

Lysander pushed open an exit door and stepped into the crisp cold air. He zipped his ski jacket up to his neck and regretted not bringing gloves as he made his way to the bus stop. The grey skies looked like they might hold snow. Lysander was looking forward to seeing snow for the first time and wondered if the temperature needed to get lower before it fell. One of these days, he should check the weather forecast before he left the house; it might save him having to stuff his hands into his jeans to keep warm.

"Hey, Lysander, right?" A voice said in Mandarin behind him.

Lysander turned and saw a slight Chinese youth, hair gelled like a bristle brush, taking up the entire bench under the bus shelter. He was wearing a brown suede jacket over a black hoodie and red T-shirt, one arm slung over the back of the bench, his jean-clad legs crossed, his expensive black boots gleaming. He held a cigarette in his right hand and was blowing smoke rings. A white plastic bag was beside him.

"It's Sander."

"Sorry. Saan…derrr."

Lysander thought Brown Jacket might be teasing him and looked down the road to see if the bus was coming.

"I've seen you around the school," Brown Jacket continued in Mandarin. "Looks like you could use someone to hang with."

Lysander ignored him. Plastic crinkled from the bench. Two girls, wearing tight sweatpants with "Juicy" prominently emblazoned over the rear, giggled their way to the bus stop and stood beside him. One of them gave him a withering look. Lysander inched back toward the

119

bus shelter. Lesser of two evils.

"My name's Brad. Here, I've got something for you." Lysander turned and saw Brad holding out a DVD, *American Gangster.* "Go on, take it."

Lysander's first reaction was to refuse but then he thought about the small allowance that his father gave him and how little there was left after he had paid for his *World of Warcraft* account and other video game paraphernalia. Why not? No harm in accepting. It *would* be kind of cool to see the movie before it hit the theatres.

"Thanks," Lysander said gruffly and quickly stepped onto the bus that had just pulled up.

Lysander flashed his pass and made his way to the back of the bus. He felt for his iPod but then remembered that he had left it on the kitchen counter during the morning rush and resigned himself to a monotonous ride. The girls settled in the seats ahead of him. He could smell the brunette's strong perfume and see the mole on the blonde's neck. When he first came to Canada, despite exposure to Western culture from Hollywood movies, he'd had trouble distinguishing between people who didn't have Asian features. Now he knew first to look at the hair colour.

The girls kept up a rapid-fire conversation, liberally sprinkled with personal disclosures of monumental importance. Lysander could only decipher about a third of the conversation. As usual, he had to take his best guess at what was being said. During the first months, his incompetence in English conversation, after years of English instruction in Taiwan, had frustrated him but now he was accustomed to that too.

He got off the bus at Dunbar and King Edward. An old lady with a bag of bright red tomatoes brushed past him onto the bus. Despite daylight savings, the afternoon sun had already disappeared. Lysander put up his hood but still shivered all the two blocks from the bus stop to the Tudor-style house his father had purchased—big lot, large rooms, enormous investment. As he unlocked the black lacquered door, he saw that the gardener had trimmed the hedges and done something to the rose bushes.

Lysander deactivated the alarm, dropped his jacket and backpack by the door, and picked up two envelopes from the bamboo floor. Bills, addressed to his father. He started to reach for the light switch but changed his mind. One of these days, he might do something to brighten up this place but not today.

Lysander walked into the storage room beside the kitchen and opened the chest freezer. Tupperware containers of stews, spaghetti sauces, blanched vegetables, and baked potatoes regularly appeared in the freezer thanks to Nancy, his guardian. The multi-hued plastic boxes made the freezer interior look like a Lite-Bright board, the only cheerful spot in the lonely, cavernous house. Scanning the choices, he saw there was no more Chinese food left.

Tamade!

He chose a container of chili and popped it into the microwave. When the microwave beeped, Lysander grabbed the container. The steam burned his hands and he dropped the Tupperware, leaving a red splotch on the ceramic tiles.

Gan!

Lysander wiped red splashes off his jeans and ran his fingers under cold water until the pain dulled. He considered cleaning up the mess on the floor but knew Nancy would do it in the morning when she came around with more food.If he didn't feel so tired, he would have done it. He hoped his mother would never find out about his house-keeping habits. Valuing privacy, he'd told Nancy he would keep his own bedroom in order. Books, papers, gum wrappers, school notices, plates, empty juice containers, and other debris littered his room. He would have to clean it before his mother's next visit . . . whenever that might be. He should probably buy a cleanser to get rid of the stain of sticky juice on the carpet beside his bed.

After he had warmed up more chili, Lysander settled into his favourite armchair in the family room, his laptop, schoolbooks, and game controllers by his side. He started the movie, gobbled his food, and read the Facebook messages from his Taiwanese friends. There was another message from Hong Li Lee. "You're so lucky," he wrote. "You can do whatever you want, whenever you want. And school is much more lax there. You don't have to study as hard." If he only knew. Lysander made a half-hearted attempt at doing his homework, played a bit of online *Warcraft*, and finally fell asleep, the TV still flickering in the dark room, his glasses still perched on his nose.

Lysander awoke to his favourite J-pop tune, *Exile's Exit*, blaring from his cell phone at 7 AM the following morning. His mother making her daily call before going to bed.

"Bai-Yi?" she said, calling him by his Chinese name, White One. "Did you eat yet?"

"Oh . . . no, soon," Lysander said groggily.

"Everything okay? Need more money?"

"No, everything's fine. Don't worry."

"Okay. You study hard. Do your homework. Be careful."

"Okay, Ma . . . don't worry."

He shifted himself off the armchair to start yet another morning. While he sometimes needed the wake-up calls, he still felt annoyed that his mother couldn't seem to stop nagging even when she was an ocean away. He wasn't a child anymore. When he finished his studies, he would have to go into National Service like all young men in Taiwan. When was she going to let go? Maybe it's a good thing she doesn't live here. She would never let me grow up.

Papers slipped off the armchair as he rose and Lysander remembered his unfinished homework. Another zero in English. Lysander sighed and hurried so he wouldn't miss the bus, steeling himself for another day of anonymity.

⌒

Sunday saw Lysander make his obligatory weekly visit to Nancy's house. Nancy's daughter, Tracy, and Tracy's five-year-old son, Patrick, welcomed him at the door of the bungalow in West Point Grey.

"I drank blood, Sander. I drank blood!" Patrick said excitedly, pulling on Lysander's arm.

"We had communion at church this morning," Tracy explained,

taking Lysander's jacket.

"It tasted like grape juice," Patrick said. "In a little, little glass." He indicated the size with his thumb and index finger.

Nancy bustled in from the kitchen bringing with her the scent of baking. "Bai-Yi, you're here. Did you eat yet?" she said in Taiwanese.

"The blood of Christ. And I ate his body too. Right, Mommy?"

Tracy nodded then shepherded the two boys into the dining room.

Lysander chose a seat across the lunch table from Tracy and her son.

"So what are you studying at school these days?" Reverend Anderson, Nancy's husband, asked from the head of the table.

"Oh, *Ma-coo-bet*," Lysander said, forking a bit of salad onto his plate. He still couldn't get used to eating raw lettuce and tomatoes. Back home, his mother cooked everything, even vegetables.

"Yuck, Shakespearean tragedies just don't do it for me," Tracy said and tried to put a bib around Patrick's neck, but he objected so strenuously that she gave up.

"Yeah, hard."

Nancy set a platter of pizza slices down on the table. "Bai-Yi, do you need a tutor? Your mother said to get you whatever you needed. You okay?" Nancy asked in Taiwanese.

"I'm okay. Don't worry."

Nancy touched Tracy's arm and mimed putting a bib around her neck but Tracy shook her head. She said to her mother, in Taiwanese, "I don't want to be a helicopter parent. He'll be fine without a bib. We don't need to hover."

I wish my mother were more like Tracy, Lysander thought. Less hovering would be an improvement. But then, aren't most Taiwanese parents like that? My parents are no different from most of my friends' parents.

Nancy sat in front of the steaming platter, spatula in hand. "Bai-Yi, I added the topping that you asked for. I made it especially for your birthday. Here, try a slice."

"My mother's pizza's the best. She makes everything from scratch,"

Tracy said.

"I want one too! I want one too!" Patrick bounced excitedly on his chair.

Nancy served everyone.

"Yeuw, what's this!?" Patrick cried, pointing to the yellow layer topping his pizza.

"Corn. That's Sander's favourite," said Tracy.

"Corn isn't a pizza flavour! Everybody knows that!" Patrick said disdainfully.

"Shh . . . don't be rude."

Lysander turned red and pushed up his glasses, pretending that he hadn't heard the little boy. He saw Tracy pick up her knife and fork so he followed suit even though he was accustomed to eating pizza with his hands. He still found the implements awkward to use. The knife clattered loudly on the plate when the pizza slipped out from under his fork. Patrick laughed. Lysander coloured and fixed his eyes determinedly on the slice. He inserted the fork deeply, made long cuts along the length of the pizza, and didn't stop until inch-wide squares covered his plate. Nobody would ever laugh at him, not even a little kid!

Lysander took a bite of the pizza. Ugh. Bland, just like so many Canadian dishes. Nancy had used creamed corn instead of corn kernels and a tomato base instead of white cheese. It was nothing like the Pizza Hut pizza in Taiwan. Good thing I didn't ask for the "French-style seafood pizza" or the "lobster abalone pizza." Who knows what she would have substituted for squid, oysters, or abalone? He washed down the pizza with a gulp of Coke.

"Patrick, corn is actually a topping at a lot of pizza restaurants in Taiwan," Nancy's husband said in a patient voice.

Lysander wondered at the indulgence of Canadians. Unlike this kindly grandfather, his hard-nosed father would never have tolerated rude behaviour from any of his children. If his younger brother had been as rude as Patrick, his father would have reprimanded him severely and made him apologize.

"It's yucky. I don't want it." Patrick turned to Lysander and ordered, "Tell about your motor scooter."

Gan! What a spoiled brat! Lysander said, "Um, I have black one and I ride every place in Taipei."

"You must miss your freedom," Tracy said. She scraped the corn off Patrick's pizza onto her own plate and returned the pasty red crust to her son.

"It's okay. I have bus."

In fact, Lysander greatly missed riding his scooter and the MRT in Taipei. In Taiwan, he could ride the express train from the north to the south of the entire island in a few hours and there wasn't a street in Taipei that he couldn't name. Here, he stayed close to home and school. The buses took him only so far and he was afraid of getting lost. Besides, it wasn't much fun exploring without a friend.

When Lysander finally finished his slice of pizza, Nancy immediately dished him a second. He gamely ate half of the second slice then left the rest on his plate next to the salad, hoping she wouldn't be offended. But then, she never spoke of the mostly untouched containers of Canadian food in his freezer; either she was unaware or didn't care that her cooking did not please him. You would think she'd have noticed that the Chinese food always disappeared first. What wouldn't he give for some pig's ears, stinky tofu, or taro ice! Even if he asked for them, she would probably not be able to make it the right way. He dreaded the thought of tasting her rice dumplings, which she had promised to make for the Dragon Boat Festival in June. His mother would never forgive him for not liking her friend's cooking, but what could he do? He supplemented his diet elsewhere. He'd tried the local McDonald's but the burgers tasted greasier than the ones at home. And he had yet to find a real Taiwanese restaurant in his neighbourhood. Lately, he'd been making do with chips and chocolate bars from the 7-11 near his school.

At the end of the meal, Tracy said, "Wait!" and went and held the door between the kitchen and dining room open. Nancy, smiling widely, brought in a cake with fifteen candles, singing "Happy birthday to you . . ."

"Now you're supposed to make a wish. If you blow out all the candles at once, your wish will come true," Tracy explained to him. Earlier in the day, in answer to one of his Facebook friends, Lysander had listed the latest models of running shoes, phones and computers as his birthday wishes. Now, Lysander closed his eyes and made his dearest wish of the day—to have close friends in Vancouver.

⌒

The following day, and for weeks after, Brad appeared at the bus stop each afternoon bearing gifts: DVDs of movies and music videos, computer games. Lysander and Brad started going to the local pool hall. Brad showed Lysander how to make double and two-rail reverse shots and Lysander decided that he would forfeit his video games for a while in order to learn billiards properly. Every weekend the pair took the bus north to Vancouver's Chinatown or south to Richmond, searching out small Chinese restaurants. Lysander couldn't contain his delight when they found an authentic Taiwanese restaurant that served oily rice and coffin bread in the heart of Richmond. Brad introduced him to T&T Supermarket where Lysander could stock up on his favourite snacks: dried squid, seasoned seaweed, and salted plums. They planned to attend the Vancouver and Richmond night markets when they opened in the spring. Lysander had found the older brother he'd never had; he'd never felt closer to anyone outside of his family before. What a relief to speak Mandarin with a friend after straining with English at school each day . . . the difference between sweetened coconut milk and the hard, brown shells of hairy palm nuts.

⌒

Six weeks after their first meeting, Brad was waiting for Lysander at the bus stop after school as usual. "Com'on." He jerked his thumb in the direction of the school's back parking lot. Lysander followed him to a black Cadillac Escalade. A ginger-headed white man a few years older than them was in the driver seat smoking a cigarette.

"Chad, this is Sander."

"Hey," Chad grinned and offered an open carton of cigarettes but Lysander shook his head.

"Let's go home," Brad said and opened the front passenger door.

Lysander climbed into the seat behind him. Chad drove across town to a quiet residential street near Commercial and Fifth. Brad led the way from the carport, across an unkempt yard, and up the back stairs of a 1970s family home. He called out "Hello?" but no one answered. Empty pizza boxes sprawled across a scuffed kitchen table, four open cans of Coke and Sprite beside them. Steel-grey appliances—fridge, stove, and dishwasher—sat on the peeling linoleum along the length of the kitchen.

Brad flipped open his cell phone and dialled the number printed on a Chinese take-out menu tacked to a small bulletin board beside the stove. "Yes, ten orders of Combo A and ten orders of Combo B. Oh yeah, and a couple of bubble teas, Taiwanese style," he said, winking at Lysander.

Chad galumphed up the stairs and disappeared.

"Let's give you a tour," Brad said.

He led Lysander through a living room, dining room, two bedrooms (avoiding Chad's), and a small den, keeping up a constant chatter in Mandarin. They arrived back downstairs at a hallway down which Lysander could see three closed doors.

"This is where I live, dude. Did I ever tell you how my folks died?"

"No." Brad opened the first door and Lysander peeked into a rec room where a pool table dominated.

"Car accident. Left me a ton of money but made my uncle guardian. I had to go live with him and his family. Got out of there pronto, believe me! Came to live with Chad. I still go to the school that my parents picked, though. Feel I owe it to them. But the Bloods are my real family now." Brad led them past the second door without stopping.

"The Bloods?"

"Mixed Blood. The name of our gang."

Lysander brushed away nascent feelings of misgiving. Brad'll take good care of me. He's done that even better than my own parents ever since I met him. No need to worry.

The door at the rear of the house had an "Open" sign on it.

"Oh good. Mike's not working." Brad knocked.

A boy their age, with spiked green and purple hair, looked up from an art magazine. "Hey Brad." He was sitting in what looked to be a leather dentist chair.

"Mike. This is Sander. The guy I was telling you about."

"Hey," Mike turned the page then seemed to remember something. "Sander . . . Oh yeah. I've got something to show you."

Mike jumped up and rummaged through the pile of books and magazines on the floor. He triumphantly extricated a red binder and started flipping through the pages.

Lysander glanced around the small room. One wall supported shelves with all sorts of odds and ends—Vaseline, pens, Sharpies, razors, bottles of different coloured inks, and skin lotion. The leather chair took up most of the room. Framed drawings of intricate leaf and floral designs filled the white spaces of the remaining walls. There was a faint odour of fried hair mixed with nail polish remover.

Mike motioned Lysander over and pointed to a laminated photo of a tattoo: a stiletto dripping four drops of blood. "You can have this one or," Mike flipped the page, "this one . . . if you make it in." The second photo had the same stiletto in a more stylized form with identically shaped drops of blood.

"Show him yours, Brad."

Brad took off his hoodie and rolled up the right sleeve of his T-shirt. The tattoo on his bicep glowed faintly and Lysander immediately longed for one of his own; he wanted to be a part of Brad's "family."

Next, Brad led Lysander to a room in the basement. Piles of brand new black and white T-shirts lay atop two long tables in the centre of the room. In one corner was a complicated-looking machine that Lysander later learned was a screen press. Two clotheslines hung with black T-shirts extended across the length of the room. Taped boxes lined the remaining walls. Lysander walked up to the drying T-shirts and examined the logo. He had seen television advertisements for that rock band all week. They were scheduled to play at GM Place next month. "Isn't this . . . "

"Yup. Don't they look real? They go for forty bucks a pop in the stores. We sell them for half that. Here, I'll show you how to work the press."

Lysander's eyes widened. That would explain all the gifts he had received from Brad—the DVDs and software were probably all counterfeit too. Oh well, so what? So many things are overpriced these days. It's good that people have a choice and can get things cheaper. My father would say it makes good business sense.

Brad took a white T-shirt off one of the tables and showed Lysander how to run the press. Lysander was eager to learn and worked diligently. They managed to print logos on twenty T-shirts before the Chinese food arrived.

Other gang members arrived for dinner, each greeting Lysander cordially. The fifteen that were there that night, most of them from the east side of Vancouver, ranged in age from fourteen to twenty-five. Mixed Blood proved to be true to its name—Lysander heard snippets of Mandarin, Russian, Cantonese, and Tagalog as well as English throughout the meal; Chad seemed to be a gifted unifier and circulated easily among the youths. Afterwards, the group chatted awhile then one by one drifted elsewhere. Lysander and Brad returned to the basement to print more T-shirts.

At 2 AM, Brad said, "Good work tonight, Sander. Keep this up and you'll be a Blood brother before you know it."

Lysander fervently hoped so.

⌒

Chad christened them the Westside Duo and, to Lysander's delight, entrusted him to Brad's tutelage. Brad turned out to be an unexpectedly good teacher, not only with gang matters but also with schoolwork, and even Shakespeare started to make sense to Lysander. Brad coasted through his own courses with perpetual comments of "Has the ability to do better..." and "Not working up to potential..." on his report cards. He laughed when he showed them to Lysander, saying, "As if what they have to teach me is going to help me in life!"

One day not long after Lysander's first meeting with the gang, Brad steered him toward the back field as school let out. Two figures were standing beside the storage building next to the soccer pitch at the far end of the field. As they drew near, Lysander saw Mike's trim form pressed up against a frail-looking boy. An open backpack was strewn on the gravel alongside textbooks and sheets of paper. Mike's fists continued to pound the boy's stomach even though he was already doubled over and blood was dribbling from his mouth and nose. Noticing the smeared blood on the boy's white shirt, Lysander recoiled. His life-long aversion to blood had greatly disappointed his father, who had previously nursed hopes of his becoming a doctor.

Brad nudged Lysander and they stopped a few metres away from the building. "Hey!" Brad shouted.

Mike raised his head at the sound and, winking at Brad, abruptly stopped the beating. He gave the boy's pack a kick then sauntered away from the field.

Brad and Lysander helped the boy retrieve his belongings. Brad handed the backpack to the boy and smoothed down the victim's jacket.

"Hey, I'm Brad and this is Sander. If you ever want protection against bullies like that guy just stick with us."

The boy shook his head and made his way past them, his head bowed, his hand on his stomach and his tongue gingerly exploring the cuts in his inner cheek. As Brad and Lysander watched him cross the field, Brad said in Mandarin, "A few more whippings from Mike and he'll be begging us to help him. We get the lonely and vulnerable. Can't wait to see his face when he shows up at the house and finds out Mike is one of us."

Lysander looked at him in astonishment, then mentally shrugged. Oh well, the kid could use a friend, it looked like. It's none of my business how Chad chooses to recruit new members.

Later on, when memories of his teen years intruded upon his staid adult life, Lysander would attribute the development of his rugged individualism to the self-loathing he felt while witnessing these beatings, though at the time they were taking place, he could not name the vague uneasiness stirring within him. He couldn't believe that he had allowed himself to follow a pack, to contribute to the pain of another. And what for? he'd ask later.

Lysander continued under Brad's guidance. "Anything for money" became his mantra. Their lives fell into a routine: full day of classes, a couple of hours of homework, and then the rest of the evening "working." Both were keen for Lysander to become a full-fledged member and Brad did his best to help him fulfill his obligations to the gang: packaging drugs; collecting debts; making copies of music, software and movies; creating fake credit cards.

Besides his duties with Lysander, Brad had recently been given the additional role as negotiator with the Titans, a rival gang based in Burnaby that had been making inroads into the Vancouver drug market. For the past five years, they had respected the Bloods' clearly marked boundaries. Recently, though, the Titans had become increasingly dissatisfied with their share of the market and tensions were mounting.

"If anyone can get them to back off, you can, Brad," Lysander said proudly. He wanted to be as savvy as Brad by the time he was seventeen.

The gang became Lysander's indulgent parents as memories of his pre-gang life started to fade. His mother persisted with her daily calls, Nancy continued to prepare her weekly meals, and Lysander kept reassuring them both, secure in the knowledge that he would no longer have to hide his report cards. They should be happy that I have friends and I'm making my own money, he thought, although he never mentioned the gang.

Three months later, when Chad finally gave Lysander permission to get the stiletto tattoo, Brad and he celebrated by buying a pack of beer and finishing the lot. "Now, you're really one of us!" Brad cheered.

Lysander would think back upon this moment and, in the quiet of a darkened cell, remember it as one of the happiest of his life. Still later, when he saw his own teenage son turn away from him toward friends of questionable repute in Taipei, Lysander would curb his urge to restrain the boy. Despite his wife's chronic worrying, he would be immovable in the belief that the boy should find his own way, for that was the only path to manhood. He would utter a proverb that his father had never taught him: *We cannot help shoots grow by yanking them taller.* His wife would frown and turn away, barely able to contain her contempt, silently thinking, "Humph. What kind of a man are you? You work as a youth counsellor but you can't even manage your own son." Lysander would read her expression and, in one of those silences that accumulate over the course of a marriage, think, "How little you know me, my wife."

A couple of weeks after Lysander got his tattoo, Chad called him at home on a Saturday morning. Lysander asked him to repeat the news. He wasn't certain that he had heard him correctly the first time.

"I'm sorry, Sander. I know the two of you were like brothers. It happened late last night. Mike got away before the cops got there. Mike said there were three Titans against the two of them. They pulled blades. Brad didn't make it. Sorry, buddy."

Lysander stared at the cell phone in his hand. Brad couldn't be dead. People don't just die like that. Especially people like Brad. They were invincible. There must be some mistake. He threw the phone down on the couch and sat down in shock, his head bowed and knees drawn, his arms wrapped around them.

Images of Brad flashed through his mind: lining up a perfect pool shot; imitating the martial arts moves of heroes in Wuxia movies; frowning with concentration as he read a difficult passage in a textbook; sketching in his notebook; plotting strategy with Chad, as he gulped down cup after cup of cappuccino; beating time to some song on his iPod. He couldn't be gone. There was no way. No way at all. Bile rose up his gullet and he choked the fluid down but rushed to the bathroom when the second wave arrived.

Lysander didn't go to school that day or the next. He couldn't imagine being there without Brad waiting for him at the bus stop at the end of the day. Lysander needed to do something. He owed it to Brad. Whoever did it had to pay. Any of the heroes in Wuxia movies would have avenged their friends' deaths. Even Westerners would act the same way . . . like Macduff, Lysander would "dispute it like a man."

When Chad called about a special assignment the following week, Lysander accepted eagerly.

"You're underaged. If anything happens, they'll go easier on you."

⌒‿

Lysander trailed the Titan to an old second-run theatre on Willingdon. A line of people a block deep anticipated the start of a *Godfather* marathon three movies long. The afternoon sun glinted off the Titan's trident earring as he waited for change at the ticket counter. Lysander made sure he sat directly behind the boy, thankful the Titan had chosen an aisle seat.

It was the first time that Lysander had ever been in a Canadian movie theatre. He had not known that velvet curtains could rise two stories high. It reminded him of the waterfalls he had seen back home, on one of those rare family outings to the countryside, when the setting sun cast its lingering glow on cascading sheets. He listened to the crinkle of popcorn bags and the slurping of drinks around him and waited for the lustrous, ruby expanse to part.

Surprisingly, Lysander found he could follow the movie even with the task at hand. He sympathized with Jack Woltz as he resisted the "offer that couldn't be refused." His pulse quickened as blood from the decapitated horse's head soaked the bedsheets. His breaths shortened and his muscles contracted.

Lysander remembered seeing blood dripped into basins of rice grains from the cut throats of chickens and his quickly spitting out the cooked, clotted blood rice afterwards. When he was five, it had been the most extraordinary sight and taste that he had ever experienced. That was dynasties ago.

Lysander took a deep breath and summoned his courage. Best to do it and not think. He ran his finger over the smooth handle of the derringer in his pocket. He felt the heft of the gun in his palm. A report sounded. Blood erupted. Lysander dropped the revolver and ran down the aisle. Someone stuck out a leg and Lysander felt the rough bristles of the floor runner attack his face before he was pulled to his feet and his arms were pinned behind him.

A crowd had gathered around the Titan. Someone was yelling into a cell phone. The movie had stopped.

"I think he's dead!" a woman was shouting into her cell phone.

"Murderer," the man pinning him hissed and tightened his hold on Lysander's arms until the boy winced. The man's rank breath hung in the space between them.

Lysander's mind began its descent into terror; he comprehended nothing. He needed to empty his bladder, his bowels, his stomach. He just wanted to lie down. He wished for someone to take him away. The noise and the heat were unbearable, the people even more so.

Most of the crowd was emptying from the theatre at the urging of the ushers, but the man had Lysander firmly in his grip. Help me, please. Someone . . . anyone. He didn't know if he said it out loud or even if he said it in Chinese or English. Sirens were approaching. Lysander prayed for salvation, but expected none.

That was when he heard it. Faintly at first, then louder and closer. He could hear it clearly—something familiar and intimate. Something inextricably melded into his core. Music, sweet music, over the sounds of the theatre.

A special song just for him, one that he had heard all his life, even before he was expelled along with the blood from his mother's womb. A song of love, shaded with fear and despair. The notes rose and descended in a mellow rhythm, willing him to follow its lead. Sunshine and warmth stole over crimson frost. Scents of salt air and flaming lilies infused his body and his limbs slackened. He hung his head and waited then, his breathing even, his mind calm, letting the melody cradle him.

After the final bars, Lysander raised his eyes but dared not look at the aftermath of his work, sediment from the roiling flood of vengeance. An eye for an eye, a tooth for a tooth, one sorrow for another. He had felt as a man and fought his battle as only a man could. Lingering strains of the song echoed in his mind. The drops of blood etched on his arm pulsed. The stiletto that would pierce his mother's heart had already found its mark. Through the blur clouding his vision, Lysander saw the dawn of manhood—the beginning of the rest of his life.

Lysander wept.

Father's Day

ON FATHER'S DAY, MY DAUGHTER eviscerated me near a signpost on the edge of a lagoon. She took a photo beforehand.

Emma has always been adept with pictures; her inventive charcoal drawings and watercolours grace the walls of the living room, kitchen, and three bedrooms in our Craftsman home in Kitsilano. At one point, her ambition was to become a graphic artist, but this month she's bent on becoming a photojournalist.

Crayon sketches of white picket fences, broccoli-like trees, and smoke spiralling up from lop-sided houses are still stored in the "Kindergarten Year" box somewhere in the garage. Adeline ceased constructing "memory boxes" of our daughter's childhood when Emma was in the Fifth Grade. Adeline ceased multifarious undertakings that year.

But now that Emma is nearing fifteen, she compiles her own collections. There are her photo albums, naturally: the posed pictures of birthdays and Christmases and Thanksgiving dinners; the school prints, Emma with and without front teeth, with and without braces; shots of snowmen built after rare Vancouver snowfalls; team photos from Emma's soccer and softball leagues; the snapshots of Emma and Adeline gliding down ski slopes; and the array of Emma in her various Halloween costumes.

Perched beside those on her bookshelf are the special vacation albums with pictures from trips to Disneyland, Disney World, Canada's Wonderland, Disney Sea, Knott's Berry Farm, and all those Six Flags theme parks. A few years ago, the ambition was to visit all the Disneyland locations worldwide. But then Emma wearied of riding on roller coasters and the family trips were suspended.

Nowadays, Emma and I take one annual vacation and Adeline and Emma take another. The arrangement just evolved and we all accept that it's efficacious. Adeline isn't well-disposed towards literary sites in England and I'm not keen on fashion malls in the States. *De gustibus non est disputandum.* I must confess that I find the procurement of material adornments shallow and wasteful. However, I indulge my daughter in her trifling pursuits.

Oh, and I mustn't forget Emma's collection of butterflies in various media: real specimens in display cases; designs on watch faces, bracelets, earrings, belts, T-shirts, scarves, skirts, and hats; replicas in clay, ceramic, crystal, and alloys. I've never failed to bring an addition to her collection from souvenir shops whenever I attend conferences in Europe, Australia, and North America.

But my secret pride is her library. A chip off the old block, one could assert. She's retained a smattering of her old favourites: *The Railway Children, The Secret Garden, Five Children and It,* and *David Copperfield.* The first time I saw *Pride and Prejudice* on those shelves, I felt the strongest wave of parental sentimentality that I'd ever experienced, topping even the moment when I first held her in my arms. Just for a fleeting second, I imagined that we could work as an academic duo—renowned father and daughter Austen specialists. Perhaps she would get a professorship at UBC before I retire and she wouldn't have to leave me. It was a capricious fancy, a product of the imagination loosed from controlled reason, fed by tender affection.

Emma and I have a ritual. Every Father's Day I select a new location for her gift-giving and she discloses a hitherto clandestine truth about herself. This year it was Stanley Park.

The day began pleasantly enough. Considerate girl that she is, Emma surprised me with reservations for brunch. We walked from the Lagoon Drive parking lot, past the tennis courts full of players lobbing and smashing, to join the queue under the green-striped awnings of the Fish House entrance.

After a short wait, we were seated at a table by a sunlit window overlooking the courts and our server presented us with a menu featuring fresh oysters and flaming prawns. Emma was attired in what I thought might be a new pair of jeans and I said, "Did you go shopping with your mother recently?"

"Yup."

Her voice sounded tight though I couldn't discern the cause; I'm certain I wasn't accusatory by any measure.

"Those are nice jeans. Did your mother pick them out?"

"No, Dad. And if you're going to start in on Mom's shopping habits again, we'd better talk about something else."

Where did that surly tone come from? I had entertained the notion that this was to be a congenial celebration. But a parent must overlook deficient behaviour from his offspring on occasion. *Sic vita est.*

The server arrived with two glasses of orange juice and a cup of coffee.

"Emma, I wasn't starting in on anything. I just asked about your jeans."

She took a sip of her orange juice. "I'm sorry, Dad. It's just that you're always putting Mom down."

"I most certainly do not do that!"

She rolled her eyes.

I couldn't fathom what had brought on her combative attitude; ordinarily, we have civil conversations and I frequently have to remind myself that Emma is only fourteen when I find myself debating her as I would a graduate student. I must admit that she is a perceptive and gifted speaker. Mature beyond her years. Even so, she still needs me and therein lies my dilemma. I cannot deprive her of a stable home environment during these crucial teen years.

In my darker moods, I imagine Emma falling prey to the seduction of ubiquitous teenage temptations, strung out on meth or Ecstacy, bullied by unscrupulous pimps on the unforgiving streets of the

Downtown East Side, turning tricks to finance her next fix or drink; a distraught Adeline unable to staunch the flow of phone calls from school administrators, police officers, and social workers. I see an unconscious Emma, marked by bruises and needle pricks, lying half-naked in a dumpster while rats run over her matted, stringy hair and flies buzz around open sores on her arms and legs.

I worry that there will be no one to save Emma from shameless reprobates who might attempt to take advantage of her; no patriarch to rescue her from infamy should she follow in the steps of a Lydia Bennet. That glamorous portrayals of teenage pregnancy in films like *Juno* will nudge Emma towards benighted acceptance of unrealistic responsibilities and I won't be there to help her avert unhappiness. That should Emma actually marry, her chances of divorcing, should I make her a child of divorce, would exceed those of children from intact families.

I also worry that I won't be there to hone her fine mind and shape her budding sense of morality. The other day, we spoke of honour. Not Arthurian, knightly codes of conduct. Not macho, "defend your honour" duels. Not Samurai, hara-kiri mutilations. Perhaps I should say, we spoke of a gentleman's word of honour—when a promise is really a promise. I've never told her that I specialized in Austen because I have always longed to be part of a society where honour was a cultural norm and I remain mum because I fear her ridicule. We questioned whether there are still societies where an Edward Ferrars will not dishonour an imprudent engagement to a Lucy Steele. I'd like to think so. Emma thought the opposite. But then she is so young. She doesn't understand how apotheoses sustain middle-aged men; everyone needs to have hope, realistic or not.

I quoted Stanhope at her. Honour is "a greatness of mind which scorns to descend to an ill and base thing." A father's job is the transmission of lofty ideals, after all. She countered with derisive laughter, blue eyes watering, blonde strands sticking to the temples of her pixie face. "Name one person who would marry someone just because they made a stupid promise when they were young," she said when she had caught her breath.

Emma unfailingly knows when she's right but is generally gracious enough not to crow. But are her assertions about my treatment of Adeline accurate?

"I don't put your mother down, do I?" I stirred sugar into my coffee.

"Look, Dad. I'm not trying to hurt you but . . . it's just that you aren't very nice to her sometimes. So what if she doesn't know as much Austen as we do? That's no reason to make her feel bad. Do you remember when she tried to teach the novels to herself?"

I recalled a time when Adeline desired to please me. She had casually commenced alluding to Austen during dinner conversations. She would ask elementary questions such as "What do you think is the theme of *Pride and Prejudice?*" and I would repeatedly be struck by her want of intellect. I would mentally scan my extensive list of publications in *Persuasions, Modern Philology,* and other literary journals and find it impossible to translate phrases such as "the complexity of signification in the correspondences between signifiers and the signified" to a level that Adeline could understand. Even so, I thought she had indeed embarked upon serious study and commended her: "Well, well. I see Adeline's been doing some reading. Keep up the good work."

Then I'd happened upon the stash of DVDs, *Sense and Sensibility, Northanger Abbey,* etcetera, movie versions of all the books she pretended to have read. "Do you mean to say that you've not read the books? Just watched these bastardized versions of her masterpieces? Shame on you!" I couldn't believe that she would compromise herself so. Although her reprehensible sham didn't turn my stomach as much as the literary desecrations, I was revolted nevertheless. I cannot abide pretenders.

Our server arrived with Emma's blueberry pancakes and my Smoked Salmon Benedict. Emma poured syrup over her pancakes and said, "You really hurt her, Dad."

"She talked to you about that?" Did the woman have no boundaries?

"No. She's never said a word. But I have ears, you know." Her steady look bore into me, her expression reproachful.

I cast a glance around the bustling restaurant. At the white cloth-covered tables, fathers ranging in age from their early thirties to what looked like late eighties were celebrating with their children, some obviously enjoying the yearly tribute, others going through the motions to preserve form. I put myself in between the two extremes, though closer to the latter at the moment. It was definitely time to change the subject.

"Remember that grad student I was telling you about yesterday?"

"Professor Newman's?" Emma's eyes lost their intensity.

"How he thought he could use plagiarized material as the basis of his thesis is beyond me. Now we'll probably have to expel him and he was so promising . . ."

"Maybe there's a good explanation?" Emma ventured.

"There's never a good explanation for dishonesty. No, he's got to go." I clamped down firmly on the piece of English muffin in my mouth.

We spoke of academic dishonesty and the role of honour in daily living. Then about the chances of my becoming English department head in the coming semester. I passed on gossip about an assistant professor in the department, up for tenure, who was unlikely to be promoted due to his dearth of publications. Perhaps she was atoning for her earlier churlishness or simply endeavouring to celebrate the occasion, but Emma seemed a more sympathetic listener now. At home, even when she's not genuinely interested in a discourse, merely having her pretend to listen is sufficient at the end of the day.

Emma suggested a walk *post jentaculum* so she could take photographs and we ambled past a busy playground with its spiderlike jungle gym, saucer-like swings, and miniature fire engine. The weather was unseasonably cold for June and both Emma and I wore fleece jackets, hers adorned with a butterfly pin and mine topped with a toque. We strolled along the banks of Lost Lagoon and pointed out bullfrog and turtle sightings to each other, stopped under weeping willows to watch raccoons forage, and kept a lookout for goldeneyes and mergansers that might have dallied past their winter stopover. Mid-morning joggers waved as they trotted past, families with small children apologized for their offspring's rambunctiousness, and lovers walked hand in hand, leaving me with a sense of loss and envy.

I've held this lake dear ever since I read Pauline Johnson's *Ode to the Lost Lagoon*. "It is dark in the Lost Lagoon . . . and gone is the golden moon." I wanted to hear the firs sing again, I wanted to see the "grouping gulls," I wanted to have someone to share moments with me during the "twilight grey."

We paused under the shade of a tall Douglas fir and Emma snapped some photos of the Jubilee Fountain. "Did you know that UBC engineers once put a Volkwagen Beetle on the fountain as a prank?" I said.

"Yeah, I think you told me. Where else? Off the Lion's Gate Bridge and on top of the library clock tower, right?" She raised her camera as she spotted a blue heron patiently waiting for prey, standing with one leg raised in the water.

"Yes. Misguided creativity."

Sounds of tooting horns from irate drivers and engine noises from passing trucks filtered down from Georgia Street. A particularly loud exhaust emission from a badly maintained motorcycle frightened the heron into sudden flight and Emma lowered her camera in frustration. We continued down the muddy gravel path. Emma cocked her head as she studied a cedar for possible composition options, a pensive look on her face, harbinger of the thoughtful woman I hoped she would one day become.

After taking a few shots of the cedar, Emma led me to a board for bird-watchers entitled "What does it all mean?" Part of the board showed a mother duck swimming in front of a row of ducklings. A series of drawings of a male goldeneye displaying courting behaviour occupied the space above the ducks.

Emma pointed to the goldeneye series and laughed. "Look, Dad. It's the male of the species making a fool of himself again."

"Excuse me, young lady. I take offence at the inference," I quipped in an injured tone.

"Well, if the shoe fits."

"Hey, just because we're male doesn't mean that we're always putting on displays. I believe that I'm an irreproachable representative of my gender," I said with my chest puffed out while Emma's clear laugh rang out.

The mention of my putting on displays reminded me of my recent interactions with members of the fair sex and I hoped that Emma would never learn of them. One of my guiding principles in parenting is "practice what you preach." I took wedding vows and I intend to keep them, otherwise how could I look Emma in the eye? "For better or for worse." Just because Adeline strayed, doesn't mean I have to follow suit. We'd started with such high hopes, Adeline and I, and even five years ago I still thought the marriage could be salvaged. How does that ant song go? "Oops, there goes another rubber tree plant..."

I'd sensed Adeline's contrition; I believe she'd tried to make amends for her transgressions. The carefully prepared meals, the attentive inquiries, the unnecessary presents. I think those gifts were what irked me the most. Each new sweater, each unwrapped shirt, each additional tie was like another pulse sent along a nerve wishing only to be deadened. Nothing so seriously militates against the growth of affection as low, superfluous advances.

So now I'm seeking female friends. *Dum spiro, spero.* As my beloved Ms Austen would say, "Friendship is certainly the finest balm for the pangs of disappointed love." Adeline and I have come to an agreement. Weekend evenings are our own, no questions asked. I'm perfectly clear about the parameters: I'm not looking for a sexual relationship, even though I crave that, but I *am* looking for an intimate friend. Thus far, Tracy is the only person I've approached.

Adeline had entrusted me to get an estimate for the value of the house; she didn't feel equal to the task. Tracy, an experienced realtor and daughter of our United Church minister, came by to do the estimate. Her warmth and sensitivity caused me to disclose more than I normally would have with an acquaintance. I shared the reason for our selling the house and a long conversation about divorces ensued.

At one juncture, Tracy said, "My mother's generation would have had a hard time with divorce. Especially being Taiwanese. It was shameful to get divorced. Not only a personal failing but shameful for the family. But nowadays, the divorce rate in Taiwan has apparently escalated to the point where divorces are quite common. I think people should find happiness where they can."

The conversation meandered to my work and my regard for Tracy's intellectual prowess rose when she made these pithy observations about the Regency era: I think the Chinese would be quite comfortable with your Jane Austen characters. Family connections and wealth are still practical considerations in Chinese courtships. The power of a father such as *Northanger Abbey's* General Tilney would not seem unusual to traditional Chinese families. Worries like Mrs Bennet's over her children's marriage prospects are commonplace among Chinese mothers. Emma's filial devotion would be admired even by Chinese youths. Put those characters into an Asian television drama and you'd probably have a hit.

Tracy made me feel listened to and respected; I found her physically attractive. She said she wanted to maintain a professional relationship. I accept that.

Last weekend, I overheard some women arguing about emotional adultery at the lounge that I frequent on Saturday nights, a nondescript place with canned piano music and middle-aged women on the prowl. "Hon, I don't care what you say. Even if he's not having sex with her, he's still being unfaithful. He shouldn't be spending that time with another woman. He should be at home with his wife." The brunette wore a silver bustier and was drinking rum and coke. Construing my stares to be a sexual invitation, she had sat down at my table and later hurriedly stalked away on her shiny stilettos, her glittery purse jammed under one arm muttering, "Why the heck would a guy come to a pick-up joint if he's just looking for friends? How screwed up is that?"

When I came home that night, a strip of light was visible under Adeline's bedroom door. I thought Adeline had relinquished the habit of waiting up for me long ago. Most weekends, by the time I returned home after midnight, she would be asleep; and by the time I rose on Sundays, she would be out on her morning run. More out of curiosity than caring, I tapped quietly on her door so I wouldn't disturb Emma in the next bedroom.

Adeline poked her head out and gestured me in. She closed the door and leaned back against it, her hands still on the doorknob. "I'm glad you're home. We need to talk." Her voice was quiet.

"I'm all ears." As I sat down at her dressing table, I caught a glimpse in the mirror of a man with a receding hairline, slight paunch, and shoulders sloping forward from too many hours spent at a desk.

"You know we can't go on like this." She crossed the room and lowered herself onto the edge of her double bed. Her athletic frame sat ramrod.

Clichés. Does the woman never stop talking in clichés? Even her affair was a cliché. Her tennis instructor for Chrissake. *O tempora, O mores!* I forced myself to be civil despite the late hour. "Did you have something in mind?"

"Now that we know how much the house is worth, maybe we should put it on the market and split the assets." She bowed her head and worried the sash of her housecoat.

I strove to keep my anger in check. "We've had this conversation before, Adeline. Your part-time job at the boutique doesn't pay enough for you to support yourself and I don't make enough to support two households at the same standard of living as we currently have. I don't want Emma to suffer if we get divorced."

We have both perfected the art of dolce arguing; any eavesdropper would have thought that we were sharing an intimate matrimonial moment from the tone of our voices. Our marriage has been devoid of emotion for years, so by and large the appearance of calm is not difficult to achieve. Our *modus vivendi*. I didn't want tonight to be the exception.

"I care about Emma, too, but how long can we go on being unhappy?"

Her blond highlights glistened and her arresting, green eyes begged but I had grown immune to her physical appeal. Comments about Adeline's preternatural beauty from admiring colleagues no longer filled me with pride. Even the thought of running my hand down her long neck filled me with revulsion. Here was territory first charted by me but conquered by another.

"I'm content with the status quo. Until you can stand on your own two feet, you'd better make the best of it. Emma comes first. It's getting late. Good night."

Yes, I am aware of my inflexibility; I know that I can be kinder to my wife. One of the curses of self-awareness is knowing when I fall short of the ideal and I fancy myself to be possessed of some emotional intelligence. In the final analysis, though, I know I'm right. We must do everything we can to maintain the family unit.

I recognize that Adeline and I no longer fulfill each other's emotional and physical needs. I love my wife and I always will but no amount of counselling will ever restore my former feelings about her. Once cuckolded, a man can never feel the same towards the culprit. *Alea iacta est.* The days when I used to croon "Sweet Adeline" to her are gone. I accept that.

In the days of our early courtship, I thought our differences were charming: her athleticism, practicality, beauty, and optimism played nicely against my dreamy, academic broodings. Now I see her for the shallow, soulless, materialistic woman that she has become or possibly always was.

Granted, I'm being a tad unfair. There is more substance to Adeline than I care to admit. She has never failed to chauffeur Emma in our family minivan to her art lessons, soccer games, or play-dates. She books her shifts at the boutique to accommodate Emma's and my schedules and is usually home in time to make dinner. Her evenings away from home are chiefly meals with other mothers. And her weekly games of cards with Emma have remained constant for the past decade.

Nevertheless, the few words that pass between us now concern Emma or the household or the divorce. Perhaps I delay the inevitable because I feel unprepared for unshackled freedom. I've been part of a married couple for so long that I need to re-establish my own identity before we make the final split. My mother used to say, "Raymond, you were the most cautious baby I ever saw. Darn if you didn't lick your food first before you took a bite."

Emma and I walked until we reached the sign and Emma posed me for a photo. "Hah! That's funny, Dad. Now hold still." I had my arms wrapped around the signpost; my right hand was covering L and my left covering A below it. Originally the sign said "Lost Lagoon," now it epitomized me. *Ecce homo!*

As we resumed our walk, Emma said, "So, Dad, I'm going to tell you something that you don't know and I hope you don't take it the wrong way." Her elfin face had an uncharacteristically serious look.

A sense of foreboding descended but I tried to look unconcerned.

"I've been talking to a counsellor at school. Sorting things out. And I think you and Mom should get a divorce," she said, with nary a trace of emotion.

"But, Emma. I thought you were happy with the way things are," I managed after an awkward pause.

"No, Dad. Nobody is happy with the way things are."

"Has your mother been talking to you?" I hoped I didn't sound accusatory.

"No. Nobody talks to anybody in our house and that's the problem. You should be talking to Mom, not me. I'm not your confidante. She's supposed to be." Emma capped the lens and slung the camera around her neck.

I gazed at the tranquil waters and prayed for serenity. This formerly sheltered cove underwent a transformation and is the better for it; I, too, should be able to. "But do you really want to live in two different places? Isn't it better to keep our family together? Don't you want to be part of a nuclear family?"

"Not like this, Dad." She looked at me in her clear-eyed way. "Besides, a lot of my friends come from divorced families. It's not a big deal these days. There's even a radio station that's giving away a "Divorce for Dad" in a Father's Day contest. 'The perfect gift for the man who has everything, and doesn't want it.' These days, they even have Hallmark cards to help people take the first step out the door."

I heard the gentle bleat of a trumpeter swan in the brush behind us. Swans work together to protect their cygnets until the clutch can venture out on their own. Cobs and pens take turns guarding the nest while their mates complete their flightless molts. A cob protecting his brood is a fearsome sight indeed. But I once saw a cob and pen beat off an intruder swan with such ferocity that their clutch became completely confused and frightened, fleeing through the rushes *away* from the nest rather than *towards* it.

The period before a cygnet is capable of flight is particularly dangerous. It's the parents' job to safeguard their offspring. At times, swans lose their young due to inclement weather—that is out of the parents' control. However, protecting the cygnet from other dangers before she becomes a fledgling is not. I feel strongly about ensuring that Emma does not take flight before she is ready; I want her feathers to be fully developed before she makes that rasping sound with her wings. But has she fledged without my noticing?

Swans mate for life. They form a perfect heart-shape with their long necks, breast-to-breast, when they perform the mating ritual and their ensuing devotion is legendary. Some cobs never mate again after losing their partners. Do swans ever get divorced?

The trumpeter swan has a resonant "French horn"-sounding honk while other swans have softer, more melodious calls. EB White wrote a story about a trumpeter swan who learned to play the trumpet in order to compensate for being mute. Maybe all Adeline and I needed to do was to learn to play each other's songs again.

I thought of the times when Adeline and I had laughed: when Adeline put a "buzz cut" sign on a freshly pruned willow in our backyard as an April Fool's joke; when Emma played Puck at her school's production of *A Midsummer's Night's Dream;* when we roasted mini-marshmallows on corn skewers over candle flames during a power outage. Adeline was always on the lookout for laughter, at herself and at me. My mind started to wander to the tender moments that we had shared. Then I caught myself and recalled the numerous arguments after Adeline's confession and the silent years after the initial tantrums, and my heart hardened once again.

"I think it's time for us to go home." I took one last look into the brush, hoping to see a bill or a feather; hoping for some visual evidence of the swans.

The Good Teacher

MR LO TAKES OFF HIS READING GLASSES and rubs the bridge of his nose; the furrows between his brows deepen. He pushes his chair back from his dilapidated teacher's desk, picks up a test paper from the pile there and goes to the homework solutions stapled to the corkboard that he had forgotten to clear the previous day.

He runs his finger down the three sheets of solutions on the corkboard and stops at question number 12. Related rates question. At what time will the snowball reach the same size as the tennis ball? Mr Lo had meant to revise his incorrect solution to the question before posting the sheets, but it had slipped his mind. It was unlike him to be so lax, but with report cards, the Christmas concert, and parent-teacher conferences, the week had rushed by.

He puts his glasses back on and peers at the solution again, just to make sure. Then he examines the paper in his hand. There's no doubt, the two are identical. The same erroneous starting values, the same error in logic, the same incorrect final answer. The only way that Aaron Curtis could have gotten the answer he did was if he had copied it from the solutions board; nobody else in the class had used the same steps or arrived at the same value. And Aaron had been sitting right next to the board during the exam.

Mr Lo throws the test paper on his desk and begins pacing the deserted room. He opens two windows despite the afternoon drizzle. He makes a circuit around the perimeter of the room: past his desk and filing cabinets in the back corner, the two adjacent walls of white boards, the television and DVD player on its cart, the recycling box, and ends up at the front of the room where the overhead projector rests on its cart. He sits down on his stool, sprays water from a dispenser onto the plastic roll draped across the overhead projector, detaches a few squares of paper towel, and starts wiping off the day's lecture notes.

Mr Lo sighs and gazes at the twenty desks in the room arranged in two rows of twos. He's had this classroom for most of his teaching career. The desks used to be in single rows but at some point, he'd conceded to the fashion of the time and allowed the students to sit next to each other, and he'd somehow never gone back. Aaron's spot is by the bulletin boards on the west side of the room, next to his friend Sean, the class wit.

The first time Mr Lo saw Aaron, two years ago in his Math 11 class, his heart had lurched. He couldn't believe the same shade of blue-green eyes could exist in two genetically unrelated people. Not only that, but Aaron had the same lean build and the same intense gaze as Cecil. Since then whenever he's looked at Aaron, he is unfailingly reminded of his early years in London with Cecil, and he hopes that his face doesn't ever betray the emotions those memories evoke; he doesn't want to think about the consequences if his expressions are misconstrued. Mr Lo decided that day not to let his feelings about Cecil ever influence his treatment of Aaron, and his resolve still holds.

Mr Lo rests one elbow on the projector and fingers his tie—a quirk of his when he's thinking. One of the students "spoofed" him at a performance years ago. Mr Lo can't remember his name any more but the student did a convincing job. He'd put on an Albert Einstein wig, short-sleeved white shirt, dark pants, and an enormous hearing aid. During the skit, the boy changed his tie five times, one for each day of the week, and made a point of repeatedly adjusting his tie. He mimicked Mr Lo's British accent perfectly and started each sentence with "And so you see, gentlemen . . . " or "And here at St Thomas Aquinas, the best school in Vancouver . . . "

Mr Lo rises and continues his restless walk as if movement will bring a quicker resolution to his problem. If it were anybody else but Aaron, he thinks. He stops in front of his "Wall of Fame," a montage consisting mostly of graduation pictures and thank you cards interspersed with the occasional ornament which students have brought back over the years from trips abroad. There's even a plaque—some boys took up a collection one year, "In honour of your continued dedication . . . " It had brought tears to his eyes.

Mr Lo is one of a nearly extinct breed of teachers who see education as a calling and devote themselves entirely to the profession. Mr Lo has no respect for teachers who take short cuts with their planning— begging and stealing resources from other teachers instead of putting in the time to create their own lessons; who only have a cursory understanding of the subjects they teach and frequently can't answer probing student questions; who still can't name all of their students midway into the school year, let alone know them well. Mr Lo scorns the public school teachers who made such a fuss about being involved in extracurricular activities during their last contract negotiations. It was fortunate that his school was not involved in such embarrassing behaviour. He gladly puts in his after-school hours coaching the debating society, the Reach for the Top team, and the math club. It gives him a chance to know the students in another context; he only wishes he had the stamina to do more with his students.

When he was first searching for employment in Canada after emigrating from Hong Kong, Mr Lo had purposely chosen a modest kindergarten to Grade 12 private school because of the smaller classes and the possibility of teaching the same students for several years in a row; he believed in developing real rapport with his students. Sometimes he regrets having been born too late to teach in a one-room schoolhouse where he is an integral part of the community. Given his private life, though, it's just as well that he's able to keep work and home separate.

He's taught thousands of boys in his thirty years . . . and now Aaron Curtis: scholarship student, born achiever with excellent grades and hundreds of school and community service hours, outstanding athlete . . . Mr Lo would wager that Aaron will be voted by his fellow graduates as "the one most likely to succeed" for the school yearbook. Mr Lo shakes his head; it's incomprehensible.

Mr Lo's favourite movie is *Stand and Deliver,* not just because he teaches Advanced Placement Calculus, but also because the film shows what a bit of hard work and dedication can achieve, even under unpromising circumstances. He shows it to his classes every September to start the year off right, and in some years, before the College Board exams as well, to inspire the students. At times they groan but Mr Lo thinks he knows what's best for them. And he usually does.

Mr Lo is noted for his thoroughness and fairness in his dealings with students; less well known is his humanity in handling difficult situations—he takes great satisfaction in having the ability to see grey instead of simply black and white, not like some of these young pups who run their classes like factories and think everything can be broken down into rules and regulations.

But the current situation troubles Mr Lo. In the past, he has tended to take a hard line because he believes that there are standards to be upheld and he sees himself as the guardian of ethical mores. Former students who cheated were given suspensions and the circumstances were recorded onto their permanent records without too many repercussions. But if he enters Aaron's offence into the official records, Aaron might lose his scholarship and not be able to finish the year. Aaron's chances of entering university might also be diminished. And Mr Lo knows that Aaron needs not just to be admitted to university, but to be admitted with a scholarship due to the family's financial circumstances. And yet, if he shows clemency, what message will he be sending, not just to Aaron, but also to other students?

Well, he isn't going to be able to decide just now. Mr Lo returns to his desk and continues grading papers. He has a reputation to maintain; in all his years, barring illness, Mr Lo has always returned test papers to the students the day directly after their exam. It's a point of pride with him.

As he enters the last score into his marks book, Mr Lo hears his favourite colleagues, Cindy Campbell and Michael Cartwright, coming up the stairs. It may have been the materials used in the construction of the building, or the architecture, or a combination of the two, but the resultant acoustics has always made conversations in the stairwell quite audible in Mr Lo's classroom when the building is nearly empty.

Throughout the years, the "stairwell conversations" have provided Mr Lo with endless entertainment. Parents who think that gossip would be a scarce commodity in an all-boys school are mistaken. Mr Lo has heard conversations centred on girl troubles, body-building tips, gripes about teachers, complaints about parents, and adolescent bravado in all guises during his tenure in this classroom. The candour of the boys when they think no one is listening dumbfounds Mr Lo, but he never lets on that he's heard anything when he sees the boys in class the next day.

Cindy and Michael are discussing some sort of basketball strategy. Both of them coach school teams—Michael the seniors and Cindy the juniors. Mr Lo isn't sure, because he has a policy of not associating with his colleagues outside of the workplace and he would never inquire directly, but he thinks the two see each other socially as well.

Despite their youth, Mr Lo respects these two thirtyish teachers. Sturdy and cheerful Michael is the athletic coordinator as well as a Grade 6 teacher; Cindy teaches math to all grades. At first, Mr Lo was uncertain about having a woman in his department, especially one straight out of teachers' college, but Cindy's knowledge of mathematics and genuine commitment to teaching won him over. He's fond of her straightforward manner and likes how she dresses professionally, her shiny brown bob and modest clothing always neatly in place, unlike some of the other teachers with their jeans and track pants. Working closely over the past seven years has allowed them to develop a friendship.

Cindy and Michael smile and wave as they pass the open door and Mr Lo returns a perfunctory wave.

Mr Lo is reminded of a conversation about cheating that he'd had with Cindy last year when she had caught a group of boys handing in copied homework. Given the prevalence and relative innocuousness of their actions, Cindy had debated whether to record the boys' infractions but had done so in the interests of fairness and consistency. At that time, Mr Lo and Cindy had passed on anecdotes from schools where teachers routinely chain their filing cabinets for fear of theft. In one school, a principal excused a student's cheating by saying "Boys will be boys" and "I cheated when I was in school. Doesn't everyone?" In another, a local private school, a parent hired a lawyer to challenge the school's discipline of his son for stealing an examination paper because the student's chances of getting into an Ivy League college had been jeopardized by the school's actions.

Cindy had said, "I sympathize with the kids to some extent. It's pretty hard to get into post-secondary now. You have to have a crazy high average to get into the best universities." Mr Lo had agreed.

She'd also said, "One of my students was complaining to me the other day about how unfair it all is. He said the ones who cheat are probably the ones who will get into university and then get ahead in their jobs later. Just because they know how to play the system. In the meantime, the honest ones get left behind."

They'd spoken of the state of morality in general and concurred that ethical lines were becoming increasingly blurred these days. "But isn't that true at any time? Haven't ethical choices always had to be made through the ages?" Cindy had asked.

"Which is why someone has to maintain some standards and teach them to the next generation," Mr Lo had stated forcefully.

Now, he wonders if he will be able to adhere to his principles. Thinking of the cheating incident, Mr Lo suddenly remembers that Aaron might have been one of those boys. He hurries down to the school's main office and flips through the "Misconducts" binder. Yes, there it is! Aaron and Sean, both of them given a warning and detention for cheating. Mr Lo closes the binder with more force than he intended.

He spends an uneasy evening at home in the bungalow that he had occupied with Cecil for fifteen years and now shares only with Euclid, his elderly Border Collie. This is one of those rare occasions when he longs for his pipe even though he gave up smoking two decades ago. He can't watch more than ten minutes of television, he can't concentrate on the Sudoku puzzle in the paper, and he can't take Euclid out for a second walk, especially since a thunderstorm has just started. He considers calling friends for a few hands of bridge but thinks the organization would be too bothersome and besides, it's already eight o'clock.

Mr Lo scrapes the remains of his mashed potatoes into Euclid's dish, washes and dries his plate and cutlery, then wanders into his study. He puts on a CD of Mozart's Symphony No. 40, the "Great G-minor Symphony," one of Cecil's favourites. Cecil always had a dark, emotional side. That's why I was attracted to him in the first place, Mr Lo thinks. He puts a log into the fireplace and coaxes a slightly smoky fire to life. As he straightens, he catches sight of Cecil's last wood carving on the mantlepiece, two male figures with arms clasped around each other. Cecil had been unable to carve once the muscular atrophy started.

Mr Lo takes his billfold from his back pocket and gazes fondly at a black and white photo—the only image of the camera-shy Cecil still in his possession. After the funeral, Cecil's daughter, Kimberley, took a box of his belongings back to England. Cecil's ex-wife had not made an appearance. Mr Lo had collected the few photographs of Cecil and packed them neatly among the framed engineering diplomas and meagre stack of cards and letters from Kimberley. During their years together, Cecil did not permit a single photograph to be taken of them with each other, and Mr Lo did not press, though he was hurt. Mr Lo knew that Cecil loved him all the more for his sensitivity. It had taken years for Cecil to speak of his daughter without tearing up.

Mr Lo extracts the photograph from the billfold and tenderly kisses it. His eyes fill with tears and an ache swells in his chest. After Cecil's death, Mr Lo cancelled their season subscriptions to the Vancouver

Symphony and the Playhouse. He stopped going to Spanish Banks and the seawall. Then he gradually got used to cooking for one, to sleeping alone, and he started taking Euclid for walks along routes where he and Cecil once strolled shoulder-to-shoulder. Last Christmas, he went to the Bach Choir's "Sing Along Messiah" after a four year absence and lost himself in the music, realizing afterwards that he'd only thought of Cecil twice the whole time.

We had thirty good years together. How many couples can claim happiness for that long? The five years since his death have been difficult but I think I've adjusted well.

Despite occasional visions of Cecil's helpless body, Mr Lo feels at peace with his partner's passing. He no longer has to engage in endless conversations with Cecil about quality of life versus the sanctity of life; the difference between murders and mercy killings; and an individual's right to self-determination. He no longer has to list Cecil's many engineering feats and point to Kimberley's personal and professional successes to cheer him up when Cecil slipped into his dark moods. He no longer has to hold back tears when Cecil asked for yet another reading of Housman's "To an Athlete Dying Young" or to choke back angry words when Cecil quoted Seneca and other Stoics arguing for the permissibility of suicide under certain circumstances. Most days, even Mr Lo's failure to convince Cecil of the rationality of Pascal's wager no longer bothers him.

He had spent weeks agonizing over Cecil's decision, trying to reconcile it with his belief that only God had the right to determine life and death. Last ditch attempts to sway Cecil by quoting Ecclesiastes passages about God's unknowable plans or, more slyly, by playing an old LP of The Byrds's *Turn! Turn! Turn!* (To Everything There is a Season) were to no avail. Cecil's track was unchangeable but he did provide liner notes: life is worth living only because there is truth, beauty, and goodness in the world—all the beauty has gone for me. If there is a God, surely he can grant me one last beautiful act—the luxury of choosing the manner of my death. By then, Cecil was so weak that Mr Lo didn't have the heart for further arguments. Mr Lo still chastised himself for not being more patient with Cecil instead of shouting at him when he'd had enough of Cecil's incessant harping on the subject: Just give me a little peace! Cecil's blue-green eyes had filled and he'd croaked: And just give me eternal peace . . .

It's done now, no point in going over it, Mr Lo thinks. He carefully restores the snapshot to his wallet.

Mr Lo considers himself past the age when he needs a partner. Euclid is company enough. The physical urges have diminished with age and he is too old to be looking now. He's very discreet with his personal life and ensures that he gives no indication of his sexual leanings at work. Not that he ever did anything untoward at school, sexual or not, even in his full-blooded prime. Teaching is a sacred trust.

He wonders if he has gradually compromised his principles over the years. Would he have considered letting a student get away with cheating thirty years ago? Why is he considering it now? What are his beliefs? Is he letting his fondness for Aaron cloud his judgment?

Then it comes to him. Mr Lo is first and foremost a teacher. And this situation is the perfect example of a teachable moment.

It's decided then. He will teach Aaron about the moral incorrectness of his actions but not initiate an official reprimand. It's much more important to develop the boy's character than to punish him for a momentary lapse in judgment. Emerson once wrote "Foolish consistency is the hobgoblin of little minds." Much better to take the long-range view than to hold fast to unbending rules.

Mr Lo feels positively giddy. Like Archimedes must have felt when he ran down the street naked, shouting "Eureka!" This is what teaching is all about.

The following day, Aaron comes after basketball practice as requested. Mr Lo thinks the boy looks nervous, understandably since he was the only person who had not had his test returned to him during class. Aaron stands awkwardly by the teacher's desk and puts his backpack on the floor. As Mr Lo starts to close the classroom door, he sees Sean lurking near the stairwell. Best to leave the door open so there will be no misunderstanding. Lately, there have been far too many stories of teachers falsely accused of sexual abuse to put oneself at risk by conducting closed-door meetings.

"Do you know why you're here, Aaron?" Mr Lo gives him a side-long look. Mr Lo has decided beforehand that he will not look at the boy directly during this whole business so that Aaron will have no physical effect on him. So far, it seems to be working.

The boy shuffles his feet and shifts his lanky frame embarrassedly. "Something about my test?"

"Yes, would you like to tell me what happened?" Mr Lo's voice is soft and encouraging. He moves a chair near the teacher's desk and motions for Aaron to sit down, careful not to touch him.

"I'm sorry, Mr Lo. I don't know what you mean." The boy runs his fingers through his newly-washed hair. He wears a defensive look.

Mr Lo perches on the edge of his desk. The kindliness he was feeling before starts to dissipate somewhat; he feels that he needs to take charge before he loses it altogether. "Aaron, I know you cheated on the test. Do you deny it?"

When the boy sees that he has no way out, he says, "No. I'm really sorry. I don't know what happened. I was up really late the night before and I studied so hard but I just blanked on the test. Then I saw the answer on the board ... I know it was a stupid thing to do and I'm really sorry. I'll never do it again."

There is no doubting the boy's sincerity and Mr Lo feels the full force of his good intentions return. "Aaron, I'm going to give you zero on this test but I will not report it. It won't go into your records. You do understand the seriousness of your actions, don't you?"

"Yes, yes. I understand. I'll never do it again. Thanks. Thanks a lot."

Mr Lo wants to drive the point home even though he is already mollified by the boy's display of contrition. "I want you to remember this later. It's your character that I'm most concerned about. Do you understand?"

"Yes. Yes. I understand. My character ... yeah."

Mr Lo expounds on his theme and only when he is satisfied that the boy has been fully converted does he allow him to leave. Mr Lo feels that in all his years at this school, he's never done a better job. He feels like Anne Sullivan after teaching Helen Keller a new word. This is his calling, his purpose in life, and after three decades of training, he has finally perfected his art.

As he sits down to finish the day's marking, Mr Lo hears them clearly as they reach the stairwell. Aaron saying, "He let me off! Gave me some shit about character. Took forever."

Mr Lo's hand freezes in the midst of reaching for his red pen. Am I hearing things right? He adjusts his hearing aid and shakes his head. Mr Lo picks up his pen and starts to uncap it, the trace of a smile still on his face. Then he hears Sean's response.

"Didn't think the old fart had it in him. I knew he was deaf but I didn't think he was dumb too. I told you the 'Sorry' act would work. Kudos, dude . . . High five!" Followed by the sound of a hand slap and a trail of gleeful laughter as the two continue down the stairs.

Mr Lo loosens his tie. For a moment his air passages become constricted, as if the tie were choking him. He is gasping, so he yanks the tie off and throws it across the room. Picking up his keys, he leaves the room, slamming the door behind him.

"Pearls before swine!" Mr Lo quickens his step. "Never try to teach a pig to sing . . . it wastes your time and annoys the pig," he mutters. As he marches the six blocks home, Mr Lo welcomes the cold rain soaking his shirt and ruining his shoes, he has forgotten his jacket and overshoes but it doesn't matter, none of it matters. He needs to be cleansed, to start afresh, to plan his retirement in earnest.

That evening, as Mr Lo takes vigorous puffs on his calabash, a thought strikes him that causes him to put down his pipe. He strokes Euclid, who's snoozing in front of the fire beside him. Then he sips his port, leans back in his recliner, and closes his eyes.

He sees Aaron in formal attire, in a crowded auditorium thirty years in the future. Aaron Curtis is accepting a Nobel Prize. His fame as a scientific researcher with exceptional integrity has spread worldwide. He has written essays on methods of educating future scientists so that the principles of intellectual honesty and unwavering dedication to the discovery of truth will be paramount. He is perennially sought after to give lectures on the subject. His name is synonymous with the authentic meaning of "pure research."

Aaron Curtis rises amid thunderous applause and makes his way to the podium to give an inspiring speech. And at the end, he says, "I especially want to thank my old math teacher, Mr Lo. He taught me the difference between right and wrong and gave me a chance that I'll never forget. Mr Lo, I'm sorry it's taken me this long but I can never thank you enough. You made me who I am today."

Mr Lo opens his eyes and laughs, a long mirthful laugh laced with a trace of cynicism, some bitterness, and no small amount of self-deprecation. Mr Lo knows he will no longer have difficulty looking directly at Aaron. He'll have to go in early in the morning, there's marking to do . .

It starts gradually. The tittering when his back is turned, the spitballs and paper airplanes that seem to come from nowhere, the smirks and knowing looks. Then the tone in his classes changes. Students who had previously been quite attentive start to chat among themselves even when Mr Lo is delivering a lesson and he can't seem to make them stop. Boys who had never challenged any of his grading judgments start to question test marks. Student greetings and farewells at the beginning and end of classes dwindle then cease completely as boys troop in and out of the room without acknowledging Mr Lo's existence. Instead of the numerous requests for university reference letters that he receives annually, there are only two students who do not turn to other staff members for recommendations. And finally, the outright disrespect when he speaks to individual students after the university "early admission" acceptance letters start reaching their homes.

"Please see me after school, Aaron," Mr Lo says after several months of "treatment" by Aaron and his cronies.

Mr Lo isn't surprised when Aaron doesn't appear. He decides to let it go, pretends that he never made the request in the first place. There are only a couple of months left in the school year anyhow.

"Hey, Mr L. Did you forget something yesterday?" Sean sneers as he's leaving class the next day. Four of his friends, including Aaron, linger by the door in anticipation.

"No, I don't think so."

"Didn't you ask a certain someone to come to a certain place?" The teasing tone was unmistakable.

"That's really none of your concern." Mr Lo vigorously wipes the overhead projector roll.

"I love how you have great control over your students, dude," Sean tosses over his shoulder as he leaves the classroom amid raucous laughter.

Mr Lo glances up in time to see Aaron's smirk of contempt.

In the days following, Mr Lo starts to see words like "deaf and dumb," "great control, man," and "wussy" on his clean overhead projector roll in the mornings. When Mr Lo first encounters the word "fag" on the plastic roll, a chill spreads through him. Suddenly, he remembers the Chinese writings on the blackboards in his first classroom in Hong Kong. He thought he had escaped the cruel homophobia of the Chinese when he emigrated. The rumours, the snubs, the outright accusations and taunts. He can't believe it's beginning again. Perhaps if he ignores them, they'll stop.

Rulers and notepads from his desk start appearing on the grounds outside his classroom window. Mr Lo speaks to the school custodian about keeping his classroom door locked after school hours but tells no one about the incidents. Even so, graffiti continues to appear on the whiteboards and overhead projector roll each day.

One afternoon, Mr Lo opens his desk drawer to find a dead snake lying in a pool of red Jello. As he scoops out the mess, Mr Lo considers informing his principal of the vandalism but sees no point in escalating the situation; the perpetrators might retaliate with worse acts. There's only a month of classes left and Mr Lo feels it will be a waste of energy to track down and discipline the culprits. Besides, his principal will no doubt speculate on possible motives; Mr Lo isn't certain that he wants anyone to probe too deeply into his affairs.

Nowadays, it takes all his energy merely to wake up in time for school, fulfill his duties, and go home to a quick supper and a short walk with Euclid before collapsing on his bed. Instead of spending time with friends on weekends, he stays in his house and reads or watches television, often remaining in his pyjamas the entire time. When he absolutely cannot avoid taking Euclid out, Mr Lo pulls on his rain pants and Gortex jacket over his pyjamas and makes the walks as brief as possible.

He stops going to the United Church that he and Cecil had attended for years (despite Cecil's uncertain religious belief). They had been attracted by the welcoming attitude of the church towards gays and lesbians; a few ordained ministers were openly gay and the church sanctioned gay marriages. The choirmaster and other choir members call him up to say they badly need his tenor voice, and Reverend Anderson himself phones to inquire about Mr Lo's health. He brushes them off politely.

The hang-up calls at home begin at about the same time as the vandalism. Mr Lo will be awoken from deep sleep at one or two AM, hear high-pitched whistles and air horns, followed by silence, then a click and the dial tone. One time, he hears what is unmistakably Aaron's voice saying, "Don't you want me, man?" followed by panting. Mr Lo arranges to have his phone number changed but does not report the calls. He starts marking off days on his wall calendar and misses work at least once a week.

The week before Victoria Day, Mr Lo opens his desk drawer after lunch break to find torn pieces of a photograph scattered among paper clips and thumb tacks emptied from their boxes. Careful to avoid the points of the tacks, Mr Lo pieces together a part of the photograph. His eyes widen and he can suddenly hear his own heart beating. He quickly withdraws the black billfold from his back pocket. His fingers tremble as he opens the billfold. It's gone! Cecil's picture is gone. He always kept his wallet with him. How did they get hold of it? The beasts! That snapshot had seen him through the first few years of his grieving.

Mr Lo retrieves as many pieces of the ripped photograph as he can, drawing blood when he jabs his thumb into a tack. He sees that it's no use. The picture is irreparable. The best thing he can do is to take the pieces home and dispose of them there. The initial surge of adrenaline is replaced by a sadness that he has not known since Cecil's funeral. He closes his eyes as he waits for the pain to subside. Mr Lo sits at his desk and, for the first time in three decades, dreads the arrival of his next class.

Mr Lo tells all his students over the next two days that for the balance of the school year he will only perform his teaching duties during class and will not be available for tutoring past the dismissal bell. He also announces to his debate, Reach for the Top and math club teams that he will be terminating sponsorship effective immediately, citing personal commitments as the reason.

The harassment continues but does not worsen.

The week after Victoria Day, Mr Lo attends the scholarship committee meeting to decide on the year's crop of academic, athletic, and service award winners. Midway through the discussions, Aaron's name comes up.

Mrs Hancock, the committee chair, is reading the criteria for a major scholarship from a private donor. "And the student must show strong character . . . Endorsements from all his academic teachers must be obtained in order for the candidate to be considered." She looks around the table at the five other teachers.

"Well, I think Aaron Curtis is the perfect candidate for this one, don't you? I'm glad because the dear boy certainly deserves and needs this money. It will pay for all of his undergraduate studies. I've been assured our school will be guaranteed one winner, so whomever we nominate is sure to get it. Aaron's mother will be so proud. It's not been easy for her."

Nods of agreement all around, except for Mr Lo.

"All right, then. Let's get all the signatures."

When the nomination form is handed to Mr Lo, he puts on his reading glasses and reads the criteria again. "Strong character . . . shows honesty, responsibility, and leadership qualities." Mr Lo fingers his tie. He takes out a pen from his shirt pocket and uncaps it. The pen is poised over the piece of paper. Mr Lo frowns then rises. The other teachers look questioningly at him.

"I'm sorry. I think I'm going to have to go for a walk. Please carry on."

Mr Lo makes himself a cup of tea in the staff room. He sits looking out at a group of students, full of chatter and friendly antics, waiting at the bus stop in front of the school. So young, so much potential . . . Mr Lo empties the rest of his tea into the sink and washes the tea cup. Then he goes back to the committee room.

"Oh, Mr Lo. Just one more signature here for Aaron," Mrs Hancock exclaims. She holds out the form to him expectantly.

Mr Lo takes the form after a slight hesitation, his brow furrowed and his expression unfathomable. He sits down, places the form on the table, and fingers his tie. He mentally recounts the events of the past few months and, just as he had when he looked into the pleading blue-green eyes of a helpless man five years ago, now knows what he must do.

⌒

A week after the nomination results are publicized, Mr Lo is called into the principal's office. Mr Davenport reveals the accusations of sexual abuse.

"They are prepared to testify if needed. The parents are outraged," Mr Davenport says grimly. "We have two choices. We can put you on indefinite leave if you want to fight this or you can resign right now. You know, it's not that long until your retirement anyway."

That evening, Mr Lo sits in his armchair with a glass of port by his side and Euclid at his feet. His head is still spinning from the accusations. He never imagined the lengths to which those boys would go. He cannot even muster the strength for indignation. They had taken away the reputation that he had worked so hard to build. What was left?

Mr Lo unscrews the cap of an unmarked pill bottle and takes out ten white tablets. Cecil had gratefully accepted his pills that day, a beatific look on his face. Forward-thinking as always, Cecil had acquired them from Mexico as soon as he was diagnosed, planning for all eventualities. Mr Lo washes down the handful with a gulp of port.

He leans back and sleeps. He is traversing a dark tunnel. Then flashes in the darkness. His father's pained face, "Think about being a good son . . . " His mother's soothing tones, "You're a good boy . . . " Students presenting him with a plaque . . . Mr Davenport's grim expression, "You're a good teacher but . . . " Eventually, the darkness is replaced by a bright light . . . then Cecil's loving countenance, "You're a good man . . . " Mr Lo feels the greatest joy he has ever experienced.

Over the next few hours, Euclid repeatedly nudges his master's limp hand. His whimpers gradually change to barks. Finally, he howls with indignation. No one hears.

Gentle Warriors

TRACY

"FOUR IS AN UNLUCKY NUMBER."

Tracy rejected the notion just as she rejected her mother's other Taiwanese beliefs, even when her mother showed her a newspaper report a few years before of the disuse of the number from license plates on Taiwanese cars and motor scooters. Natural resistance to her mother's prejudices and opinions had become so ingrained in Tracy by then—she was thirty-five and her son, Patrick, was just turning four—that she dismissed almost all her mother's irrational pronouncements out of hand. Fear of the number was another subject about which Tracy could tease her mother; she took pleasure in pointing to her mother's degrees in chemistry and challenging her to produce scientific proof for her belief. Tracy continued her indulgent and mildly supercilious taunting for years—until she encountered Becky and the four legal documents.

The problem started the summer Tracy turned forty-four. She had reached a nexus of means and clarity that allowed her to enter seminary school as a mature student, much to her father's delight. A sense of predestination pervaded all she did that summer. She had ended her lacklustre career as a realtor at long last; her final act as an agent had been to purchase—enabled by her parents' down payment—a house in Grandview-Woodland. She'd felt the hand of divinity at

167

work when it occurred to her that she could rent out the lower floor of the Vancouver Special. Taking out a home renovation loan, Tracy managed to convert the lower floor into two self-contained rental suites.

The renting was easy. First, Tracy's father, David, a minister in West Point Grey, introduced a congregant: a recent Chinese immigrant in her late twenties who was studying engineering at BCIT. Alice was Tracy's idea of the stereotypical Chinese woman: quiet, shy, and eager to please—someone who would seem young even as she aged because of her petite figure and girlish manner, the sort to giggle into her hands. When Alice handed over a cheque for damage deposit and first month's rent, Tracy was certain she would be an ideal tenant.

Even better, Alice recruited her friend, Becky, to rent the second suite. Becky and her husband, John, came for a viewing in early August. John Crawford, a heavy-set twenty-eight-year-old with a sonorous voice, did most of the talking. He was jovial and polite. Tracy liked him immediately. His neatly dressed Chinese wife stood beside him, occasionally nodding and smiling in agreement.

"Becky and me, we just got married last week. We're gonna have a baby right away." John grinned, showing a gap where his two front teeth should have been.

"Um, maybe . . . I'm almost forty, you know?" Becky said, embarrassed, worrying the small cross on her necklace.

Tracy was charmed by their frankness. And, of course, the cross was the clincher. When John boomed their acceptance, Becky passed him an envelope stuffed with bills. Renting out two suites without advertising was a godsend, Tracy thought—further testament to the correctness of her new calling.

Tracy invited her parents for Thanksgiving dinner that fall—the first family event in her new home. Though the turkey was dry and the mashed potatoes lumpy, Tracy's mother, Nancy, made no comment. Likewise, her father, David, kept the conversation light and praised her projects for the downtown eastside church where she was interning. Even her twelve-year-old son, Patrick, did not complain about the food. Tracy detailed her work: care packages for the homeless, clothing drives for the destitute, shelter and employment for unwed mothers. "I feel like I've found my true calling after so many years of aimless wandering. I'm so glad I'm finally able to make a difference," she said.

Midway through the meal, sudden shouting blasted up through the dining room air ducts. "Stop it! I've had enough! Shut up!" Tracy and her family froze. It was John's distinctive voice.

It wasn't the first time that Tracy had heard foul language from her tenants. On one occasion, she had awoken to John's strident bass shouting obscenities and was forced to call the couple at four AM.

"I'm sorry. But you don't hear the stuff she whispers to me. I'm loud but it's not just me . . . but I'll be quiet. Sorry, Tracy."

Tracy hoped the Crawfords weren't going to have a lengthy argument today.

The diners pretended they hadn't heard and raised their own voices in their conversation. But as John's voice got louder, they stopped eating and listened to the abuse coming up from the vents. "I can do whatever I want, you controlling bitch. Just shut the fuck up, I don't need your nagging; I *can't* get a job. I'm going to start an *apprenticeship* program, what the fuck do you want from me?"

John seemed to spend much of his time gambling online and going to pubs. The shouting usually came on Friday nights after he had been out with his drinking buddies. Once, Tracy thought she heard John yelling about a baby but the bellowing was short-lived; she couldn't be certain that she had heard him correctly. John's occasional absences were noticeable; there was no shouting during those weeks. Becky said he sometimes travelled elsewhere to find work.

Tracy and her family looked at each other. Nancy said, "See? What I tell you? He white trash. I saw first time." After nearly forty years in Canada, Nancy's Taiwanese accent had diminished significantly but nobody would ever mistake her for anything but an immigrant.

Tracy bristled then took a deep breath and, glancing at Patrick who was following the conversation attentively, turned to her father.

David returned Tracy's gaze then turned to Nancy and said, "Every couple has their moments."

Tracy saw him tap a finger against his jaw as he looked at Nancy—giving her their private signal against imprudence.

"Lazy. So many white people too lazy," Nancy said. She took a sip of water from her glass and frowned at her husband in annoyance.

"Ma, I'm half white, remember?" Tracy threw a worried look at her father and ignored the grin spreading across Patrick's face.

Nancy set the glass down and gave Tracy one of her looks. "No, you half Chinese—more important." Then she asked, "And how is other *guah seung lung*, Alice?" Nancy always referred to Chinese who were not Taiwanese natives as "out-of-province people."

"My tenants are all fine. I wish you would stop speaking of people in such racist ways, Ma. You're educated and you're supposed to be a Christian. You can do better."

"Not racist. Just truthful. People from Mainland different from Taiwanese. Like rice dumplings. Taiwanese bah-zan is triangle shape. Cantonese zongzi, rectangle. Meat filling inside is not same. Different. Inside and out."

Tracy could never understand how her mother presented such a polite exterior to the world and yet harboured such dark thoughts. The Taiwanese, she thought, had too many layers for her to ever penetrate and she shrank from digging too deeply for fear of discovering even more unsavoury thoughts. Tracy knew her mother had suffered discrimination both in Taiwan and Canada—her own gran had been unkind to Nancy at times, but still . . .

"People are people, Ma. You can't make generalizations. There are good and bad people everywhere," Tracy said in exasperation.

Patrick turned toward Nancy expectantly, a bemused grin on his face. David was now tapping pointedly against his jaw.

"You naïve, Tracy. Life been too easy for you. You don't know black heart of society."

"You're too hard on people, Ma. We need to treat people with tolerance and respect. And *definitely* not discriminate on the basis of things they can't help. Let's not contribute to the woes of the world. Be kind."

Patrick seemed to be eagerly waiting for his grandmother's next response. Tracy threw her father a plea.

"Nancy, *please!*"

Without another word, Nancy sniffed and carried on with the remainder of her dinner.

Tracy couldn't say exactly when her impression of Becky changed. When she tried to remember later, she thought it might have started on that clear November day when Becky stopped her as she carried a bag of groceries and a bucket of fried chicken up the back stairs.

Tracy heard "Psst . . . " and saw Becky motion for her to go to the partially open door. Becky had been to the hair salon again—this time it was a shoulder-length hime cut with a reddish rinse. She wore a yellow dress with bright red flowers and her fingernails were painted crimson.

Becky squeezed herself out through the opening and closed the door behind her. She presented her usual ingratiating smile. "You have chicken take out, Tracy? Smell good."

"Yeah. It's been a long day. I don't feel up to cooking tonight."

Becky lowered her voice and said, "Can you make late rent note for us again?" She made a rectangle in the air with her index fingers.

"But you paid yesterday. I don't need to give you a notice for unpaid rent if you've already paid." Tracy scowled.

"Shh . . . he sleeping," Becky pointed toward the suite. "I need it. To scare him. I need that money."

Tracy hesitated. "Okay. I guess I can do that. If he's not pulling his weight and this is the only way to get him to contribute."

Or Tracy's new opinion of Becky could have been formed on that cold morning in January, when Becky knocked on her kitchen door, dressed in a ratty overcoat and old boots.

"Please give mail from Immigration Canada to me. Don't let John know. Just call me okay?" Her usually glossy hair was greasy and shadows rimmed her eyes.

"Yeah, okay." The woman had suffered enough and this was the least she could do, Tracy thought.

The shouting had increased of late and Tracy often heard Becky crying downstairs after John had slammed the door and left for the night. Afterwards, there were invariably sounds of furniture being dragged across tiles and wood and Tracy dreaded the day when she would have to make an inspection of the suite. She imagined streaks across the flooring and dents in the walls. Tracy thought Becky was fortunate to have a friend like Alice; the aggrieved woman could always be found in Alice's suite after her physical exertions, no matter what the hour.

"John, he says terrible things to me." Becky lowered her voice conspiratorially. "Lazy. So lazy. Not like Chinese man. I want him get job. I not suppose to work until I get paper. But I pay rent. Wendy's and bingo. You go there you see me work. You know what he say to me? He say I spread my legs, make money. Pig! I hate that guy. When I get paper, I divorce him. Then I want him move out."

"Well, you can stay but he has to go. And let me know if I can help with the immigration process."

"Thank you. Thank you so much, Tracy. Just call me for mail okay? Use my cell phone. Just call me, okay?" She almost bowed as she went down the back stairs.

To Tracy's relief and mild surprise, John quietly moved out in the middle of February. The household settled into an uncustomary calm. Visits between Alice and Becky increased. At the end of February, Becky climbed the stairs to Tracy's kitchen for a protracted discussion about her damage deposit.

"I sure when we move in, we give you one month rent deposit," Becky repeated, shifting on the kitchen chair. She fingered the cross on her necklace and looked directly into Tracy's eyes.

Tracy felt an explosion of heat spread from her midriff to her face and struggled to keep from yelling. "It's not possible. I only ever ask for half a month's rent as a deposit. By law, that's all I'm allowed to take. I'm very careful about things like this and unless you can show me some paper documentation, I just don't believe it."

"I tell you this how we did in China. I give you cash. Half month rent and one month for damage deposit. I have in bankbook."

"I'm sorry, Becky. I'm getting angry. I'm going to have to ask you to leave. There's no point in going over this again. I'll look for my copy of the receipt when I have a chance." She pushed her chair back.

As Becky stalked from the kitchen table to the back door, Tracy thought to ask, "Do you know when you'll be moving out?"

"I not know yet."

"Well, make sure you give me some paper when you make up your mind."

"Sure." The screen door slammed behind her.

Tracy considered giving Becky notice but couldn't think of a valid reason for evicting her. As long as Becky paid her rent and behaved herself, Tracy didn't have legal recourse so she decided to wait and see.

Three days later, Tracy glanced out of her kitchen window and saw two men carrying furniture from Becky's suite. She ran down the back stairs.

"It's March first. You're moving out now?" Tracy gasped for breath.

"Yeah. I need deposit money," Becky said with an open palm outstretched.

"No! You didn't give me any notice. Our agreement says if you don't give notice, you owe me the damage deposit and a month's rent. I can't give it back." Tracy's heart was still pounding.

"We will see." Becky went back into the suite to bring out more boxes.

Fortunately, Tracy managed to find another renter for the beginning of April. The loss of a month's rent and the work she had to put in to repair the damaged walls and floors was a reasonable price for finally being rid of Becky.

On March 30, a notice arrived from the Residential Tenancy Branch. Becky had filed for the return of double her alleged damage deposit, the equivalent of two months' rent. That was the first legal document.

"She's still saying she paid a full month's rent as deposit even though she's included my receipt as part of her evidence. The receipt says only half a month's rent was collected as a damage deposit. And she's submitting a picture dated March 1 to show that she left the suite in good condition. Can you believe it?" Tracy said angrily to her mother.

"Renter so stupid. You have agreement. No notice. So clear. You win," Tracy's mother declared.

Tracy looked forward to being vindicated at the dispute resolution hearing.

The following week, Tracy sat at the writing desk in her small study and phoned the Dispute Resolution office for a scheduled conference call. She confidently answered the officer's questions, occasionally referring to the papers spread out in front of her, and tried not to interrupt when Becky recounted her version of the events.

At the end of the hearing, the dispute resolution officer said, "I'm afraid your rental agreement isn't valid. The damage deposit is only to cover damage to the unit, so if you had wanted to keep the deposit you needed to make an application to the Tenancy Branch by the mid-March deadline. But I don't see evidence that more than half a month's rent was paid as a deposit. The landlord will have to pay the $50 filing fee, double the damage deposit, and the interest on the deposit."

Almost as an afterthought, he added, "But the landlord can file for the lost rental income if she wishes."

Tracy put down the phone in disbelief. Damn! Now she was out two months' rent. She reproached herself for not reading the Tenancy Act carefully before drafting the rental agreement or withholding the damage deposit. Well, live and learn.

Tracy gathered the rental papers and put them into a file folder. She stacked the file on top of the other "in progress" folders in her desk tray: papers dealing with her mortgage, Patrick's soccer team and dental fees, and her credit card bills. She rested her elbows on the desk, her head between her hands. Should she fight for the lost rental income? She could use the money and it was only fair that she should partially recoup her losses. She drew her shoulders back and sat up in determination.

Then she caught sight of the corkboard mounted on the wall directly above her desk. The mock-up for a flyer advertising some of her internship projects met her eye—her efforts to help the homeless and the poor. Tracy slumped in her chair. Maybe this would be a good time to stop the battle. If Becky felt she was getting a good bargain, Tracy would never have to deal with her again.

She thought of the last time she had seen her—a few days after Becky's unexpected departure. It was a rainy afternoon and Tracy was stopped at a red light a few blocks away from home when she saw her. She tried not look but some inexplicable force made her. Becky, shivering in a thin blue uniform and light windbreaker, was reaching into a trashcan next to the bus shelter. She retrieved a pop can, poured out the remains onto the pavement, and quickly jammed the tin into her shoulder bag. As she looked around furtively, Becky caught Tracy's eye. She flushed, glared at Tracy, and turned away. Tracy had driven off feeling as if she had just stepped on a banana slug in her bare feet.

Tracy sighed. What would Derek do? Even though she had lost her husband a decade ago, when faced with uncertainty, Tracy still thought of the compassionate realtor who was always so sensible. Would Derek continue the fight? No, he would move on. He used to say life is too short to bother with trifles. Look at the big picture. With a sigh, Tracy tucked the folder of rental papers into the filing cabinet next to her desk. She had an assignment due for one of her courses and she still had to take Patrick to a dental appointment.

The following Sunday, while helping her mother with the gardening at her parents' West Point Grey home, Tracy informed her of the outcome of the hearing. Nancy thought it all stemmed from associating with Mainlanders. She'd taught Tracy from infancy not to trust *guah seung lung*, knowing from her experiences in Taiwan that they were liable to turn on you at any time.

"Corrupt, grasping, ruthless Mainlanders are everywhere in Taiwan. They would be no different here," she said. She conceded there might be exceptions but asserted they were rare.

"But Ma, it's been so long since you've been there and maybe things have changed. Besides, this is Canada and the woman has never been to Taiwan. She would only know it as the name of a province from geography class, if that," Tracy said.

"Bad seeds promulgate regardless of where they are planted," Nancy declared in perfect Taiwanese.

She bent back a hydrangea stem and took a cutting from one of her thriving shrubs, instructing Tracy to keep the clipping indoors until it had rooted and to weed diligently after planting it outside. Tracy accepted reluctantly, for she was not possessed of a green thumb, but later found the hydrangea to be one of the few plants that flourished in her garden and was even more pleased when the shrub first yielded, not the cobalt blue flowers in her mother's garden, but brilliant pink blossoms. In succeeding years, whenever she saw the hydrangea bush, Tracy would be reminded of the four documents and her sermons the following Sunday would again touch on themes of tolerance, prejudice, justice, legacies, and independence of thought, though it would never be clear to the congregation what Tracy's personal feelings were on the subjects.

"Let's ask Dad what he thinks," Tracy said, taking the stem into her mother's kitchen so she could put the cutting into water.

To her surprise, even Tracy's normally conciliatory father thought she should fight. As Tracy, Patrick, and her parents sat around a hotpot in the small dining room of her parents' bungalow that evening, Reverend Anderson said, "We've talked about gentle warriors before. Turning the other cheek doesn't mean we invite abuse. It means our confidence is such that we are not afraid to turn the other cheek toward those who trespass against us. But that doesn't mean we unquestioningly offer ourselves up."

This coming from a United Church minister!

"Yes, gentle warriors stand their ground when injustice occurs," Tracy's father said, pouring a bowl of peeled prawns into the hotpot.

"I don't know. Maybe I should just let it go. The dispute resolution officer said I could file for the lost month's rent because Becky didn't give notice. I'd probably win but she needs the money more than I do."

"She give you much trouble. You fight!" Nancy said. She set out some vinegar in small bowls for Patrick and her husband then sat at the head of the table.

"Yeah, Mom. You should get some of your money back," Patrick chimed in.

"I don't feel quite right about it but you guys have a point. Injustice is injustice."

Tracy filed for damages the following day and was awarded the lost month's rent.

She could hear tears in Becky's voice when the officer asked if they both understood the judgment. A copy of the order arrived three days later; that was the second document.

A week after the decision, Tracy got a call from the Vancouver city permits department.

"We've received a complaint about the two illegal suites in your house, ma'am. Can we come by for an inspection?"

The inspector who came said, "You're going to have to tear down one of the kitchens and ask the tenant to leave. As for the other suite, you'll have to apply to get a permit to use it as a rental unit."

After the inspector left, Tracy stood in Alice's suite for several minutes. How was she going to manage with the loss of rental income? Not to mention the costs of the renovation, the permit application, and the yearly permit fee. This couldn't be happening. How could Becky do this to me? And she still hasn't paid the lost month's rent. The anger that arose surprised Tracy with its intensity; she wanted to find Becky so she could give her a good shake. After the compassion that she'd shown the woman this was the repayment she got! So much for common decency! What her mother said about Mainlanders was right!

Tracy scrutinized the inspector's list. West suite: Dismantle the kitchen sink and counter, tear down the overhead cupboards, remove the stove and ventilating hood, get rid of the refrigerator . . . in short, no trace of a kitchen was to remain. East suite: upgrade the smoke detectors, put in self-closing hinges for the doors, install a peep-hole for the outer door, refit the plumbing to new standards . . . Tracy put the paper down on the counter; she couldn't bear to read on.

Damn! Damn! Damn! Tracy gripped the edge of the counter and tried to calm herself. She had known the risks of building two suites when she did the renovation but she also knew there were many houses like hers in the city. Most landlords with illegal suites were not reported. Heck, MLS realtor listings often cited the existence of "unauthorized suites" as selling points.

Why didn't I just let Becky have the deposit in the first place? I could have stopped this earlier.

But she tried to cheat me. I couldn't let her get away with that.

Tracy had never thought of herself as vindictive. She was trying to raise Patrick to be a kind and loving person. Turn the other cheek. Isn't that what she was supposed to do? It was just money after all. How did things get so out of hand? And if Becky didn't pay? What would she do then?

She just wanted the whole thing to go away.

Then there was the matter with the City. If she evicted Alice, the poor woman was going to have difficulty finding another apartment with the city's vacancy rate at close to zero. But if she kept Alice, what message would that send to Patrick about her regard for the law? Even though the law was questionable given the need for affordable housing in Vancouver, there were consequences for those who disregarded rules. It would have been easy to hide these matters from Patrick a few years ago but his twelve-year-old antennae sensed everything these days.

Later that day, her father said, "Honey, the only way to deal with people like this is to show them that you're not afraid of them. You did the right thing. And if she doesn't pay, take her to Small Claims court. As for the suites, do whatever you think is right. Just don't get into trouble."

After the third document, an official order from the City to legalize her suite, arrived in the mail two months later, Tracy regretfully gave Alice notice to vacate. It cost Tracy $2000 (borrowed from her parents) for the repairs. Hoping for a home-stay student for the new west suite, she put herself on waiting lists with local colleges and posted ads on Craigslist. It would mean more work, preparing meals and looking after the student's needs, but at least it would be legal. Only the collection of the lost rent from Becky remained. As she filled in the service order (the fourth document), Tracy sighed with relief. Grateful release from the strain of battle overshadowed her sense of vindication; the money had become almost meaningless.

When Tracy first saw the returned service order marked MOVED, she didn't open the envelope, thinking she might need it later as evidence in Small Claims court. Becky had evidently cancelled her mail box number and not provided a forwarding address.

The Small Claims clerk told Tracy she would not be able to file an order for enforcement if she did not have Becky's contact information. The good news was that Tracy would have ten years to enforce it.

"Honey, you have two choices. You can let it go or you can try and track her down," Tracy's father said at dinner that night. Nancy had prepared his favourite daikon soup and he slurped with pleasure.

"You find her. Money belong to you!" Nancy snapped her chopsticks together as she picked up a piece of broccoli from the communal plate and gestured to Tracy to fill Patrick's bowl with more rice.

"But I don't know how to track her down. All I have is her email address which might or might not be current. I don't even know if it's worth my time to pursue this." Tracy spooned some garlic pork onto the rice in Patrick's bowl and handed it to him. He held his hand over the rice when she attempted to add broccoli.

"She doesn't work at the bingo hall or Wendy's anymore and they don't know how to reach her or won't tell me if they do. Alice claims she doesn't have information to give me. I called her ex and he told me that he doesn't know where she is and he wants to keep it that way. She was going after him for spousal support at one point but he thinks she's finally left him alone." Tracy sighed.

"I have idea. Pat, you show Grandma how to use computer."

After Patrick finished his second helping of apple crumble, the four of them went into his grandfather's study. Patrick turned on the computer.

"Now, make new email. Make company name."

"Grandma, don't make me do anything illegal."

"No worry. Legal. Make company name."

Nancy had Patrick send an email to Becky informing her she was the winner of a $100 gift certificate. All Becky had to do was provide her address for the certificate to be mailed.

"You wait. Greedy people always greedy."

Tracy checked the email account the following day.

"Gotcha!"

As Tracy started to copy down Becky's new address, she put the pen down, sat back in her chair and let the triumphant tide wash over her. She should savour this moment. Now she would be able to file for order enforcement in Small Claims court and receive $700. Small comfort after all the money that she had lost in this fiasco, not to mention the time and energy.

Despite a twinge of guilt, Tracy copied down the address, relieved that the ordeal was finally over.

A few years later, after Tracy had graduated from seminary school with honours, including a certificate of merit for her work with single mothers, she came across a returned letter addressed to Becky in a desk drawer in her study, and her fingers tightened. Resentment still lingered. It was the service order that she'd sent in an attempt to collect that last month's rent. Becky had disappeared by the time the case got to Small Claims court and Tracy had felt too embattled to continue the legal dispute. For months afterwards, she had carried the envelope in her purse on the chance that she would accidentally meet Becky. A year after the dispute, John had called asking if Tracy would act as a reference for his application to a new apartment (he was planning to marry a fellow carpentry apprentice) and mentioned that Becky was working at a Chinese restaurant on Fraser. Tracy made a last attempt to collect the money but Becky had quit by the time she visited the restaurant. Though some of Becky's feints and parries weren't intentional, Tracy had winced each time she found herself bested by the new immigrant. She vowed not to let the matter taint her view of Mainlanders, though she never rented to another Chinese tenant again, other candidates always being more suitable. She continued to defend Mainlanders whenever the topic arose in conversations with her mother, albeit not as vociferously as before, and she no longer challenged her mother's belief in the inauspiciousness of the number four.

Tracy tapped the envelope on the edge of the desk. There were still a few more years left for her to enforce the order.

She sat down and stared at the bulletin board above her desk. The flyers for Downtown East Side clothing drives had been replaced with notes for her new church duties. To her family's joy, she had taken over her father's West Point Grey ministry upon his retirement. Tracy looked again at the envelope and was tempted to continue the fight. At the same time, it irked her that she was unable to let the matter rest; she had never thought of herself as petty. It was only a month's rent, a pittance, really. Still, the injustice. She fiddled with the envelope and considered. Finally, with clenched jaws and a lingering sense of disappointment in herself, Tracy looked one last time at the envelope then put it through the shredder beside her desk.

ALICE

ALICE STOOD BESIDE THE HOSPITAL BED and tried not to cry out as Becky squeezed her hand. She'd promised herself she would be a source of support for the duration of Becky's pregnancy and she wasn't going to pull back now, in the final hours. Her parents would have been proud, satisfied that all those decades of secret "house church" meetings, held even during the Cultural Revolution, had been worthwhile. Their daughter had fully absorbed the gospel lessons and was acting as a true Christian, a committed "warrior of Christ," even in a foreign land.

Becky's face contorted as she let out a scream. Alice withdrew her hand and rubbed it after the contraction passed. Becky leaned back on the half-raised bed and closed her eyes. Alice wiped her friend's forehead with a damp sponge, turning her face away from Becky's sour breath.

Alice first met Becky at an English language class in Vancouver—part of her church's outreach program. It was her landlord at the time who had introduced her to the free English classes at the United Church in West Point Grey. Though it meant an hour's bus ride from her apartment on Main and 21st, Alice had attended the classes faithfully.

"Go to the services. It'll be a good way to practice what you've learned," Mrs Woods, her white-haired English teacher, had suggested. The retired elementary school teacher had a convincing manner and Alice thought more conversation practice couldn't hurt.

Alice found Reverend Anderson to be genial and particularly sympathetic to Asians; his wife was Chinese and Alice heard that he had done missionary work in Southeast Asia during his youth. Although Mrs Anderson was polite, Alice often thought she heard faint notes of disdain in the older woman's voice. Alice put it down to oversensitivity on her part and continued to attend the services; she was determined to take advantage of the opportunity to learn English—even if it was the United Church, and the congregants were not as zealous in spreading the Good Word as she.

The first time Becky appeared in the basement classroom, she made an immediate impression on the group of six Chinese women and two Korean men. Alice had never seen anyone so eager to speak and so quick to learn. Judging from Becky's above-average height and long face, Alice had pegged her as a Northerner and was surprised to learn that Becky, like herself, came from Shenzhen. It was only later that Becky revealed that her family actually lived on a farm in Henan. Had Alice known this beforehand, she probably would not have befriended Becky; she was not in the habit of associating with uneducated women from the countryside. Becky had boasted of a degree in economics from Nanjing University. It turned out the degree was a fake, as so many other things about Becky turned out to be. Alice thought she had to give the woman credit. It takes a great deal of intelligence to be able to bluff your way through life. Becky seemed to make up for her lack of schooling by reading books and newspapers, always coming up with the most surprising facts.

Becky's face contorted again, and Alice gave her a towel to squeeze. "Breathe," Alice told her in Mandarin. "Remember what you learned in prenatal class." Becky drew a ragged breath and panted unevenly.

The young, dark-haired doctor at the foot of the bed said, "You're almost fully dilated. Don't push yet."

"Tamade! I need to push!" Becky screamed.

"Don't push. You might tear too much," Dr Weinstein said.

"Can't you do something for her pain?" Alice asked him.

"She's doing fine. I'll give her some nitrous oxide soon. Breathe, Becky. Breathe!"

Becky took another ragged breath and squeezed the towel harder. Alice wiped her face with the sponge again.

Over the past year, Alice was given many occasions to feel sorry for Becky but this surpassed them all. Alice had never attended a birth before and the experience was making her dread pregnancy. She and her parents had agreed that she would concentrate on emigration and studies abroad before getting married. Now that she was twenty-nine and nearing the end of her degree program at BCIT, Alice's thoughts turned increasingly to marriage and children. Even though she did not envy Becky's lot most of the time, Alice sometimes thought she could use a bit of Becky's fearlessness when it came to men.

Alice remembered the time the two of them had rented *Lust, Caution* when they were sharing Alice's basement suite, a few months after Becky had first appeared in English class. Alice had blushed through the sex scenes while Becky took note of the lovers' positions.

"Do you think you could have done what she did? Sleep with the enemy? Do you think you would have gotten emotionally involved like she did?" Alice asked.

"You're talking to someone who has sex like a man, remember?" Becky said. "She was weak. I would have done my job and walked away."

"Such a sad fate . . . "

"We make our own fates. She made her choice and it was a bad one. End of story," Becky said and shrugged.

Alice now looked at Becky's exhausted face—who wouldn't be tired after fifteen hours of labour?—and wondered what Becky thought of her fate now. Alice had always known Becky to be the mistress of her own fate despite difficult circumstances. Born into a rural family, Becky had made her way to Shenzhen and found work in one of the city's many factories. But she had ambitions and the determination to carry them through. Becky had left China on a visitor's visa and, when her visa expired, gone underground to find work and even to marry a Canadian. Alice was astounded by her resourcefulness. When Becky first moved in with her, Alice knew little about her. The common bond of being from Shenzhen and the struggles of immigration had been enough to ensure their intimacy. Gradually, Becky confessed about herself as her trust in Alice grew. Alice forgave Becky the lies about her origins and her education, knowing that many women not born into urban families faced great hardships in China. She couldn't blame Becky for wanting to get ahead; Becky's impoverished parents and younger brothers could not have survived without her earnings. Several years later, for a very brief period, Alice would look back and remember the unflagging regularity of Becky's monthly cheques to China, then try not to think of the verse "Judge not, lest ye be judged."

Becky's next spasms seemed even more painful. When Dr Weinstein completed the next exam, his worried look unsettled Alice. "Is everything all right?" she whispered.

"Not sure yet," Dr Weinstein muttered.

"Doctor, hurting bad. Please, drug . . . " Becky begged.

"Yes, I'm getting some nitrous oxide for you. Just hang on."

Alice hurried back to Becky's side and offered her some water. Becky shook her head and writhed in pain. A nurse wheeled a gas tank into the room. Dr Weinstein handed Alice a mask and told her to hold it to Becky's face. Alice rushed to obey but the mask slipped and fell onto Becky's chest. She tried to retrieve the mask but Becky angrily pushed her hand away. Becky inhaled hungrily then screamed into the mask as another wave of contractions hit. When Becky slumped back onto the bed, Alice let out her breath.

Oh, Becky, what have you gotten yourself into now?

Alice said this to herself whenever Becky introduced a new suitor. During the few months that she and Becky had been roommates, Alice had met several "boyfriends" (Fred, Tim, Andy—all of them white Canadians well past fifty). Becky had collected John Crawford as one of her beaux when he appeared at Planet Bingo one evening. Though he was uneducated and ten years Becky's junior, Alice thought John's youth made him the best prospect. Becky herself didn't have a preference for any of the candidates.

"Whoever asks me to marry first will win."

Becky asked Alice to be her maid of honour at the simple civil ceremony held at Mrs Woods' home a year ago. Even though she knew little about John Crawford, Alice thought he was friendly and accommodating, albeit a bit crude. "Hey, good lookin'. How's tricks?" he'd say each time they met. Becky didn't seem to mind the flirting though Alice would turn red each time. Once, John had helped install a new showerhead at Alice's apartment and when he was done, suggested the three of them take a group shower to mark the occasion. Becky just laughed but Alice blushed and couldn't look John in the eye for days afterwards.

After she and the Crawfords moved into Tracy's house, Alice thought Becky's troubles were finally over. Becky would become a landed immigrant and be able to work legally; John would take care of her. Unfortunately, the quarrels started almost immediately. The walls separating Alice's suite from the Crawfords' were thin, and Alice was spared few details. It was after one of her arguments with John, when she had sought refuge in Alice's suite, that Becky confessed the paternity of the unborn child.

"But how can you be sure that it's Fred?" Alice asked in Mandarin as she stirred the instant noodles in her bowl.

"The timing. John was away with his brother in Alberta that month." Becky took out a nail file from Alice's purse.

"How are you going to tell him?" Alice lifted some strands of noodles from the bowl.

"He doesn't have to know," Becky said. She blew on the ends of her fingers and continued filing.

"But that's wrong!"

"Alice, I know you're into being a good person, but really . . . did you know that in Germany it's not legal for fathers to get DNA tests in paternity suits? The courts think it's better if men don't know if they're the real fathers. They think it's better for the child to be in a stable family."

Where does she pick up these choice bits of information? Alice tried again, "But don't you feel guilty about lying to him? It's paternity fraud."

"Look, women do it all the time. Even animals. I read that with Western bluebirds, forty-five percent have babies that are not fathered by the mother's partner. The rate in humans is probably not much better."

"I'm just worried about his reaction when he finds out the truth . . . and it's wrong!"

"You know, Alice, sometimes you can be really judgmental." Becky stood up and put her hands on her hips. "Look, he wants a family and I'm giving him one. End of story. His mother thinks it's his baby. Who am I to ruin things for him? I've had too many abortions in my life. I don't want to go through another. And I'm not getting any younger. This might be my last chance to have a child. Anyway, it's really none of your business."

After a few more failed attempts to persuade Becky in the weeks following, Alice thought it best to stay with safe conversations like who was doing the scripture reading at church the following Sunday or which movie to watch. Alice often wondered why Becky would have jeopardized her marriage with loose behaviour, and brooded on the matter for some time, but she didn't bring the subject up again.

After John moved out and Becky became embroiled in a rental dispute with Tracy, Becky had asked Alice to go to prenatal classes with her.

"I don't have anyone else, Alice."

Alice had tried to stay out of Becky's rental dispute with Tracy. Though it surprised her when Tracy wouldn't return Becky's damage deposit, and the thought had crossed her mind that Becky might not always be entirely truthful, Alice had relied on Becky's report out of loyalty. Becky was adamant—she deserved to get her damage deposit back. (One of the patrons at Planet Bingo had once worked for the Tenancy Branch and was coaching her through the dispute process.) She was glad when Becky won her deposit and the whole thing had blown over; she had been uncomfortable disavowing knowledge of Becky's whereabouts when Tracy queried her.

Later, after Tracy gave Alice notice, Becky and Alice had set up house together in a rundown apartment near Fraser and Marine. At the time of her eviction, Alice asked Becky if she had anything to do with the changes in Tracy's suites and Becky denied involvement. The two women were easily able to manage the rent on the apartment with Alice's educational allowance and Becky's new job as a server at a Chinese restaurant.

After the baby's birth, though, they would have to live on Alice's paltry allowance and the little money that Becky had saved from her previous jobs. It wouldn't be easy but they had planned for it. The arrangement would last for six months. By then, Alice would have graduated and the baby would be weaned, allowing Becky to return to work. Since Alice didn't know where she would find an engineering job, she had been reluctant to commit to a longer term.

Alice's parents had praised her good deed, though they questioned whether it was necessary to support Becky financially.

"It's only temporary. I would want someone to help me too if I were in her position," Alice told them.

"Well, you're a true warrior, no question. She sounds like a difficult case but I think you can win her to Christ eventually," her father said. "It's really encouraging that she still wears the cross you gave her. I'm sure she'll be a convert soon. I'm proud of how you are sowing seeds of faith. I'm sure you'll reap her soul in due time. Devotion takes time to flower."

Now, as she watched Becky straining with each contraction, Alice felt both pity and envy. Only Becky could face the prospect of single parenthood with such equanimity. Strong as bamboo. Constantly sprouting new shoots. The baby would probably be just as strong. Alice couldn't wait to hold the baby in her arms. Since she couldn't yet be a mother herself, this was the next best thing.

"Okay, Becky. When the next contraction comes, I'll tell you when to push and you push as hard as you can, okay?" Dr Weinstein waited for the next wave of contractions. "Okay, push!"

Becky grimaced with the effort until the contraction passed. Her hospital gown was damp. "I feel like I'm going to pass out," she said in Mandarin.

"She feel faint, doctor," Alice said.

Dr Weinstein was too distracted by the fetal heart monitor to reply. "It's not coming back to baseline. Give her an IV," he said to the nurse.

To Becky, he said, "Can you turn over on your left side?"

Alice turned the exhausted Becky over. Dr Weinstein's gaze was focussed on the heart monitor. Frowning, he performed a vaginal examination. His eyes widened as the baby's heart rate decelerated even more and he immediately withdrew his hand. Dr Weinstein turned to the nurse and said breathlessly, "Call Anesthesia and get an operating room ready! Stat C-section." The nurse quickly left the delivery room.

Alice felt her heart thumping and asked, "What's happening? What's wrong?"

"We're going to have to perform a C-section. The baby is in distress."

Becky groaned but appeared not to have heard. Alice leaned closer to her and said as calmly as she could in Mandarin, "They're going to do a Caesarean section. Everything will be okay."

Becky nodded groggily and sucked on her mask. The nurse came back with two women in scrubs. They wheeled the bed out of the room and rushed down the hall; Dr Weinstein kept telling Becky not to push as he ran alongside.

Alice sat on a straight-back chair beside the space left behind by the bed and ragdolled back, breathing in the smell of antiseptic and sweat. Becky was right to come to a hospital, she thought. A few months ago, Becky had told her the women in her village still gave birth with the aid of midwives but she was determined to renounce the old ways. Becky had adopted Western practices wholeheartedly when she arrived in Canada—even to the point of throwing her own baby shower before the baby's birth. Alice thought her friend had gone too far in doing so; Becky was tempting fate in her departure from the age-old Chinese tradition of welcoming a newborn only after he had survived the first month. Becky also planned to hold the red egg ceremony when the baby was a month old. "Be modern, Alice. Blend the old with the new."

Becky had invited Mrs Woods and the five women from English class as well as a few coworkers to the shower.

"The more people, the more presents."

Alice had spent two weeks looking for the perfect gift and finally settled on a delicate porcelain figurine of a baby lying on a white camellia. She had inserted a card onto which she had copied "The White Camellia Japonica," a poem by the English evangelist Charlotte Elizabeth Tonna which began, "Thou beauteous child of purity and grace . . . " Alice saw the offering as emblematic of her friendship with Becky: fragile and costly.

In their cramped apartment, Alice held her breath when Becky reached for the gift. Becky's face fell when she lifted the figurine out of the white tissue paper. She read the card and turned toward Alice.

"Thank you, Alice. I'm sure I'll find some place to put it," she said in Mandarin.

Alice managed a weak smile and it suddenly dawned on her that perhaps Becky would see the figurine as just a dust-collector when what she wanted and probably needed was something utilitarian.

When all the wrapping paper and boxes had been cleared away, the women were given paper plates and napkins while Alice brought in platters of chicken wings and spring rolls. An awkward moment ensued when Alice insisted on silence while many of the women were in mid-bite. Alice prayed on their behalf: For what we are about to receive, may the Lord make us truly thankful. The conversation then turned to baby names. Becky was thinking of names with meanings, such as Odelia (wealthy), Almeta (ambitious), or Jewel.

Later, as Alice was washing mugs and cutlery in the kitchen sink, Becky asked, "Do you think you can return the statue for a refund?"

Alice swished the dishcloth around the inside of a mug, avoiding Becky's eyes. "Yes, I suppose so. Do you want the cash or do you want me to buy something else instead?"

"No. Cash is good. If I refund the mobile from Mary and the clothes from Sandy, I can get a stroller instead. Sometimes, I don't know if these showers are all they're cracked up to be. You never get anything you want and with the food that I put out, who knows how much I'm actually making."

Alice looked up when a nurse wheeled in a new bed. "I'm sorry, dear, you're going to have to go to the waiting room. Just down the hall on the right."

Alice found the last empty seat in the waiting room and picked up an outdated fashion magazine from the low table in front of her. She flipped through a few pages before her thoughts turned to what was happening in the operating room. She wondered how many babies the young doctor had delivered. He looked like he was barely out of medical school. What if there were complications with the surgery? Would he be able to handle it? Of course he would. He was a trained doctor, wasn't he?

Alice relinquished her seat to a pregnant woman who had just come through the sliding doors. The woman's male companion joined the line in front of the admissions desk. The woman adjusted the wet towel between her legs. Suddenly, she cried out, "Mark! There's blood coming out!" The admissions attendant called someone on the phone. A few minutes later, a nurse ran out from one of the delivery rooms and escorted the couple down the hall.

Alice bowed her head and prayed, "Please God, help Becky through this. No matter what she's done, she doesn't deserve to die. And please help the baby. In Jesus' name. Amen."

Eight years later, Alice sat on a bench watching her two young sons cavorting at a playground in Toronto. A tall woman resembling Becky walked by pushing a stroller and Alice was reminded of her friend. Alice had not seen her since she moved to Toronto for her first engineering job. She had felt guilty about leaving when the baby was only a month old but her job search had ended earlier than expected and she didn't want to risk losing the position. She'd paid three months of advance rent on the apartment and Becky had been grateful. It was one of the few times that Becky had smiled after being released from the hospital. Alice had attributed Becky's post-partum moodiness to the strain of parenthood—who wouldn't be short-tempered with a colicky baby?—and the painful recovery from the surgery.

Alice's parents congratulated her on the successful conversion. "Waahh . . . she even named the baby after Christ? Incredible! We can't believe it's your first convert! You're like a professional!" Alice glowed and told them how much more she had done to save Becky's soul. They still bragged about her success at evangelical meetings.

Alice believed Becky never learned why John started questioning the paternity of the baby—at least Becky never confronted her if she had any suspicions. Alice had made sure her note was typed and printed at the public library. She had prayed on it for weeks and knew to her core that God's amazing grace was flowing through her.

Alice had never meant for things to go so far. "But what did you expect would happen?" she chided herself. She always thought it was unfair of Becky to burden her with that confidence; it made her resentful, if not downright angry. And it wasn't as if she hadn't tried to talk to Becky about it. Who knew how long that marriage would have lasted, even without her intervention?

It had turned out well enough for Becky in the end. God moves in mysterious ways. Alice heard from Mrs Woods that Becky had found some man to live with. She was somewhere in Saskatchewan. If nothing else, Alice thought, Becky's new relationship was based on honesty. A better fate awaited her. Alice's conscience was clear.

She recalled the words of San Zi Jing, the Three-Character Classic that her parents had made her recite daily when she was first learning to read:

ren zhi chu
xing ben shan
xing xiang jin
xi xiang yuan

"People are all born good, only their habits make them different."

If Confucius could believe in the essential goodness of people, who was she to believe otherwise? Alice hoped that she had been able to help Becky be a better person, get closer to her true nature. She took pride in having been the one to bring Becky to the Light. It would have been terrible for Becky to live in deceit the rest of her life, not to mention for the child. Though many women had done it, she wanted better for her friend. She felt responsible for her soul. Alice found that becoming a mother herself had affirmed the aptness of a decision taken during a time when she acted on instinct rather than experience. These days, being a stay-at-home mom to two toddlers, her days occupied with family and True Gospel Church activities, Alice couldn't imagine a more joyous existence. She didn't blame Becky for wanting to bring a precious innocent into the world—a babe to love and protect.

The baby in the stroller started to cry and the tall woman stopped in annoyance. Alice noticed the frayed cuffs on the woman's coat as she took a pacifier out of her pocket and jammed it in the baby's mouth. The baby sucked a few moments before resuming his cries.

"Damn it! I've had enough of you, you little brat! You're just like your no-good deadbeat father!" The woman violently shook the stroller handle and tramped away from the playground.

Alice stared after her. There but for the grace of God . . . but Becky must have turned out to be a caring mother. Her family life must be happy and complete now. It *had* to be.

Although Alice continued to attend the same evangelical church for the rest of her life, and even went on a church-sponsored goodwill mission with her husband to Botswana after the children were grown, she never managed to convert anyone else to Christianity. Alice put her friendship with Becky behind her even though her parents still occasionally referred to the "conversion" decades after Alice had lost contact with Becky. By Alice's reckoning, one soul saved was more than sufficient. The residual sense of responsibility and worry, which almost verged on guilt at times was too high a price to pay. Despite the life-long spiritual link she felt with Becky, Alice never attempted to track her down; even curiosity was insufficient inducement. Whenever she thought of her old friend, Alice imagined only the best scenarios: birthday parties, family barbecues, mother-daughter lunches, until the imaginings gradually became facts in her mind. She would see a radiant Becky surrounded by a loving family, her hand still wandering up at times to finger the cross at her neck. A sense of satisfaction would come over Alice then, and without any trace of irony she would congratulate herself on a job well done.

BECKY

BECKY WOKE TO MORNING RAIN pelting her grimy bedroom window. She shrugged on an old sweater and stepped into her slippers, then rearranged the quilt so the sleeping baby on the double bed would be covered. Bright yellow chrysanthemums sparkled on the embroidered cotton quilt. The quilt cover had been one of the few things that she had brought from China. When she was preparing to leave for Vancouver, her mother had insisted on seeing her one last time and pressed the hand-made quilt cover on her as she walked off the farm. Though it did not quite fit in with her plans, the cotton cover did not take up much room when properly folded and Becky had packed it during a weak moment of sentimentality.

It was unlike her. She was accustomed to packing only essentials whenever she moved—when she first left her home village in Henan, each time she "jumped factories" in Shenzhen, and for her various apartment changes in Vancouver. She didn't like excess baggage. Once, when she didn't want to arouse suspicion at her old factory as she "jumped" to a better job, she had left everything behind, down to her toothbrush.

Becky went into the outmoded kitchen and warmed up a bowl of rice gruel. She stirred in some shredded pork floss and sat at the slightly wobbly kitchen table. Today was the day. She was going to finalize everything. Most of the boxes were already packed. Alice had paid for her to stay for three months but Becky had given the landlord notice and recouped two months' rent. It didn't make sense to stay here when she could find a cheaper apartment in Surrey.

She didn't expect to keep in contact with Alice much longer. Becky rarely continued friendships after parting. She changed her cell phone numbers and addresses too often for sustained friendships. There were many girls from her old factories who had been deleted from her life that way. No matter. There were always new people to fit in with her plans. Alice had been useful, though a bit dim-witted when she spouted her Christian beliefs. Useless superstitions. Becky blamed it on Alice's parents. They should have passed on Chairman Mao's teaching: "religion is spiritual opium." Instead, Alice and her parents held fanatical beliefs and worshipped a god. Not only that, they insisted on converting others to their superstitions. Chairman

Mao would not have been pleased. Becky's only belief was in making a better life for herself. It was an ongoing battle but Becky thought she was making progress. From a farm girl to landed immigrant in two decades. Not bad. But she wasn't done yet.

Becky put the bowl into the sink, found a pen and pad of paper in one of the open boxes, and sat back down.

My father and mother,
Thank you for your recent letter. I am glad to hear you are well.

Becky stared down at the paper for a few minutes then decided the letter would have to be finished later. She stood and walked into the bathroom. Opening the medicine cabinet above the sink, she rummaged among jars and tubes and retrieved a pair of nail scissors before stepping into the bedroom where the baby was still sleeping soundly, her hands curled in loose fists.

Becky climbed onto the bed and knelt beside two-month-old Chrys. Alice had assumed "Chrys" was a shortened form of Christina and rejoiced at Becky's conversion. Becky had let Alice believe what she wanted. It seemed to make her open her wallet more easily. As soon as Alice left for Toronto, Becky had removed the cross Alice had given her from the necklace and sold it to a pawn shop. Becky would never tell her friends why she had chosen Chrys as the baby's name. They would not believe that she had a romantic streak in her. Who would believe that she, a forty-year-old mother, had chosen Chrysanthemum because the flower bloomed in autumn? Or that she had always admired the flower's ability to thrive in cold, hostile climates? But Becky had chosen the name before the baby's birth. These days, she only associated the baby with duty and exhaustion. She should have named her "bothersome egg."

Becky watched the rhythmic rise and fall of the baby's chest. The colicky baby usually slept for only an hour or two at a stretch. The rest of the time, she was either hungry or crying. Becky refused to pick her up at each whimper; she was not going to spoil the child. So she sometimes cried for extended periods. It was enough to drive anyone crazy. Becky hoped she would sleep longer today. It would give her a chance to do what she needed to do. She felt strong; her caesarean incision was almost healed and she had gotten five hours of sleep last night.

Becky reached out and pinched the bridge of the baby's nose. She tightened her pincer-like grip on the cartilage and pulled hard. The baby grimaced but did not wake. Becky pinched the bridge again, pulling the nose higher. She repeated this a few more times. Next, Becky took the scissors and, using her left index finger to protect Chrys's face, clipped her eyelashes close. Then she clipped her finger and toenails. Still, she slept.

Becky disposed of the nail clippings and returned to the letter.

The baby is well. I am glad to hear that you can take her. I know you will take good care of her. I will bring her to you in a few weeks.

Becky paused again. It was a good plan. All her projects had been successful so far: her jobs, studies in English, visa applications, and pursuit of Canadian citizenship. This one was no different. She would work hard and make enough money to bring Chrys back to Canada when the girl was ready for school. Becky planned for Chrys to become a successful woman and support her in old age. If she played the angles right, she would get child support from Chrys's father, Fred, as well as spousal support from her soon-to-be ex-husband, John. Of course, she would ensure that neither men got anywhere near the child. Financial support was all that was required.

Alice had gone into her preachy rants when she found out about Fred. The simple-minded woman didn't know anything about choosing good stock. Fred was better-looking, smarter, and had more money than John. Why wouldn't Becky want to give her child the best start in life?

Becky thought about including a list of baby care instructions with the letter but decided to wait until she saw her mother in person. She should start the list now, though, before she forgot. Becky ripped the letter off the pad and started on a fresh page.

BABY CARE:
Bathe daily
Clip nails as needed
Clip eyelashes weekly (for full lashes)
Pinch nose daily (for high bridge and slender nose)

Her mother would probably laugh at her instructions but Becky wanted to make sure Chrys had as many advantages as possible. She would have to insist that her mother follow directions or risk losing her monthly allowance. Not that she would really withhold the money, but it might be a good threat.

The one thing Becky regretted was not being able to breast-feed the child much longer. She'd read that nursing babies for at least six months is the ideal. Three months would have to do. It was more important to go back to work.

Chrys's cries interrupted Becky's thoughts. Becky let her wail for a few minutes before getting up. By the time Becky picked her up, the baby's face was turning red. Becky sat cross-legged on the bed, wrapped the quilt around her shoulders, unbuttoned her pyjama top, and put the baby to her breast. The baby suckled hungrily as the milk let down. She wrapped her tiny hands around her mother's breast. Becky looked down at the baby's wavy black hair and a sense of loss overwhelmed her.

Don't be impractical. You're doing the best thing. She's a nuisance anyway.

Becky finished nursing Chrys and put her on the bed. Looking down at her, Becky saw a toothless grin spread across the baby's face as she recognized her mother for the first time.

It couldn't be. It's just gas. Babies don't recognize people at this age. I know. I read it in a parenting book.

Chrys continued smiling and gurgling. Becky turned her gaze away and quickly changed the baby's diapers. She wrapped the quilt around the child and carried her into the living room. Becky cleared the floor of some boxes with her feet, spread the quilt in the space, and put the baby down on it. Chrys was unusually placid. Becky returned to the kitchen and began packing glassware. After sealing a couple of boxes, Becky sat down at the table again.

I am finalizing my plane ticket today and will call you in a couple of weeks to give you the details.

Her cell phone rang. Becky ran into the living room and picked up the phone from the coffee table. She concluded her arrangements with the cook from her former job at a Chinese restaurant. He would help her move in two days. Becky sat on the couch and looked down at her daughter wriggling on the floor in front of her. Then, out of curiosity, she crouched down and moved towards the baby's face. Chrys smiled as soon as her mother got near. Becky could smell the baby's sweet breath as she leaned in. The baby's smile grew wider. Becky folded the quilt around her daughter and held her close, blinking furiously. She climbed back onto the couch and cradled the baby. Becky rocked the cooing baby until Chrys's uneven eyelashes started fluttering and she fell asleep.

In a few weeks, Becky would be parted from her daughter for four years. She would miss Chrys's first steps, her first words. When they met again, the girl would not recognize her.

Becky quelled impending tears.

There is no other way. It must be done. For everyone's sake.

Becky stroked an embroidered chrysanthemum. Her mother would teach Chrys to make chrysanthemum tea from local flowers. She would take her granddaughter to the Kaifeng Chrysanthemum Festival in town each fall. She might even teach Chrys some poems about chrysanthemums. No, that would have to be Becky's job.

When Chrys came back to her, Becky would teach her the many poems Chinese scholars had written about the noble flower. She would tell her the Han Dynasty story about the village in Henan called Gangu. It was said that Gangu villagers drank from a mountain stream filled with chrysanthemum petals and all lived to be one hundred and thirty. Becky thought her own village might well be on the site of old Gangu; she knew several villagers over eighty. There would be many years for Chrys to be with her.

Getting soft! Poems and stories! What next? Maybe the baby should be sent away sooner rather than later.

Becky hurriedly carried the baby to her bed and dragged out a carry-on bag from the closet. Breathing quickly, she overturned a dresser drawer full of baby clothing into the suitcase. Remembering that her cell phone was still in the living room, Becky ran back to the couch. She called the travel agent and found that changing the departure date would cost at least a hundred dollars. Becky resignedly told the agent to reserve the original date; she would be in to pay for the ticket in the afternoon if the rain let up.

Stick to the plan. Don't go soft.

Becky walked up to the sliding door of the balcony entrance. She put her forehead and hands against the glass, grateful for the coolness against her skin. She closed her eyes and willed the weight in her heart to lift. She listened to the rapid ticking of raindrops against the glass, her sadness increasing with each tap. When her breath had made a white circle on the door and her hands had warmed the glass, she shuffled back to the couch and flopped down. Becky leaned back and stared listlessly at the wall of glass.

She watched the raindrops run down the glass door like water down a mountain. She thought she could see the outline of a chrysanthemum in the imprints she had left on the glass. She imagined chrysanthemum petals floating down mountain streams. Some people eat chrysanthemum petals to prolong life. Connoisseurs say inferior petals taste bitter but good quality chrysanthemums always taste sweet. Her Chrysanthemum was sweet . . . Becky shook her head in disgust and drew herself up. She brushed away tears and, despite the stream still coursing down her face, vowed not to cry over useless flowers for the next four years.

Acknowledgements

Sincere thanks to my "constant readers" for their ongoing support: Jenny Coyle, Lu Kim, Tracy Wong, Tanya Dubick, Chris Barber, Mary Anne Girard, Margaret Fulton, Rebecca Ward, P.W. Ferguson, and Deirdre Nowicki. Love and thanks to my family for never doubting me. You help me to continue writing.

Many thanks to Hiromi Goto for her advice and encouragement during her terms as Writer-in-Residence at the Vancouver Public Library and Simon Fraser University. Thank you for telling me that being "stubborn" is an essential quality for being a writer. Your lessons remain with me.

Heartfelt thanks to Margaret Hart and Nurjehan Aziz for guidance in navigating the unfamiliar route to publication.

Most of all, profound gratitude to M G Vassanji, my writing mentor at the Humber School of Creative Writing, for his teaching, encouragement, and generosity during the program. Thank you especially for insightful and sensitive editing of the manuscript during pre-publication. Truly, this collection would not have been possible without you.

Julia Lin was born in Taiwan and lived there and in Vietnam before her family immigrated to Canada when she was nine. Since then, Julia has lived in Vancouver and its environs, Toronto, and northern British Columbia. She holds a graduate degree in Immunology (M.Sc., University of Toronto) and a post-graduate degree in computing education (University of British Columbia) and has taught high school math, science, and computing science in British Columbia for a number of years. Julia lives in Vancouver.